DON'T YOU KNOW THERE'S A WAR ON?

JANET TODD is a novelist, biographer, literary critic and internationally renowned scholar, known for her work on women's writing and feminism. Her most recent books include *Jane Austen's Sanditon*; *Radiation Diaries: Cancer, Memory and Fragments of a Life in Words*; *Aphra Behn: A Secret Life* and *A Man of Genius*. A co-founder of the journal *Women's Writing*, she has published biographies and critical work on many authors, including Jane Austen, Aphra Behn, Mary Wollstonecraft and her daughters, Mary (Shelley) and Fanny, and the Irish-Republican sympathiser, traveller and medical student, Lady Mount Cashell.

Born in Wales, Janet Todd grew up in Britain, Bermuda and Ceylon/Sri Lanka and has worked at schools and universities in Ghana, Puerto Rico, India, the US (Douglass College, Rutgers, Florida), Scotland (Glasgow, Aberdeen) and England (Cambridge, UEA). A former President of Lucy Cavendish College, Cambridge, she is now an Honorary Fellow of Newnham College. Close to her home in Cambridge, the College's gardens provide a pleasant interruption from the other pleasure of writing novels.

T0126121

Radiation Diaries

'Janet Todd's pain-filled interweaving of life and literature is a good book written against the odds – it is frank, wry and unexpectedly heartening.' Hilary Mantel

'Beautifully written, viscerally honest, horribly funny.' Miriam Margolyes

'A stunningly good, tight, intelligent truthful book and one of the most touching love letters to literature I have ever read. Ah, so that's why we write, I thought.' Maggie Gee

'I read it avidly, unable to stop. I love the voice, especially the tension between restraint and candour in its brevities – and yet endearingly warm and honest. It's an original voice and utterly convincing in its blend of confession, quirkiness, humour, intimacy. It's nothing short of a literary masterpiece, inventing a genre. A delight too is the embeddedness of books in the character of a lifelong reader; it is fascinating to learn of Todd's variegated past. How gallant (like the verbal gallop against mortality at the close of *The Waves*).' Lyndall Gordon

A Man of Genius

'Strange and haunting, a gothic novel with a modern consciousness.' Philippa Gregory

'A quirky, darkly mischievous novel about love, obsession and the burden of charisma, played out against the backdrop of Venice's watery, decadent glory.' Sarah Dunant

'A mesmerising story of love and obsession: dark and utterly compelling.' Natasha Solomons

'Intriguing and entertaining; clever, beguiling.' Salley Vickers

'A real knack for language with some jaw-droppingly luscious dialogue. I can see the author's pedigree in the story, style, and substance of the book. It seems like a wonderful sleeper: think *Elegance of the Hedgehog*.' Geoffrey Jennings, Rainy Day Books

'A haunting, sophisticated story about a woman slowly discovering the truth about herself and the elusive, possibly illusive, nature of genius.' *Sunday Times*

'Mesmerising, haunting pages from a gothic-driven imagination.' *Times Literary Supplement*

'Gripping, original, with abundant thrills, spills and revelations.' *The Lady*

Aphra Behn: A Secret Life

'Genuinely original.' Antonia Fraser, *The Times*

'Janet Todd has a good ear for tone and a deep understanding.' Emma Donoghue

'Todd is one of the foremost feminist literary historians writing in this country. She has devoted her literary career to recovering the lives and works of women writers overlooked and disparaged by generations of male literary scholars.' *Independent on Sunday*

'Thorough and stimulating.' Maureen Duffy, *Literary Review*

'Todd has an enjoyably satirical style; she writes with shrewdness, humour and compassion.' Miranda Seymour, *Sunday Times*

'A rip-roaring read.' Michèle Roberts, *Sunday Times*

Mary Wollstonecraft: A Revolutionary Life

Death and the Maidens: Fanny Wollstonecraft and the Shelley Circle

'Todd is an extraordinary researcher and sophisticated critic. This biography conjures a vivid sense of a revolutionary who is a woman, and offers precise insights into the progress of one writer's life.' *Ruminator*

'A juicy portrait, reconstructed with insight and wit.' *Entertainment Weekly*

'Terrific insight . . . Todd soundly and generously reimagines women's lives.' *Publishers' Weekly* (Starred)

'Janet Todd brilliantly captures the absurdity in Wollstonecraft while defending the view that her life was both important and revolutionary. Like Virginia Woolf, Todd interprets this life as a daring experiment. Wollstonecraft is all but resurrected in Janet Todd's distinguished book: brave, reckless and wide open to life. Virginia Woolf claimed for Wollstonecraft a special kind of immortality. Janet Todd has strengthened the case.' Ruth Scurr, *The Times*

'The great strength of Janet Todd's biography lies in her willingness to unpick the feminist frame on which earlier lives of Wollstonecraft were stretched to fit.' Kathryn Hughes, *Literary Review*

'Janet Todd, a feminist, has done ground-breaking scholarship on women writers. Her work reads quickly and lightly . . . Even Todd's throwaway lines are steeped in learning and observation. Todd has documented so ably the daring attempt of a woman to write, both for her daily bread and for immortal fame.' Ruth Perry, MIT, *Women's Review of Books*

Don't You Know There's a War On?

Janet Todd

Fentum
Press

First published in Great Britain by Fentum Press, 2019

Sold and distributed by Global Book Sales/Macmillan
Distribution and in North America by Consortium Book Sales
and Distribution, Inc., part of the Ingram Content Group

Janet Todd asserts the moral right to be
identified as the author of this work

A CIP catalogue record for this book is
available from the British Library

ISBN (paperback) 978-1-909572-072
ISBN (Ebook) 978-1-909572-201

Typeset in Albertina

Printed and bound in Great Britain by
CPI Group (UK) Ltd, Croydon CR0 4YY

DON'T YOU KNOW THERE'S A WAR ON?

A telephone rings in the dark waking Phyllis Payne. She picks up the receiver in the kitchen, hears nothing. Moments pass, then a dull wailing too dry for sobs.

'Maud,' she says. 'Maudie, is that you?'

Choking words: 'I can't, Phylly . . . I can't . . .'

A thud. The receiver's fallen. Phyllis hears fingers dragging round a twirled lead.

'Maudie, what on earth? Tell me.' Cold rises from the floor into her bare feet. 'What is it?'

Heavy, hitched breathing. 'Come, I can't . . .'

'Shhh, calm yourself. Nothing can be so bad.'

A whimpering, then silence.

'Dearest, you're ill. Of course, I'll come. As quick as ever. But it'll take best part of an hour. Sit down, make a hot drink.' She refrains from the obvious: 'Wake your mother!'

Good reason: the mother's a monster.

Renewed wailing, no kind way to interrupt. Phyllis drops the receiver on to its cradle. The abrupt sound risks alarming Maud, but no help for it. She pads upstairs, curling her chilled toes against the lumpy carpet. She dresses in the bathroom to avoid waking Ray, then scribbles a note: 'Gone to Maud's. Emergency. Px.' She won't telephone again – the mother might answer in her ice-cold voice.

She starts her red Anglia, disturbing the night. Behind floral curtains, a bulb flashes on. Old Mrs Hennegan sleeps lightly beside her cold cocoa.

3

The streets are nearly empty – it's not yet 4.30 – but Phyllis adjusts her speed; she likes rules. By the time she reaches the outskirts of Norton, she feels a prickle of satisfaction that her friend has wanted her so urgently. Now, at last.

Next to 14 Ackroyd Close, the yellow mini she'd persuaded Maud to buy is tucked in like a mothballed ship. It couldn't be more rooted if draped in ivy. In the sitting room, facing the cul-de-sac, curtains are open, the central light on. Maud's not in the window frame.

Once parked, Phyllis is aware she's been blanking out possibilities. She jerks her keys from the ignition, jumps out, and dashes up the path past the neglected garden.

The front door gives way. Strange since Joan – Mrs Kite as Phyllis is obliged to call her to her face, even after so many years – is particular about locking up at night. She steps quickly into the sitting room.

In the cruel light a skeleton rocks back and forth on the sofa, eyes wide in sunken sockets. Phyllis blinks against the glare, then stares.

Maud was always slim, but this figure is Belsen-like; bones push against taut skin. Horrified, Phyllis sees the mouth is stretched in a grin.

'Maud, love, Maudie, dearest,' she cries, 'what's happening? You're starving!'

The rocking figure is unresponsive. Breath scarcely moves the chest.

'My God, Maudie, what is it?'

Phyllis bends down to touch the blank, swaying face. As expected in early morning, air is chilly, but the thin cheek is colder.

The room smells musty: Mrs Kite's standards have slipped. Phyllis glances at the grandfather clock, surprised by its silence.

She sits on the sofa, one arm hugging the bony shoulders. The rocking body carries her with it, then shudders. Still the open eyes seek no contact.

'Maudie,' she urges, 'what is it?' No answer. 'Let me fetch you some water, then we'll find a doctor.'

A hand springs out to clutch her arm. The grasp pinches.

'All right, all right. I won't leave you. But we must get you to hospital. My car's outside. Just a few steps.'

The wailing resumes, more muted and throaty than down the telephone. 'I can't . . .'

Moving with the jerks, Phyllis notes the strangeness of Maud's being fully dressed in skirt, blouse and grey cardigan in the dark early morning.

'We must take you to hospital,' she says again.

Understanding flickers on Maud's face. 'No, no,' she moans, adding something indistinct.

Phyllis has no time for this. If Maud – as close to death as Phyllis has seen a person outside a geriatric bed – thinks she shouldn't leave her mother, there's more than one lunatic here. 'We're going now,' she says firmly. 'You need help, dearest, at once. You must see a doctor.'

With surprising strength, Maud recoils. She clutches Phyllis's arm, preventing her getting a proper grip, then jerks her shoulders away.

Phyllis gulps, bewildered. She's cold and suddenly very thirsty. She's missing the morning tea Ray brings her in bed.

What sort of private hell have the two women created in this house?

'Come,' she says, grabbing the thin arms and pulling Maud upright. She could carry her to the car if she'd relax, but, though sturdier than her friend, she can't take the weight of a resisting body.

The struggle ceases. Maud is tentatively upright. Phyllis winces as she catches foul breath.

With more force than she'd expected to need, she propels Maud towards the door. Dragging the reluctant feet along the carpet, she scatters a pile of blue notebooks neatly stacked by the grandfather clock.

Abruptly Maud bends towards them, clutching at Phyllis. 'I haven't . . .'

'It's OK. I'll tidy them later. When I come back for your things.'

Maud continues to pull towards the notebooks but, now standing,

Phyllis is stronger. She urges Maud outside, ignoring her whimpering.

She leaves the front door slightly ajar. Why close it? If the house were on fire, she doubts she'd bother to wake Mrs Kite until she'd felt the lick of flames. Even then?

As she turns the ignition, Phyllis glances over at Maud, aghast to see the mouth is falling open. She recalls her own mother after a hysterectomy, before she'd shaken off the anaesthetic.

She manoeuvres Maud into the hospital's shabby, brightly lit reception area. Not as busy as on drunken weekend nights, so there's no delay. A pretty young nurse questions Maud in vain. Phyllis tries to answer in her place. The nurse regards her coldly: Phyllis feels herself being blamed.

She doesn't demur, for, as Maud is pressed into a wheelchair, guilt stabs her. She's let the lazy, deckchair summer go by without simply ignoring Joan Kite and storming her way into that house, knocking the woman down if necessary.

She pulls herself up: she's no good at self-reproach. Maud's dreadful state isn't her fault. Far from it. Nothing can be laid at Phyllis's door, not even in part. She's tried her best. You can't force your way into a monster's lair.

Despite overcrowding, a bed is found. Maud is wheeled through the swinging plastic divide. The nurse follows. Neither mother nor sister, Phyllis is left behind. 'I'll bring you some things,' she calls after the retreating chair.

She hopes to erase any lingering self-reproach by chatting to the receptionist. She's interrupted by the return of the pretty nurse, who remarks, 'I've never seen anything like it.'

Probably true. Thirty years since war ended.

'Me neither, Linda,' says the receptionist.

As Phyllis prepares to leave, the nurse turns to her with the same disapproving look. 'One question: has your friend' – she stresses the word as if it covers heaven knows what – 'ever been in a mental institution?'

'No,' says Phyllis, 'of course not. There's nothing mentally wrong with Maud.'

'Hmm,' says the nurse and grimaces to the receptionist.

She must return to Ackroyd Close, get nightclothes and sponge bag for Maud, to show the hospital she's not friendless. She might even write a note to Joan Kite.

Saying what?

'Maud's starving. I've taken her away, you witch.'

Driving back to Norton, she has time to reflect. An illness has touched Maud's mind and body. But what and how? Even a mother as unnatural as Mrs Kite must have noticed her daughter's dwindling.

Unless, of course, she too is ill, and mother and daughter are suffering together.

Phyllis represses the thought as she passes along the still sleeping streets. Maud needs good diet and care. Phyllis will invite her to Coventry to convalesce. Mrs Kite will protest but Phyllis will overrule her this time. She doesn't consider Ray's response, though well aware she lives in his home now.

The house in Ackroyd Close is still lit, the door ajar. Everything looks as before. Joan Kite is a great sleeper when drugged with sleeping pills. Never needing them, Phyllis has an exaggerated belief in their power.

Again she notices the unpleasant smell. The women must have kept their windows closed this long, stifling summer, breathing the same stale air day after day. It will be an effort to mount the stairs and pass the mother's bedroom to Maud's smaller one.

Before she can summon the energy and courage, she returns to the sitting room. She almost stumbles over the scattered notebooks.

She leans down, picks one up and opens it. Blood surges to her face as she spies her own name. Written in Joan Kite's affected hand.

Holding the first notebook, she sinks on to the sofa, on the spot where Maud had been rocking.

August 1975

'Why not write something of your life?'

'I have no life.'

'Phyllis says . . .' Maud stopped as she heard me expel breath.

'Right,' I said after a pause. 'I'll be disciplined. Just occasionally. Not everything.' I smiled.

She turned away, giving no answering smile.

Writing is diuretic: it shouldn't be undertaken if you aren't near a lavatory. 'No, siree,' as the Yank said to Rachel when he went off unsatisfied, refusing to hand over the nylons.

It's like taking a dose of salts.

Why did she suggest it? Maud rarely initiates. Does she want me to reflect on *us*, on mother and daughter? Her widdershins way of asking? We're not that sort of family. We don't wear our hearts on our sleeve.

Does she wish to know about herself – at the beginning? Or does she want to know about me? I doubt the latter. Children are so self-centred. Besides, it would be unseemly.

No getting away, though, there's been a change these last weeks. Something's a little different. She's not introspective, no point interrogating.

The notebooks she's brought home for me are cheap and lined, with pale-blue covers. From Woolworths? Pinched from school?

'I'll get more if you need them,' she says.

Why is she encouraging me? It's not her place.

'Shall I start with birth?'

'If you like.' Maud shrugs.

'Don't you have an opinion, dear?'

'Begin with the war. You often mention it.'

'Do I? Maybe I do. Yes, the early years, before the Americans.'

'No, the later part.'

Is she mocking me? If she is, Phyllis taught her the trick.

'That's not the real war.'

'So, start with yourself.'

She's silent. Then, with her back turned to me, she says, 'Phyllis is getting married.'

I sit down. 'She can't be.'

September 1975

'Some more cake, Maud?' says Phyllis.

'No thank you.' Maud wipes her mouth with a serviette and smears it with lipstick.

I'd suggested she wear some – such a pale, insipid face. She took no notice till Phyllis gave her a tube of pinky-orange, 'coral' they called it. I'd not have chosen that colour for her.

I glance at the soiled linen on the table, then at Maud. I fold up my serviette and put it by my plate. No ring provided for either of us; no future teas anticipated. I dare say it's as well.

Phyllis takes another piece of Victoria sponge cake, protruding her reptilian tongue to lick the oozing cream. A spot attaches to the side of her nose. Out of Maud's range but not mine. I say nothing.

Maud wanted to move in with Phyllis. She brought it up with me a few times. The last one a year or so ago. She was rubbing her finger across her gums to dislodge an apple pip – I've trained her to eat the skin and core. Unusual for her to talk and draw attention to herself. I expected the gums to be pale but they were scarlet. So I remember the moment.

'You wouldn't like it,' I said. Spinster schoolteachers perched on that hideous butterfly-wing settee by the gas fire. Doing what? *The Times* crossword puzzle, watching *Dixon of Dock Green* on a rented television?

Phyllis would have scratched her raw, then cauterised the wounds with a simper.

Maud even said – just once, 'Perhaps all three of us . . .' then stopped. She saw my lips curl.

To be sure, Phyllis might have relished it. Skirmishing, retreating, sniping, snarling whenever the two of us were alone. Then buttering her face as Maud approached. Touching a hand or arm or shoulder whenever she could. So insolently.

Too late now. Maud lives here. At 14 Ackroyd Close. Always will.

And you, Phyllis, stay in Coventry. You should have been sent there long ago.

Maud's silent, but I see what's going on.

'Self-pity butters no parsnips.'

Say nothing: 'Loose talk costs lives.'

Early October 1975

'Start with birth,' I think she said. Why not?

My Life as 'Child'

1922 was a good year for some. David Lloyd George ruled England and no one declared war.

Mother said to Father she'd never suffer *that* again. Repeated the remark in a burst of giggly loquacity to cousin Clare and me over the teacups one afternoon just after Clare was evacuated on to us.

'You really must not,' Father responded. 'I forbid it.'

Yet she'd enjoyed the fuss made over her 'bulge'. Looking fresh and nice in the diaphanous surplice frocks in gingham a friend persuaded her to order from the local dressmaker and which she'd found – another little giggle here – were really quite becoming, as well as concealing. Especially a pale lilac and white striped one Father adored.

'You look like a luscious boiled sweet,' she said he said. 'Good enough to lick and eat.'

Pop it in your mouth right now, I say. Swallow the whole farce to come, me and Clare and Maud. And Phyllis. All of it. Without stopping to chew.

She loved the baby things: the lace and crochet work on soft, patterned wool. Gifts from the Hereford family of which she saw so little once married. She ordered Megan to lay the caps and bootees flat on the dining-room table for inspection by her friends, their ribbons smoothed and glossy. The wicker cradle had a white blanket, the silk edging stitched by adoring sister

Gertie when her fingers were still supple. A shiny black perambulator with huge spoked wheels stood in the hallway.

'He too,' she added turning to me, 'your Father, took as much joy. He wasn't one who thought it manly to despise pretty things.'

I shrugged, while Clare smiled and cocked her head. Mother sniffed. I got on her nerves, she said.

My nerves jangled at the pair of them.

I was born in a soft double featherbed on a birch-wood frame. People say you can't recall that far back, but infant eyes see more than you think. I remember the warmth and snugness from walls of pink and green whirling flowers and dappled orange fruit. Sleepily feeding from the softest, prettiest breast; pink lips pursing and dissolving at each suck, thin milk trickling in and washing against the soft, furred mouth.

Then one day it hurt. The rubbery gums – there couldn't have been teeth – pressed harder than they should, and Mother exclaimed. She'd been carelessly eating a ripe golden plum, its juice dropping like melted jelly on to the wrinkled forehead and running along fleshy folds, seeping into tender skin.

Hearing her cry out, Father dashed into the bedroom, 'You must stop at once, darling Isobel, your lovely breasts mustn't be harmed. After all, they're mine first and I enjoy them most.'

Clare liked the story as Mother told it; slyly she looked at me, 'Bully for Uncle Jack.'

Father said my birthday was really Mother's day as much as mine; so he'd give her a present. Sometimes there were small parties with Aunty Gertie looking on benignly, spraying into soft clouds the excess face powder from her whiskers.

13

One year, when staying nearby, Uncle Harry visited with pretty, ailing Aunt Laura, a 'martyr to migraine', and the child Clare, already employing her demure, come-hither look. (Children without siblings are supposed not to know how to vie for admiration, but she knew tricks from the cradle.) When Uncle Harry, Aunt Laura and cousin Clare came by, there was no Aunty Gertie: Mother's and Father's families didn't mix. Uncle Harry had married up, though getting precious little from it except an indolent wife and a few pieces of grand furniture.

Once I begged Mother and Father to take me to the talkies for a birthday treat. Father mildly disapproved. Moving pictures at the Empress Cinema weren't quite genteel. He poured his eyes over his wife and said, 'If you really wish to do that, Isobel.'

So affectionately he spoke that she grew winsome. 'We do,' she said. She knew a trip to a cinema would have no bearing on our status.

Off we went, the three of us. I wanted *King Kong*, but we travelled to a little cinema in Birmingham to see *The Blue Angel*. I couldn't understand the words which didn't fit the mouths saying them and didn't much like it. Mother chose it because she admired Marlene Dietrich's cool expression and never-ending legs.

Father sat through it, then said quietly that it was unsuitable for a child, but he doubted I'd understood it.

What was there to understand? Just pictures, just shadows, make-believe, real people pretending. What harm in that?

I'd have judged better had I been allowed to go to Saturday matinées with common children, eating crisps and spilling blue packets of salt into the pleats of a ruffled skirt watching Tarzan and Mae West. Father thought infection lurked in the plush purple seats, even though you could smell the lemon disinfectant as soon as your head passed the door, infection which might come back to contaminate a fragrant home.

So many dangers out there from *other* people.

What was Father like? I don't think I ever knew.

Once he must have wanted some widening of horizons. When I brought home my prize from Sunday School, he said he'd read *Pilgrim's Progress* as a child, but he didn't search my book for a special page. Do I believe him? Possibly. Such reading fits that Methodist home which put its pennies in the Friendly Society, lived cleanly and bred two ambitious boys.

Before he married, he bought fifteen encyclopaedia volumes from a catalogue, bound in imitation leather. Using coupons from a newspaper, he acquired a fat dictionary; on its inside cover he'd copied out two verses of W.E. Henley's poem, 'Invictus'.

> Out of the night that covers me,
>   Black as the pit from pole to pole,
> I thank whatever gods may be
>   For my unconquerable soul.
>
> It matters not how strait the gate,
>   How charged with punishments the scroll,
> I am the master of my fate,
>   I am the captain of my soul.

It tickled Mother pink when she spied the poem one day when the great book thudded open on to the floor.

He owned an Everyman, too, in red and green jacket: Boswell's

Life of Samuel Johnson, inscribed with Milton's words in swirly patterns, 'A good book is the precious life-blood of a master-spirit, embalmed and treasured beyond purpose to a life beyond life.' I puzzled over this bloody master atop his embalmed body. Everyman was the previous owner, I assumed – I wished he'd had a more inviting book to sell on.

Mother discouraged Father from further purchases: though so feckless at housekeeping, she understood about gentility (heaven knows how). She made him play golf instead of hiking with the Rambling Club. No need to spend time on dictionary or encyclopaedia, just imitate the Better Sort of People – though only well-off Masons, when all's said.

So, together they moved from their lowly starting place into the middle class – not the upper-middle, mind, not well off enough for that. Sometimes Mother adopted a haughty, high-heeled walk, though her childish expressions modified the effect. In new company she made stylish work with her eyes and limited herself to a few brittle, adaptable remarks and abrupt strategic laughs. She stopped herself declaring she was 'in a pickle' or that someone was 'no spring chicken'. She had afternoon frocks for visiting and a beaded silk gown for the Masonic dinner-dance in the year Father was Worshipful Master. She wore hat and gloves to go to town.

For Sunday lunch and weekday dinners Father put on a jacket; at work he wore a stiff collar and a bowler hat which marked his forehead. He liked Mother to rub it smooth when he came home. She did this from behind him where he sat in the ladder-back chair. He didn't see her slight grimace as she kept the nail of her middle finger clear in the air for fear of damaging it. He was as proud of his appearance as any Horse Guardsman on parade.

Both changed their voices, mimicking the classier Masons, probably the Harrisons, who used to live in Leamington Spa; then mimicry grew natural. Now, thinking back, I see Father avoided treacherous vowels and never opened his mouth too wide. When at a loss, he let his lips form a condescending smirk round his pipe – like a public-school chap, he must have thought. With all this, there'd be no knowing he'd been running grocer's errands in Dudley at thirteen, his widowed mother finding fewer pennies than expected in the Friendly Society when her husband, a mere foot soldier of Empire, was lost in Black Week, somewhere unnamed in South Africa.

Unlike Mother, Father had no siblings to let him down, just Uncle Harry back from a term in India, a military man called Major ever after. (Father served in the reserve trenches on the Western Front in the Great War, dealing with supplies – not heroic, but he claimed a bit of shrapnel somewhere inside.) The rank of major suited Uncle Harry's bearing. He'd confidence in spades. In India he'd earned money enough for a detached house when hardly anyone we knew owned their own home. It had a half-timbered Tudor top and, on the stairway, a stained-glass window depicting St Michael with a defeated dragon: I thought it a lord's mansion.

Fair enough. He'd made what he had. Only upper classes have legacies, though one might say that, like Father, he'd inherited a habit of striving. Methodists were supposed to be humble, but Father and Uncle Harry weren't. I suppose they'd 'mastered their fate' – I suspect Uncle Harry also knew 'Invictus'.

'You make your bed,' he said to me as if it were the First Commandment. 'You reap what you sow.'

*

Perhaps Father was fond of me in his way, but never as a girl needing fine underclothes or compliments.

Did he ever touch me intentionally?

I can think of only two occasions.

I was in the pond near the old house in our straggly overgrown village. A lovely day. Newly unfurled lily pads rolled around and were refolded by a blustery wind; squawking mallard ducks and geese screeched on the rippling water, coming and going, changing places with no obvious purpose, just a flapping irritation with each other as they swooped and strutted. No swans about, though a few of their pale feathers shone on the pond's muddy edge.

I stood in shallow water, my feet in soft mud, socks and sandals on the grass verge, frock hitched up, liking to watch the white toes under cold liquid as mud settled and water cleared. I stretched my fingers down through the surface to touch them, but I made everything murky and my frock wet. When the water cleared again, I spied little minnows swimming over the white feet. As if these feet belonged to a dead body.

Then, like a bird of prey on a quiet rabbit, Father burst on me and pulled me out. Dragged on to the muddy grass, I saw the toes weren't so white. They were pink and wrinkled, probably with chilblains from the hot brick we used to take to school wrapped in a little blanket. (But that would be in winter and this was late spring.) While I stood swaying on the bank, boys with scabbed knees and home-made fishing rods went by snickering.

'Really!' said Mother when he brought me home. 'Your bottom in the water for anyone to see!'

Father added something else.

'She never!' said Mother falling back into her old voice.

Confined to a room for punishment with only a full chamber pot as human trace. Left there a whole day and night for calling Mother 'she' in the uproar that followed.

Shhh. 'Careless Words Cost Lives.'

And the second time?

Father was flying a kite on the common with Mother and me. I clutched its tugging lead until the blue and orange tail snagged on a high blackberry hedge, Mother giggling. The tail came away when Father pulled. There the kite remained: later, rain dissolved the paper leaving the woody skeleton on the brambles. (The common's gone, to make way for estate houses. Such a post-war boom of babies they'll have to burn not bury bodies when this cohort has trampled through the world.)

Thinking back, I recall that, when Father took the kite string from me, he didn't touch my hand. So, there *is* only the pond and my wet frock and skin in his fingers.

He spoke to me though. Don't fidget, don't fiddle-faddle, don't dawdle, don't cough, don't harrumph, don't disturb, don't bother. Don't Upset Your Mother.

Father stroked Mother, her hair and the stuff of her frocks. I was too big for caresses, he said when once I pushed up to them.

Uncle Harry often touched 'my Clary'. Aunt Laura left them to it; she'd retired from the family long before.

Late October 1975

My life in theatre

Mother and Father were in the chorus of an amateur production of *The Gondoliers* at the Masonic Hall. Neither sang or acted well, but both were fine looking enough to be stared at. Father delighted to watch Mother dressed up in full white lacy gown with red apron; puffed sleeves showed off elegant arms; glossy ribbons twined in her hair. She held a tambourine with red and white streamers, ready to dance a fandango, though she never did.

I was made to sit near the front of the auditorium to watch. Aunty Gertie should have been with me but she'd been disinvited when she hinted at a chesty cold; they didn't want her coughing and hawking and spoiling the show. So I sat with the Harrisons and Thompsons, Father's Masonic friends, and their wives, and one or two children.

At the end, in high spirits from so much admiration – for she was the prettiest on stage – Mother thought it a frolic to lean out from the make-believe, to wave and call to her daughter, her eyes skimming the smart couples beside me.

A silence followed. I was supposed to say something charming and complimentary in a childish voice that would make people smile.

Mother had Megan cut down the Spanish gown into a gypsy skirt and blouse because she was tired of it – she always grew bored with things once loved – and I was invited to a fancy-dress party at the Hall. It was my birthday and would do for celebration. There's a photo where I don't look out of place in my gypsy costume, though, amongst the eight little girls standing upright before the camera that took so long to get us in focus, I alone hadn't cocked my head to right or left.

Girls being looked at should do this – to show they know they're being looked at. Don't unnerve a man with a straight-headed, unwomanly stare.

'Best to fit in,' cackled Aunty Gertie when she saw the snap-shot.

So sniffy about cinema, Father respected theatre as Culture, though he rarely saw a play. 'When I was watching *Abraham Lincoln* at the Birmingham Prince of Wales . . .' he used to begin, and Mother would stifle a yawn by stretching her chin.

In 1941 the Prince of Wales was bombed.

The jealous postman, who had to carry his heavy bundle on a bicycle instead of a horse, told Clare and me that the 'yampy' carter slept with Cedric the station horse at nights. I didn't laugh for I loved Cedric and always scampered out to watch him trudge slowly past. Clare hooted when I said it was a grand thing to sleep between the four legs of a sturdy horse, lying up against that soft warm chestnut belly and steamy flanks. Clare never watched that marvellous creature. Not theatre, no cruelty.

Real theatre's always a menace. On a whim, actors may cross the limelight and humiliate mute spectators, like a magician with his butt in a magic show. Of course. It's their business to show off. How show off without a victim?

There's a victim in any act, onstage or off. Do you know that, Maud? Phyllis knows it: you should have asked her what *exactly* she is doing when she waltzes off to Coventry with (I suspect) hardly a by-your-leave.

Did you anticipate that twist to the drama, Maud?

Young Joe, dapper, Brylcreemed, shaven face like a shorn sheep. Taking me to a touring production of the *White Horse Inn*. He paid for the best seats in the stuffy wartime theatre, where he hotly held my hand as his legs squirmed. Later he put his dry lips on mine.

Clare, in her feather hat, spied him at the interval, then came upon us like an actress through the curtains to steal the scene, launching a grimace into the air of the foyer. Always the exhibitor of herself. The feathers on her hat danced such devastating amusement that it was all up.

'My heart is broken, but what care I?' So they sang.

The last time I went to the theatre was as a 'Poor Relation', the kind a humourist called the 'indigent she-relative' – unlike the shabby male sort who pays for his scones and whisky by amusing children, quacking like a duck or whistling wild bird songs.

Invited to the Royal Court because – I assume – some friend of Clare and Nick's couldn't make the performance despite free tickets, or, on second thoughts, face high culture, I was available at the last minute.

'How nice but I wouldn't want to be a bother.'

'No, you'd be doing us a favour. Don't like an empty seat.'

When Clare saw me in the lobby, almost everything I said got up her powdered nose.

Endgame, a play of parents as dustbins. The old people were fed soft biscuits or the wrong biscuits. At one line – 'This is not much fun' – only I laughed.

The holes in the dustbins for breathing were too big. I could have written that play: a child could have written it.

'The two main characters are master and servant,' Nick explained when I ventured an off-kilter remark.

A few people walked noisily out of the theatre. They thought it the middle. In fact, we were five minutes from the end.

Afterwards, Nick and Clare (and I) were joined by their friends for a drink in the theatre bar. One man actually said 'existentialist'. Aloud!

A woman screeched out across the crowd to a man dressed as if for the opera, 'Darling, did you see *Godot*? You know he writes these things in French first. It's all about politics. He's Irish after all.'

Rubbish. It was about ageing and being stuck at home.

In an aside to Clare – I was not to be talking to the whole company – I hinted that there was just a teeny bit of analogy.

Clare sniffed. 'Try not thinking of yourself for a change.'

'How simply exquisite,' I overheard one of their friends say about Clare's frock. No ripple of discomfort in that foyer. (The silk hugged her figure. She always looked ravishing in silk – and knew it.)

'*Fin de partie*,' said Maud when I mentioned the play yesterday.

'It was no party,' I said. Just thrown-away lives.

Everyone went to chapel or church on Sunday mornings, Mother and I in gloves and hats, as inevitable as brushing teeth or Father donning his jacket for the 'tea' that one day became 'dinner'.

On the hard, shiny pew, I sat between them like a slice of ham in a sandwich. I must keep my hands on my lap and not let them fall to the sides of my kilt. Cosy squashed there, though

23

the chapel was chilly. An old oil stove in the back delivered more smell than heat.

Most Sundays, ordinary people read the lesson. Once, the reader was the knife-sharpener, the wizened man who came to our house and stared at Mother while whisking our knives through the little device slung on his back or grazing them against the stone step at the side door. He'd whistle in a common trilling way Mother said grated on her ear.

In chapel he read the sonorous words of Ezekiel and his valley of dry bones in a deep, dense voice. Father gave Mother a mocking glance as the Black Country vowels boomed out; she answered with a coquettish smile. I could feel the looks flipping and uniting over my head, knowing without giving the matter words that I stopped them squeezing hands, right there on the pew.

Those cosy chapel Sundays of Father, me and Mother rest like warmed treacle in memory. Treacle and runny rice pudding. Yes, even jelly (the puddings crowd in on me today). Before I was expelled.

After some years, Mother made Father move from the chapel near the rough crossing to the C of E at the end of the High Street to worship with the Harrisons and Thompsons and sing to a proper organ. The churchyard had fatter graves than the municipal cemetery where chapel folk and other excluded bodies went underground. In church I sat by Mother alone. Father said he liked the pattern of descending heights in his 'girls'. Mother was now the child in the middle.

I'd look up at the angel wings in the church roof, then stare at the huge brass eagle lectern, pointing its malevolent curved beak at the wooden feathers high out of reach, and finally end at a brass plaque of a skeleton wearing its pelvic bone like a ballerina's tutu, one leg forward in elegant pose. A huge stained-glass shepherd was caught in the window surrounded by sheep: I imagined him shearing off their woolly coats and wrapping himself in the pelts. In *Pilgrim's Progress*, the shepherds on the Delectable Mountains are called Knowledge, Experience, Watchful and Sincere. The sheep have no proper names. Like our flop-eared dog, who was never anything but 'Spaniel'.

Mother left chapel with never a look back, but Father? Something Methodist may have lingered. Though he brought home a bottle of Harvey's Bristol Cream sherry at Christmas, he was no drinker: a bottle of sloe gin presented by Mr Harrison lay untouched in the dining-room sideboard for months, maybe years.

'Not gin like poor fat people gulp to become senseless,' he said, the colour refined it. He still didn't drink it.

Unlike Uncle Harry, at heart Father was always a Temperance man, despite admiration for C of E golfing chaps with silver hip flasks of malt whisky. Always on the tip of his tongue to say 'use' instead of 'drink' alcohol.

He had an especial horror of inebriated women. 'Thank heavens Gertie doesn't drink,' he said after Mother added a further eccentricity to her sister's inelegant habits. 'We have that to be grateful for.'

Early November 1975

'I'm tired of writing,' I say to Maud.

I'm lying of course. It's not fatigue, more like apprehension. I've never kept a diary, I'm not the sort of woman to look in chance mirrors to catch sight of myself or bare my soul to strangers in a railway carriage. That kind feels better for her spillage, never fearing – or realising – she's addicted.

I know the damage unleashed writing can cause. I hinted as much when Maud first brought home the notebooks.

'Diuretic,' I'd said. She didn't take the hint. 'Besides, it's a dangerous habit like confessing; it's self-indulgent. Catholics never amount to anything.'

She doesn't look at me. Then she says without elation, 'Write of pleasant things. We had some good times with Aunty Clare and Uncle Nick.'

As she speaks, she leaves the room.

Just as well. She knows what she says.

By the time she returns, I'm irritated only that I've allowed myself to be disturbed by anything she could say. Mothers and daughters are so tied, so glued, so predictable there are no surprises; most expressed irritations are just practised repetitions.

'No,' I say, knowing she knows what I'm answering. 'Aunty Gertie.'

Aunty Gertie

The grandfather clock had its bottom portion sawn off to fit the low-ceilinged farmhouse where Mother's lackadaisical clan lived. It descended to Aunty Gertie, the eldest girl; she left it to me.

To the bequest she should have added the contentment she usually achieved beneath its tick and tock in the fuzz of her unkempt sitting room: not 'easy cast up, easy cast down', as people used to say. Every other day I wind the clock, so there's never complete silence. Aunty Gertie sways in each tick-tock.

'God has made the back to the burden.' For her, the burden of time and gnarling fingers.

She had many homilies. Trite of course, but delivered with a smile and a little laugh, so you could take or leave them – unlike Uncle Harry's. She knew such sayings might come in handy later. They'd been passed down from her Hereford family and helped her through life. Beyond the grandfather clock and dampened hopes, what else had they given her?

As I write, I see her before me: plain, almost ugly, in sturdy countrified style, a human station horse. The type that lets itself go to fat, pushing against wider and wider corsets, the type that makes little effort to disguise hairy moles on face or neck.

Clare would have shuddered, then smirked, if she'd seen her. Aunty Gertie would have answered with a warm, inclusive smile. 'How are you, dear,' she'd have said and, understanding the girl doted on compliments, have added, 'what a very pretty frock you have on.'

Her rooms were in an old Victorian building, reached through a brown-tiled hallway. They smelt dingy from long stored dirt. When wind gusted through cracks along the window frames, it made cobwebs, thickened with dust and dead daddy-long-legs, wave in corners. In a tarnished copper vase beside the grandfather clock, peacock feathers swayed and shed little bundles of friendly fluff into the room.

Where we had gas jets at home, she used oil lamps. A paraffin stove gently leaked and thickened the air. Sometimes ice furred the inside and outside of the windows: yet the room felt as cosy as if warmed by an iron kitchen range with bright brass handles and thickening milk puddings. Mother and Father had a polished range with brass handles, but we didn't sit by it, only

Megan. Aunty Gertie fried Welsh cakes in a none-too-clean pan and toasted hot crumpets on the end of a long brass fork against the open mouth of her paraffin stove.

Sunshine never entered the bedroom where she kept her upright piano with its stately candle holders. There, by the window, where normal people put their dressing table and mirror; as Mother once remarked with a little laugh: 'So eccentric.'

On her piano she played Chopin and Liszt, and Mendelssohn's Preludes and Sonatas, above all his *Songs Without Words*, over and over. Though she lamented mistakes as her fingers stiffened, I listened and noticed none. Sometimes in dismay she left off halfway, but, when I begged her, she'd start again. I had her thick green dressing-gown over my shoulders for warmth. It smelt of camphor.

She had no skill in singing but I pressed her, and, while playing, she sang in a trembly voice her one song,

> 'Come into the garden, Maud,
> For the black bat, night, has flown,
> Come into the garden, Maud,
> I am here at the gate alone;
> And the woodbine spices are wafted abroad,
> And the musk of the rose is blown.'

Only the first verse: we never got beyond 'the gate' to the flowers.

Neither have you, Maud. Not in over thirty years. I don't count irises. Besides, there were no irises in that rosy-posy garden under the daffodil sky. You don't know about the enchanted place, do you? I've never sung you the song.

*

Kindly, whiskery spinsters are almost extinct, left over from wars in Mother's and Aunty Gertie's time, those 'little wars', then the Great War. Alone or in sisterly pairs they collected floral china, pressed roses and honeysuckle in books of poetry; they sucked Ely toffees in the morning and had pyramid-shaped humbugs last thing at night to keep regular; they kept cats they loved to bits or hung up silk birds in painted wicker cages, put feathers or dry grasses in tall vases. A few did missionary work or collected money for missionaries to go out and be eaten by cannibals. Some reached for the gin bottle to ease the pain of solitude and dropsical legs.

Aunty Gertie was one of those leftover women. Not craving attention like spinsters now. (So unlike you, Phyllis, entitled – you think – to anyone and anything your heart desires.) She smiled at random people on path or pavement and gave out sweets to small children with runny noses. She collected dark green mosses from walls and stones, traipsing about hour by hour in hail and drizzle to find the thirsty stuff where it clung; then she studied it through spectacles – Mother and Father said 'glasses' – then through a little microscope, comparing her findings to black-and-white pictures in *The Student's Handbook of British Mosses*. She made careful notes of what excited her as strange.

'Moss is ancient,' she'd tell me, 'the oldest lineage on land. It can survive what we can't. It'll be here when we're long gone.'

'Stars lurk deep inside it,' she said. 'Moss in trees or stone walls makes a world of unseen power.'

One day she carried over to our house some dried and brittle samples in a brown envelope for me to see. The stuff was intricately structured and rare. Dust spilled on to our polished dining table. Mother primped and frowned a smile over to Father, who raised his eyebrows and went out to smoke his pipe in the garden. Megan swept away the lingering dust, tutting.

'Well, if she enjoys her tomfoolery,' said Mother when Father reappeared once her ungainly sister had left.

'At least she doesn't drink,' said Father for the umpteenth time, as if doubting the proposition.

'Mosses!' they laughed, sharing the joke with their Masonic friends. Even more ridiculous when she called them 'bryophytes'. Imagine! A woman using such terms! Piano playing was one thing, pretending to learning quite another. For that sort.

Gertie was the bogey of my parents in those five years we lived near her in our half-suburban village on the edge of the dull Midland town she came to love. As she must have loved her picturesque Weobley when a girl. She was fiercely patriotic about England, more so as her Methodism waned – easier for Mother, who replaced it with Father's Masons and the C of E, neither requiring strenuous faith.

When she visited us and was inescapable, Father, courteous to any woman however blubbery, would be excessively so to her. He hid his distaste and wonder that such a grotesque being could emerge from the same two parents as his delicate wife. She spoke rurally with a sort of Hereford version of a Midland accent. From the same stable, Mother must have spoken like this once, before she accompanied her husband into gentility. (I can't blame her. This is what 'bettering yourself' meant then as now, despite post-war pretence. 'Proof of the pudding,' as Mother would have said had she been alive.)

'If you go on that way, reading so much, you'll end up like my sister,' or, 'You sound like her when you come back from visiting,' or, most of all, 'Poor Gertie, at that dull job of hers; of course she'd love to have been married, she's so fond of children.'

With this last sentiment Father and Mother would warm themselves, though Father, an accountant of a sort and never (to his sorrow) chartered, was not so clearly beyond her, and Mother, excited by trinkets and pretty frocks, couldn't have reached on tiptoes to her mind. And I was all the children they proposed to have. (Those breasts were Father's, not to be wasted on more babies.)

Aunty Gertie was untidy in person and place, her drawers and cupboards disordered as though the thief my parents dreaded in their neat house rifled her nightly. Mother suspected fleas in her wardrobe. I said there weren't any; otherwise she'd put them under her microscope and marvel.

'Fleas can live for nearly three months without biting and eating,' said Aunty Gertie.

I didn't tell Mother. She'd have stopped me visiting for fear of bringing home a family of starving fleas from the disordered wardrobe.

'She's not happy,' Father'd say. 'We should allow for that.'

'If she'd only take more care of herself,' Mother would reply. 'She really does smell.'

Father would look shocked at the naked word, then loving. The naughty knowledge brought them closer.

'She's a bad influence on the child,' Mother would say then.

Aunty Gertie took me on her knee even when I was big, at least ten or eleven. I smelt then her sweet acrid smell. She had a weakness and always a damp stale odour clung to her, faint but noticeable. Not so unpleasant to me.

When she found it difficult to bend for fear of snapping the huge stiff corset that held the soft fat of her, I had to get down on my knees to retrieve the fancy tasselled bookmark with its uplifting saying about home or kindness or England. Well, then I might be a little overcome by the sweetly sick, ammonia smell of her and spy the edges of those voluminous drawers in flesh-colour pink.

Yet I would be a long time bending there. And when once more she held the dropped bookmark and was about to place it between the pages where she'd stopped reading, to her surprise I had to stand up and rush home.

I ran all the way to the bus, gulping in the coldest air. Strange since the last thing I wanted to do was get away from her. On the way I saw everything in bright light: an old woman pushing a wheelchair, a young one cuffing a child struggling against reins in its pram, a man with no legs pulling himself along on a cart with his strong bony arms, a traction engine stuck in the shallow pool. Everything with such startling clarity.

When I echoed a denigrating remark I'd heard at home about vagrants, Aunty Gertie said, 'No, child. Do you see those lame soldiers leaning against walls in the square? With empty sleeves and placards hanging from their necks? Their war record. So shaming.' The shame wasn't theirs.

Once I had to write her a letter. I can't now remember why but it was not long before she died, so she may have been ill. I wrote about a new friend. I must have used expressions I'd heard between Mother and Father or spied in Mills and Boon romances Mother left about the place.

She replied oddly: she said people must always hold tight to independence. Her words made my head whizz.

Aunty Gertie worked in a government office in town. I went to see her there twice. A disagreeable building but jobs were scarce after the Great War and she was grateful. The corridor smelt of sharp Lysol. Its walls had a stripe in the middle to separate different shades of muted green. When walking along, if you stopped and turned, you forgot the way you were going.

A dull job moving town-planning applications from one desk to another for decisions by more significant people.

'Don't work in an office, child,' she once said to me.

But what use is advice to the young when they don't feel high walls pressing on them?

'Don't be a schoolteacher,' I'd said to Maud. 'They do no good. They always get things wrong.'

She didn't argue, simply did what she wanted. Or had to do, she'd have said. Well, it was her funeral. Like mine.

Aunty Gertie had seen kingfishers and heard them singing in royal blue and gold. I saw the very bush – though, when I looked, I noticed no startling birds. She told me of the murmuration of starlings, the murder of crows and a bittern's mating boom. See, she knew special words. She saw clouds called cirrus, nimbus and stratus.

Once I walked with her among bluebells in a little wood not far from her rooms. Dark-blue sky laid out greenly on earth. Their beauty striated my eyes; their subtle smell surged up my nose.

She pointed out other flowers: honeysuckle, dog rose, violets, moth-winged salvia, all wonderful. Just the idea of them brought tears to my eyes, but never tears that ran down my cheeks. And underneath, behind the tearing eye, something troubling and warm.

33

She read old books, new books, books from the second-hand stall in the market, botanical books with diagrams of plants and insects, novels too, but especially poetry. She'd sit in her musty flat and hold the volume upright in hands stiffened by arthritis but strong enough to let her enter other worlds. Occasionally she gazed through her spectacles at Millais's *Ophelia* on her wall or some picture of intricate weeds. ('He who can draw a joy from rocks or woods or weeds is wise,' she quoted when my eyes followed hers.)

She rarely glanced at two certificates stating she came first and second in national piano competitions. She'd won a scholarship to a music college in Manchester but never went: grown girls must bring home money. Other children needed to be fed and clothed, one of them a beauty.

She read me patriotic excerpts about Sceptered Isles and Happy People from Shakespeare, then long narrative poems like *Sohrab and Rustum* and *Philip and Mildred*. She knew *The Eve of St Agnes* by heart but kept her eyes on the page when repeating the magic words about the far-off lovers, Madeline and Porphyro:

> And still she slept an azure-lidded sleep,
> In blanched linen, smooth, and lavender'd,
> While he from forth the closet brought a heap
> Of candied apple, quince, and plum, and gourd;
> With jellies soother than the creamy curd,
> And lucent syrops, tinct with cinnamon;
> Manna and dates, in argosy transferr'd
> From Fez; and spiced dainties, every one,
> From silken Samarcand to cedar'd Lebanon.

These delicates he heap'd with glowing hand
On golden dishes and in baskets bright
Of wreathed silver: sumptuous they stand
In the retired quiet of the night,
Filling the chilly room with perfume light.

Soon I had the sumptuous, gluttonous lines in my mind too, so often she recited them.

Sometimes she mentioned a poem I might read, then left the open book on her side table while she pored over her mossy diagrams.

I took her my *Pilgrim's Progress* from Sunday School, the prize for reading 'audibly'. The frontispiece was a drawing of Pilgrim with a burden like a vast untidy tumour on his bent back.

'Every house had a copy when I was a girl,' she said.

I can't imagine Mother looking inside it – she'd smirked when I carried my prize home – even less than Father, who might just have managed to. Aunty Gertie had really read it: she once told me I must be in the Enchanted Ground, my eyes so near to closing in her fuzzy room.

I've used Aunty Gertie's repulsiveness to berate Maud for sloppy appearance or an unmannerly way of leaving shoes unaligned at the door or, when damp, without shoe trees to keep shape and avoid odour. Or for sneezing wetly and being uncontained. 'You really remind me of my aunt,' I'd say. 'It's so easy to let yourself go and so hard to prod yourself in again.'

Then, one day, Maud answered back, 'You told me not to be like her, not to be slovenly.'

I slapped her face hard. The blow stung her cheek and my hand.

35

Who was *your* Aunty Gertie, Maud? Did you need one? Why would you? I was enough. I didn't place *The Golden Treasury* by your elbow, but the book was in the house: it could have been opened at any time.

'Aunty' Clare never featured for you; that much I know.

And you, Phyllis? Was it the lax 'mum' who bred you a predator? Did you prey on her for loving her boy more – for she must have done, mothers always do, don't they?

Did you spy on her as you've spied on Maud and me, wanting her to watch only you and applaud?

You and Maud spiral in a void now, not young but not old enough to know everything's already happened. I can't unsee what I've seen, you can't see what you haven't. No cascades of flowery words, no magic snow will ever fall on your strange lands. Just irises, you say: half dead under that false French sun.

Our generation's memories have formed you. What pitfalls will you tumble into? Or do you think you've clambered out of your pit, Phyllis, stamping on Maud's pale head in your haste?

'Have you written what you wanted?' Maud asks as she sees me pick up the cap of my fountain pen.

'I never *wanted* to write anything. It was your idea.'

She doesn't reply or even look at me.

A sudden thought: has it been Phyllis's idea? Like the yellow car. A way of tossing Maud back to me and this house, now she's finished with her? All that education must have taught Phyllis refined ways of cruelty. No need for open declared war, for honest guns, bombs and gas.

'I shall go on all the same,' I add. 'I'd thought you might be curious, but I see you aren't.'

'What about?'

I uncapped my pen.

Aunty Gertie with me

Snow came to our Midlands mainly in February when we'd nearly been fooled out of our winter felt or fur overcoats by a sight of spring crocuses. One January day it lay thick. I'd gone to Aunty Gertie's house. She'd thought me moody. 'After-Christmas dumps,' she said in her eccentric accent.

Then, following the box of photos and cards of Hereford scenes, a few stanzas of poetry, some details about sporophytes, crumpets toasted and a little burnt against the paraffin stove, she said, 'I've got a treat for you, a real Christmas card.'

I waited. Aunty Gertie didn't tease.

'We'll go by train. Only a little way out of town, just one stop. That halt, you know, where no one gets off. You remember?'

I nodded.

'Just up the road there's a little wood, several rows of planted Sitka spruce, with a gap in the middle. I haven't seen the place in years. I used to go there when the trees were younger to search out haircap moss.' She chuckled. 'The green so green it was almost blue. They must look magic now with snow.' After a pause, she added, 'Your mother wouldn't come. She's not a walker.' She chuckled again. 'Someone's always there to drive her. What would she want to walk for? With her face and figure.'

She caught my glum expression. 'No one's especially pretty at eleven. An in-between sort of age, neither one thing nor t'other. The story of the Ugly Duckling is all about it.'

Too young then to answer, What of a misplaced duckling among swans waddling into adult duckhood? Tell me that. Swans are cruel, snobby birds.

The next day, a Saturday, we set out in early afternoon, Aunty Gertie needing to do her 'chores' in the morning. My throat was a bit raspy, probably from her stove; my hands and ankles felt oddly cold.

Thick snow lay on the ground, sun shining frostily, refracting gold, crimson and tawny light. Small holes grew in the whiteness; a glistening in the air where fresh water had passed. Snow on slate roofs, but, around chimneys, slates were clear and wet. Every so often a chunk of ice splattered on to the pavement from overhanging eaves.

Organ-pipe icicles hung from the station sign. Inside, the wobbly wooden floor steamed. Framed yellow and ochre posters of Skegness and Brighton ran wet from the breath of passengers and gusts of heat from a squat iron stove with lions' feet.

The engine chugged into the station, lining up the end coaches against our platform. The smoke and noise were Christmassy, more than Christmas.

We climbed into an empty third-class compartment without a corridor. Aunty Gertie could be sociable but didn't seek out people. The air was thick, so she let down the leather window strap to freshen it from outside, then with an effort pulled it back to fit the metal prong in its hole. The air still smelt like the station horse.

We didn't talk. On the dirty glass, diagonal streams of water from snow or ice melting above it; through their clear paths I glimpsed the day sparkling. My eyes sprang open as if on silver springs.

The ride to the halt was so quick Aunty Gertie said we could almost have walked, though we both knew we couldn't.

'The train was fun.'

She smiled. 'You're a good girl.'

We stepped out on to the short empty platform. No one to collect our tickets; all day I clutched mine inside a mitten, remembering how Aunty Gertie once said that was what mittens were for; otherwise 'why make kiddies' hands into paddles?'

The road we walked along was almost untouched. Some vehicle or perhaps two motorbikes had gone along it a little way; beyond this double track, all was smooth. No footprints, so our feet marked and packed untrodden snow.

After a short way we turned up a steeper, narrower path. Over the slight rise at the end I could see the black and white silhouette of trees.

'It's here, isn't it?' I said, excited.

Aunty Gertie was amused as older people are when they think they've pleased a child. 'Cold?' she asked and squeezed my arm.

'No. Not even my feet.'

But they were. When we'd left the road, the snow had been thicker and some of it slipped over the top of my short boots, seeping into my socks. Aunty Gertie wore her old black wellies.

'Good. Let's go on quickly. It's already getting late and the days are so short. I've brought along some slices of bread and butter.'

We crunched our way to the first row of trees, entered the

wood, looked behind at the thick zigzag, then moved towards the clearing beyond.

All was white and sparkly. The trees were tall but, except at the edge of the wood against the central path, they'd lost many of their lower branches. If dead pieces protruded farther down, at their tops they were full and snow-covered, the thick white stuff stopping just where it ought – white sauce on Christmas-card plum-pudding trees. Skeletal grasses in the clearing stuck up through the snow.

As we went into the wood, Aunty Gertie drew back. 'You can walk faster,' she said. 'I know you want to go on. Young people always do. Young legs.'

'No, I'll walk with you.'

I was surprised, she'd been quick enough earlier. She chuckled, her plain round face merry.

'Go on,' she said.

So I did.

It was magic. On the trees the white was absolute, but, on the ground under the outside branches where snow had fallen only thinly on dark pine needles, it was more a paleness.

The sun was trundling along to its early setting. Some fir trees were dripping snow, the sound emphasising the quiet. Occasionally a streak of red sunlight would catch the snow-drip, turning it blood-red. When it hit the whiteness below, it grew clear as crystal. No wind worried the needles of the higher branches, caught in heavy snow. Under the trees, I still felt the whiteness from layers above my head. A canopied light.

I wanted to be lost, a Babe in a Wood, Red Riding Hood or Goldilocks, some little girl trapped in a soft, dark place, at once safe and precarious, a place where she shouldn't be but might want to stay for ever and ever. A cosy, threatening hideaway.

I felt the tang of ice cold on my teeth as I trudged along, though I tried to breathe only through my numbed nose.

Did I see a hare in a space between lines of trees? Have I inserted the hare now, from Aunty Gertie's *St Agnes* poem? I know nothing of their winter habits. Perhaps they hibernate or just lurk in forests, or avoid them as cold, drafty places.

If it *were* there, then its fur would have glittered in the low sun and its eyelashes jangled with frost. A lean, golden, tuft-eared hare with shining amber eyes like a barn-owl, sitting on its hind legs on the enchanted, ruby-tinted snow. It would hear no wind, no muttering and crackling in the branches, and see no scribbling across the sky, even when it 'limped trembling' away, hiding its unspotted belly and private bits as it did on that magic Eve when I wasn't there.

There was no barn owl: I know that much. Nothing ridiculous like a deer or wolf, angel or dwarf.

Tracks of a happy bird? I think so.

I must have been yearning to see a feral, wordy world. Why think to find or add a hare or fox or deer or yellow-eyed wolf? Something at the time encouraged them to come, then and later.

How far down did the winter go? Was it warm and always late spring six inches below the snow? I don't want to believe it. The glinting and glistening shouldn't just be surface, covering the same old moist mess. As the sky turned from silver to grey, the grass under its white prettiness would be growing dull, but I like to imagine the earth farther down strange, frozen and uncanny, so that something one day just might erupt and transform the upper world.

I remembered the bluebells. I'd picked some when Aunty

Gertie wasn't looking. They had white liquid roots: they reminded me of the graceful feathery swan above ugly rumpled grey feet, so I dropped them.

Not like that. Something more wonderful here. I thought that even then.

As the day darkened, it didn't grow colder; it might even have been warming. The thinning light made the dripping snow translucent. Even under the trees, in this intimate place water was seeping through black-green needles. The snowy beauty, held too long, was crumbling.

Like an infant beautiful with no effort, with no control, no need of control.

When I came back into the clearing, I saw Aunty Gertie almost upon me. She'd walked slowly through the snow in her capacious wellies, making a wide track beside mine. Occasionally she'd overwhelmed my smaller footprints, but mostly she'd broken the snow for herself.

She was out of place.

'I thought you'd got lost,' she said. 'I didn't see you.'

'I went inside the trees for a while. It's warm there, at least in the beginning.'

'I'm sure it is. But it's not warm here.' She chuckled. 'We'll have to go soon. The sun's setting.'

'Just a moment. I want to walk to the end of the wood.'

I marched off quickly, needing to be without her. I felt the wetness inside my short boots travelling up to my ankles. At first, I feared she'd try to catch me up. But instead she followed slowly. I was alone again.

The sun was just above the horizon, darting reddish rays

across the whiteness, making shadows with the white-clad trees, licking trunks with orange. Outside their dimming, I was again in Christmas-card land. The dark and dripping inside of the wood was beyond the glittery display, but here on the wide path the trees were pretty and flat as in a picture. Impassive, they whispered between themselves.

Do poems remember the trees they once were? Do trees already know the words? Are our poems dead because they killed their trees? No matter, the wind and rain give trees even better poems than *The Eve of St Agnes*, much better than 'Invictus'.

> 'In the fell clutch of circumstance
> I have not winced nor cried aloud.
> Under the bludgeonings of chance
> My head is bloody, but unbowed.'

No tree would ever say anything so stupid.

At the end of the wood was a thread of barbed wire, strung on haphazardly leaning wooden posts. I'd not noticed it earlier. Beyond it were bare fields and a few ordinary trees, now stark, black and naked against the darkening sky. Trees biding their time.

I shivered, even more aware now that my socks were sodden, my toes numb. I was giddy, as if the world were spinning faster. I grabbed the barbed wire and felt its sharp points pierce through my mittens into my skin; closed my eyes, then opened them to find shadows deepening.

I turned back the way I'd come. I walked hurriedly on the edge of the clearing between the trees, looking straight ahead, expecting and fearing to see Aunty Gertie on the open path.

In the dimness I missed her.

'You're in a great hurry now,' she said. 'Are you tired of it?'

I stopped, a little breathless, hearing her voice but not seeing her at once. Then I spied her standing still under a tree. 'No, no, I'm not. It's beautiful, it really is. It's getting dark though.'

'I'd noticed that.'

She came out of the shadows, her laughter too loud amidst the silence. I waited until she was by me. The fir trees were still almost white, yet now growing sombre. The paleness was ominous, tinged with grey.

'Was it worth it?' she asked as we regained the road.

'Yes. I loved it.'

She saw me shiver. My feet were burning blocks of ice.

'Cold? You should have put on two pair of socks. I always do in winter. No doubt your mam didn't tell you.' She smiled thinking of her pretty, helpless sister. 'You've cut yourself,' she added as she saw blood seeping through my woolly mitten. 'We'll find a leaf and you can spit on it to stop the bleeding.'

By the time we took the train home, the sky was black where there were no urban lights. We sat cosy in the dimly lit compartment, eating the pieces of bread and butter we'd forgotten till we smelled them in the heated carriage.

As we chugged away, I felt the trees in the dark mirror of the window pane, cool and lovely in their private night. In the cold of real blackness, the drips would have stiffened into stillness and the wood be silent.

While I saw the trees in the mirror of the window where the weather rubbed against the pane, I thought of Aunty Gertie chuckling and smelling so definite. She was despised so thoughtlessly by Mother and Father – and me sometimes. As I considered her and all her movements that day, I saw at once that, when we'd arrived, she'd sent me on because she needed as usual to look for 'a spot'. She hadn't cared to expose her massive silk bloomers and naked buttocks to my child's eyes.

Yet she needn't have hidden, for, though I might have stared, I wouldn't have been shocked. Indeed, I saw her then in my dark window as clearly as if I'd stood by her, watching her hitch up her thick felt skirt above her boots, then hole the snow with hot yellow. She'd been making the place her own like any other large animal.

The wood will be gone now. Trees were all cut down for fuel and building in the war.

Remember what you're fighting for.

The day after our excursion I coughed and sneezed and thought only of breathing. By evening my temperature had climbed to 103 and I was away in a fitful sleep where trees swished and swooped through my burning head. The doctor hinted pneumonia. An old man, he regarded Mother as a rare flower and was prepared to come often to contemplate her. For the next three days he visited morning and early afternoon.

My parents were harsh on Aunty Gertie. She'd been selfish and thoughtless. She should have known better, traipsing round in that silly way of hers on such a bitter day. She'd been well wrapped up herself, they'd be bound, mouths going prim, and no one else mattered.

Once, Aunty Gertie travelled to see me but didn't stay. She suggested the usual – warmed goose grease on a flannel clamped to the chest. She was ignored, then frozen out by Father's looks, for she'd had to come after work when he too was at home. She didn't visit again, though she sent round some treacle toffee.

'Hardly the sort of thing for a sick child,' remarked Father.

'It makes an ugly mouth,' said Mother.

Aunty Gertie's long dead. She died of diphtheria – an illness that suggests one doesn't always wash one's hands afterwards.

'In some ways it was a blessing,' I heard Father say the day before the funeral. 'Gertie couldn't have stayed alone much longer, with the arthritis crippling her hands. Who'd have looked after her if she'd lived to a great age like your grandmother, Isobel? Gerald wouldn't have had room to take her in.'

She could have come to live with me. Somewhere in the middle of a wood in a gypsy caravan, with her piano in one corner, playing though her fingers were growing stiffer and stiffer, so that only the slow movements would be left her, then perhaps just right-handed pieces. But I would go on listening in that caravan in the wood of plum and lemon trees, where branches tap-tapped on the window, and she in her spare time, between playing the piano, toasting crumpets just right on a brass fork, and looking at mosses on wet tree trunks in the early morning when the light's best for studying things in their natural place, would be telling me that I was so good and clever and should read this and that and might become – what?

I can't remember what I might have become had she been there to tell me over and over – and stop me giving myself away in a rush like a badly wrapped parcel.

I'd have sat on her coffin to eat my sandwiches. Or, better still, lain down with her in the pinewood box. She'd have filled it snugly, but I'd have found room.

Lying there alone, did she feel guilt for taking me down to the woods, then disappearing?

My nose dripped through the chapel funeral: tears ran from my eyes, sloshed along the bridge of my nose, then fell off the end. Crying, I thought dramatically, for Aunty Gertie and me and all the whole wide world.

Perhaps, though still at school, I knew then I'd never be really clever again, nor the earth so beautiful and full of soft moss, gush, snow and bluebells – and strange, strange smells. I'd never become the sort of person who finds snail's slime lustrous.

'Oh, for goodness' sake,' hissed Mother, handing me the small handkerchief she didn't need. Father looked into the dignified distance.

The undertakers, Meredith & Son, owned a horse-drawn hearse. I often watched it going along the High Street. I'd stand stock still on the pavement out of respect for the dead, as one was supposed to do while the horse clip-clopped by even more slowly than Cedric. This year they'd acquired a black motor hearse. It banged and jerked along with far less gravity than the old horse neighing and tossing its shaggy mane against flies, or even defecating at unseemly moments (when it did, mourners averted their eyes and studied the sky). The motor was more expensive and, thinking back, I understand why Father paid extra for it.

Indeed, he paid for the whole funeral, the cemetery stone and glass dome of white shell flowers. To show Mother's relatives, Gerald and Sally and Floss and others whose names have slipped my memory, that Mother had done better in marrying than they had.

Why didn't Mother, Father and I go to the funeral breakfast?

It was attended by all sorts of shabby people from her office and from a nonconformist choir for which she used once to play the piano, all people who'd liked Gertie. They must have, for, between hymns and while wiping my wet face, I heard snuffling that rolled over the pews from the back rows.

A reason beyond snobbery why Mother, Father and I weren't there, but I don't recall it. No offence obviously, for more than once by the chapel door, behind the minister's back, Gerald thanked Father for paying for everything.

But still, why didn't he and Sally and Floss and all the people they left at home in Hereford shout to the heavens at the rudeness of our not going back to drink tea and eat cold-meat sandwiches and fruit cake in honour of their sister?

Truly, I was glad not to go. I'd have been looked at and remarked on – 'You must be Isobel's girl. How old are you now, dear? Really? Same age as our Daphne. Look, Floss, like our Daphne.' Feeling the oddity of our not knowing them.

And I'd cried so much through that dirge of a hymn 'Abide with Me' – even then not really crediting a for-ever realm where Aunty Gertie and I would be united in cosiness as Heaven's morning broke – that I looked a fright and would have been noticed for my blotchy face as well as my existence.

Why didn't we sing 'Come into the Garden, Maud'? We could just have done the first verse.

'Do pull yourself together,' Mother said when I tried to give back the wet handkerchief but was still jerking with sobs. 'It's really not helping.'

I've forgotten Aunty Gertie's deathday. Each year it comes round and I don't notice it. Not now, not before. We make such a fuss of birthdays: how do we not observe deathdays – after of course, but even before they've happened? You'd think there'd be fore-shadowing as well as remembering, time being what it is.

A friend from her choir took the old upright piano. Where did her other things go? Her sheet music kept in the hollow stool, her moulting peacock feathers, her music certificates, her second-hand books of poems, her microscope, her pages of notes about moss on walls and trees? Thrown on to the rag-and-bone-man's cart? Mother and Father would have thought them grubby.

Only the grandfather clock, the sewing machine and the framed picture of Ophelia were stored for me, things that could be wiped down with disinfectant. She'd put the bequest in a let-ter to brother Gerald. The clock and picture were wrapped in a grey blanket, the sewing machine was left to gather dust. All were kept free of charge, for Father had a friend with a furniture warehouse.

The rooms were simply cleared, Mother said. 'Your Father has taken care of everything.'

In all the years that followed, she hardly ever spoke of the dead sister who'd done so much for her: a sister who adored my pretty silly mother, light years younger than she'd ever been.

I shouldn't have let this pen stir memories. All Maud's fault. I've allowed words, written words, to bring back bluebells and snowy firs when they should have stayed trampled and cut down for all the good they did and do. For Aunty Gertie or me.

Late November 1975

'Why did you leave school so early, Mrs Kite?' asked Phyllis in that bold way of hers, 'and you so keen on reading!'

'You don't need education to appreciate books,' I said. Irritated, I added, 'You yourself have had many extra years of education and remain largely ignorant of literature.'

She snorted. 'I always wanted to teach, Mrs Kite. I stayed in school to do so. Like Maud.'

I bridled at that. 'You have no idea,' I said, cutting off the talk.

'Growing up'

I did better than cousin Clare in her fancy private school. But here's the thing: I did it through hard work, not with ease, not carelessly. In class they called me Swottypotty.

I was not the *very* best. Nobody minds how one does unless one's best all the time – or so bad it shouts for comment. You can boast about coming last – or top, as long as you didn't work. If not first, one might as well be forty-fifth.

Swots aren't smart. Proof of the pudding.

The English teacher took an interest in me. At least I thought so. Usually spanking clean, I came dirty to class, wafting a musty, sweaty-knickers smell, then sat on purpose close to her, arms and legs spread. Until Miss Carrington had to say, 'We need more air here. Someone's not taking baths.'

Man-faced Miss Carrington. Sweet Miss Carrington.

I knew the contempt of the games teacher, vulpine teeth and frog torso, breathing a mist of misery over the hockey field, but I'd expected better from an English mistress, even one with big, outstanding bones and chalk clinging to her wiry hair. Yet Miss Carrington never took Mother aside to whisper I should stay on in school, despite my reading extra books beyond boring old *Julius Caesar* and *Marmion* and knowing *The Eve of St Agnes* by heart. No word from her about compositions that were applauded in red ink and given stars.

Was it that mute, unwashed time I sat before her with the tearing feeling inside that kept her silent? Was she stupid? Or did she, despite some little praise, think I was?

Only the two smelly gypsies from the forest ever wanted to be my partner for anything in council school: no one would be seen dead with them. Then here in high school came Maria, my 'best friend', who got no stars from Miss Carrington.

Big wide foreign face, large eyes set below a forehead where you'd expect depth but got only flatness. Eyebrows looking plucked even then, high cheekbones growing raw on icy days. Something doll-like, yet the face could light up with a smile. Now, on the edge of old, I see Maria's sort among voluptuous waitresses, shop cleaners and scantily clad starlets displaying clefts in tabloid newspapers.

We used to sit by the white war memorial, quartz sparkling in the sun, and push the gravel around with our feet or watch beetles and pale-pink slugs in the nearby flowerbeds. We gave each other little presents: from me a small green and white beaded purse, from her a red-felt heart-shaped sewing case.

She was chubby and, later, skinny boys would jostle her on the cinder track or in the street to make her drop her schoolbooks. Then they'd watch her bend down to pick them up.

We were both neat in ourselves. Her uniform was always

clean and looked oddly stylish on her, the tie falling straight despite being loose at the knot. By now I pressed my gymslip pleats every morning, heating the iron before breakfast. Maria's mother did the same for her. It helped keep the line as we developed. (With deft sewing I avoided this in Maud's second-hand uniform, though with little to fear there. Unlike Phyllis, no doubt swollen out of her gymslip for all to see.)

Maria wasn't talkative (as I was if given half a chance, sharpish sometimes without anticipating the effect – Mother's thin leather strap on my palms never taught me – how could it?) but, when she spoke, she caught attention with her slow, husky voice. Occasionally she'd imitate her stout mother, adding vowels to our consonants – 'stoppa your noisea' or 'I makea you nicea cakea, darlingsa' – though she herself had good English. Better than her father with his tricycle of ice-cream cornets.

Through several weeks I waited and watched for Maria. At first, she'd run off giggling round the games field with Molly, a red-faced, papery-skinned country girl with ringlets – like a weasel peering through laburnum. I'd chase her, coming close enough to see her breath whiten the air. Soon I grew slyer, sauntering out of sight or behind an abandoned military box until she returned and I could pounce. I wanted her to tell me her name, though I knew it well enough.

At first, she was haughty, especially when guarded by her ginger friend. Then one day I got her alone and was, just that once, cunning and confident.

'Maria, what's your name?' I asked softly.

'Maria,' she said and smiled.

I was quick at arithmetic, while Maria panicked if two numbers came together on a page. To pay for her company, I let her see my answers. Ineptly she'd copy only the results, leaving out workings. I knew she'd be caught and that I'd be publicly blamed for kindness. It took a surprisingly long time.

Though her father sold his ice cream in the streets, she created a nobler calling for him before they came to England from – the place differed but was always immensely hot, beautiful, and richly endowed with all the splendours of *The Arabian Nights*. Later, I found the family came from an Italian industrial town, which wasn't that hot or bejewelled. She fantasised poorly and perhaps I won her by pretending to assent to her make-believe. That and my correct sums.

We grew close and for a few months absorbed each other. But I suspected her even then. I'd stand inside a stout hawthorn hedge by the path, watching her and anyone with her, trying my hardest not to crack dead brittle branches and alert her. I'd trail behind her on dark moonless nights to discover if another girl stopped at her house near the station crossing after she'd gone through her front door. Easy enough to see, for the door opened right on to the pavement.

We talked about God and the universe, as young girls do. Being Catholic she had a head full of virgins, blood and leaking bodies.

Her lush, crazy faith tinged her with glamour. 'I'm named after the Mother of God,' she'd say. 'She has the most beautiful oval face and a rich red bleeding heart.'

In the C of E we did blood even less than in the old chapel, just that gently bleeding Lamb. So I linked Maria with fresh crimson human blood – flowing from a huge pulsating pincushion feminine heart. I imagined her Virgin with wide, open-eyed face and a body bursting with blood and milk.

'A penny for your thoughts,' we used to say, Maria and I, pushing stones with our feet inside the chain-linked fence by the war memorial. We never told them. We couldn't have begun.

Maria was proud of her thick, weighty hair. At first, it fell like smooth ribbon across the top of her head. As she grew lighter in body, shedding puppy fat, it became darker and fuller, emphasising and framing her moon-face. I wasn't ugly but not so pretty neither – the sort of girl who'd be better at thirty, as a friend of Mother's once said in my hearing. (Why not say I had good eyes, hair, mouth, legs, backbone, any feature?)

I brought Maria home, regretting it as soon as Mother turned on her that seducing smile. I told Aunty Gertie about this 'best friend' and what I felt. Hold on to independence, she'd said. What did she mean? What could an ugly old spinster know? Little time to learn.

I know now. Don't have expectations. Don't *need* anything anyone else must give.

I accused Maria of making her voice soft to attract boys, even though we were too young to think of them. We fell to wrangling.

'I like a friend who's loyal,' I'd say.

'Who's talking of loyalty?' she'd reply.

'I am. You're always after that Molly Donoghue. You took her for a partner though you knew I was there.'

'She asked me. There's no rule to stop me.'

'I thought we were friends.'

So comfortable with herself that in the beginning she'd give in with a click in her throat, be encouraging and apologetic, promise that next time and for always we'd be partners and 'best friends'.

But I wore her down. Until she'd say, 'Oh go and find someone else,' throwing out her new harsh verb, so comic issuing from her wide, perfect face: 'You *bore* me.' When, underneath, it was I who was a little bored by everything she said, unless affectionate. We swiped at fantasies and families.

From then on, we rarely spoke, but I threw her bitter looks. One Friday we were in the only spare period of the week. Cutting out paper for painted Christmas cards: a rare extravagance in that penny-pinching school, where we even drew extra lines in exercise books to make them last twice as long.

'My five cousins are coming from Wolverhampton for Christmas and New Year,' Maria told someone, perhaps Molly. Yes, homely Molly with her ginger ringlets made from twisted rags at night. 'The eldest, Edward, has an English name, you know. He'll bring me chocolates and flowers, I expect. He's been sweet on me since I was ten. Mama's noticed it. He can't keep his eyes off me. He's afraid to say anything. Such a chump.'

'Go on,' said Molly in her cheerful, admiring way.

'It's true though.'

Maria caught sight of me close by on the next desk. Her flat eyes grew shrewd. She chuckled, nodding her head towards me, 'For Swotty it'd have to be in the dark when her mam's not by.'

Molly sniggered.

Maria had the scissors for our group. 'Can I have them?' I said turning towards her.

'I'm not finished.'

I grabbed them too forcefully and they opened, so that one sharp blade scratched Maria's arm, then plunged in. The cut bled on to her blouse and jumper, the blood dripping on to her desk, more profusely than I could have imagined. Perhaps the blade had hit a vein or artery.

The art teacher, Miss Simpson, a hollow-cheeked S-shaped woman whose striped tie flapped on a flat chest, pushed Maria on to the long front desk where she bound the arm with a large white handkerchief. It was too thin and stained crimson at once, then soiled Miss Simpson's dangling tie. Form monitor, Molly Donoghue was sent to find the first-aid box in the staffroom.

By the time she returned with gauze and cotton wool, the blood had stopped flowing. The carved initials of dead children on the wood desk where Maria's arm had lain were filled in darkening red. A lot of blood, but not enough for piercing a vein.

I was punished for carelessness, knuckles on both hands rapped with the thick birch-wood ruler; one hand stayed red and raw for a week before healing to stiff scabs.

The incident washed away much of Maria's meanness, much of Maria. Maria, the Mother of God.

When I came second in the class after Edith Penny, Maria was forty-first. Lucky not to be bottom without my sums. She never did School Cert.

'Why bother, with *her* looks,' Mother said when I told her Maria was leaving school. She'd never wanted her visiting. 'Catholic,' she'd said, 'from by the railway crossing. Can't you make some better sort of friends?'

Come into the garden, Maria, and I'll show you hemlock, nightshade and aconite.

(Never read this, Maud – just silly girlish feelings. Nothing real. Like you and Phyllis, nothing real.)

*

In my bedroom I'd only small nail scissors, Mother's Florentine pair with the filigreed handle being out of bounds. Although I forced myself to press, at first I merely grazed the arm. Blood oozed out in little drops, not even flowing.

Later, at night, going to fetch a drink of water from the scullery jug, I took the carving knife and held my arm over the sink. Then blood flowed as it should.

Only bombers' moonlight to see it by: the silvery light turned red into purple.

Less pain with the knife – though the pain was always quite small, mainly acute in the moment before cutting, when the sharp point pressed to puncture the taut surface.

My first slashes were short and irregular. They were etched above pale blue veins just below the elbow, sometimes closer to the wrist. Over the weeks they grew longer and straighter. Yet, when they dried, however adroit I'd been, they came out crooked and uneven. I never pressed deeply; was this why the cuts failed to keep long sleek lines?

Just before wounding and while the skin was being punctured, I felt the edges of my head dissolve into a sugary sweet mass – me and not me. That's a thing that's stayed into grown-up years, accommodating the smell of ether from a dentist's chair. I imagine taking the white, sparkling stuff and rubbing it into the streaking gashes. The sensation would be good.

Cutting felt neither good nor bad. It was simply what I was doing. Sometimes I must have hoped Miss Carrington might notice the cuts nearer the wrist, but mostly I dreaded anyone seeing, so I covered them with my blouse and navy cardigan. The marks stayed for an impressive number of days. Had I been asked in school, I'd have shrugged and muttered something about a cat we never had. Or said nonchalantly, 'Oh that! It's nothing.' But I wasn't asked.

Since the weather was mainly cold, my arms were shielded by the grey jumper I changed into when I got home. A few times a little blood stained the green blouse; Mother caught it when she sorted laundry for the Monday wash.

'It happened in games,' I said, though those of us not picked for rounders or hockey teams rarely played.

Mother wasn't curious. Aunty Gertie would have noticed. Maybe I couldn't even have explained to her. But she'd not have needed words. The best conversations don't happen. She'd never said what she meant by 'independence'.

The cuts on my arms brought the end of Jesus and Fountains filled, never mind his bleeding mother (the curse might have been a better moment for apostasy – such a well-kept secret till blood seeped down my legs and I learnt it would do this every month till, as Mother put it, 'you stop being a woman'). I tested Him up in the sky, telling Him, if He indeed existed, to draw a line across the scratch marks by my elbow. They'd look like numbers prisoners gouge into rough walls to show how many days and months they've been in solitary.

He did nothing. You'd need more humility than I mustered to go on begging for daily bread and forgiven trespasses.

'Count your blessings and thank the Lord,' the Sunday School teacher used to say. None of us did. Prayers were about what you wanted, not what you had.

In my final school year, the first prize was an outsize blue book called *Character Sketches from Dickens*. The words were illustrated

with glossily finished, pastel pictures by Harold Copping pre-
served by translucent paper from touching ordinary wordy
pages. Gangly Edith Penny, beloved by teachers unaware she
smoked every day behind the outside lavatories, passed round
the book for us to admire but not turn the pages. So we saw only
Peggotty and Little Em'ly with her red cheeks and light-brown
ringlets sitting on the steps of an upturned houseboat on clean
beige sand.

Edith Penny left the book in the cloakroom, where I found it
and moved it, just a little. Even then I never looked at the other
pictures.

The second prize was mine: *Palgrave's Golden Treasury*. Only
one coloured illustration inside the soft cover, a lady playing
the piano with closed eyes to a man who slept – or was dead.
Alfred Lord Tennyson, appearing like an elderly Jesus, formed
a black-and-white frontispiece. He wrote *Idylls of the King* – por-
traits, I imagined, of King George V lying lazily on a couch in
soft curly-toed shoes. On the very last page was Father's poem:
'I am the captain of my soul', 'Invictus'.

> Beyond this place of wrath and tears
> Looms but the Horror of the shade.

Righty-oh.

The prize with its dream of idleness and pleasure mingled
with the bright-moon tunes from Aunty Gertie's upright piano,
even though 'Come into the Garden, Maud' was only a poem
there and never sang out; even though *The Eve of St Agnes* was
omitted; even though 'Invictus' brought up the end, like Hol-
man Hunt's predatory Jesus in *The Light of the World* barring the

way to pleasant syrupy lands. Sometimes – but rarely – you can ignore the end of a book.

Second is nowhere.

Edith Penny left for a better school in Birmingham, smoking her way through Highers. She must have found her Peggotty and Little Em'ly – or sauntered off uncaring – she never loved books, despite their doing well by her.

And I?

I passed the School Certificate with Credit.

What does this certify?

You've finished thinking.

Leaving saves the three guineas a term your Mother has to pay. 'School Cert's more than enough for any girl.'

I went to work in an office, checking addresses of ratepayers for the Council, though Aunty Gertie told me never to do this and I'd promised faithfully not to.

Early this year, I did the Whitsun sale at Rackhams. Usually I walk briskly up the left side of the escalator, not slouching on to the first step and lazily leaning on the handrail. But this time I happened to stand still while my feet carried me through Household Linen and Kitchen Items to 'Fashions'. Coming down the other escalator was a stout woman with brown, satisfied face framed by permed ginger hair. I saw her tight, splay-ribbed yellow jumper but nothing below the escalator rail. Eyes locked. Something familiar.

'Hello,' she said as we rattled past. 'Swottypotty, is it you?'

'Molly Donoghue,' I said.

No time for more. She spoke over her shoulder to a tall young couple, who swivelled their heads. I heard her say, 'A girl from school yonks ago; smart.'

Yonks?

I could have dashed down the other side to catch her, ask what and how she did. Had she kept her badge as form monitor, and did I hear 'smart'?

She too could have turned and returned: then I'd have seen she was wearing a leather mini-skirt around bulgy thighs. No sense of what's appropriate to her age.

Early December 1975

'Nights are drawing in,' remarks an old man in the bus shelter. The immigrant Pakistani women turn away, hidden in their scarves and frippery. 'It's cold enough for Christmas.'

As mindless as comment on early Easter, Whit, cool August Bank Holiday, Guy Fawkes again.

I say nothing. I'm not one for small talk.

According to Phyllis, I mention the war too often. I make it sound like a fairground lark, fun on the big-dipper.

'No one wants a war,' I said. 'We had no choice.'

Phyllis gave me her arch look, then rested demanding eyes on Maud.

'It wasn't all japes,' I said. 'I doubt you young people would have stood it a week.'

Is this the past Maud thinks I should recapture, what the notebooks are for? Doubtful: she's shown hardly any interest, her long education taught her nothing.

The whole nation with her in that. You'd think the war never happened, the little it's remembered, the little good it did us. Better to have lost the war, have done with it there and then. We could still have gone on moaning about the weather.

War isn't the only violence: surely you know, Maud?

Not the only type, but the cleanest.

My war

War was women's as much as men's. Allocating and filing ration books and coupons wasn't the agitation of a fighter pilot, but it was *war*-work demanded by the nation. Fighter pilot, Spitfire Woman and office menial might be blasted to smithereens in the air or on the earth.

Welsh Muriel sat beside me in the Ministry of Food Office. We'd both been conscripted into the work. Pleasant on the bench, making quiet chat as she prepared special ration books for bombed-out families and counted out points, while I separated buff from blue and checked for illegal duplicates. We enjoyed a smoke and a joke then – what was the sausage made of when there was no meat?

Laughing ourselves silly at a car driving along with a great gas balloon in a wooden cradle on its roof. Any minute we expected it to rise from the road and flee to the stars.

Once we watched a bomb whoosh out of the purple-black night sky. We saw the Bull Ring in flames in the distance.

Muriel was good company at the time. Why wouldn't she be? Young, cheery, and shallow, she greeted any nasty gossip with 'it takes all sorts'. She hadn't read *How Green Was My Valley* – I thought everyone Welsh read that. Couldn't get away from Ebbw Vale fast enough, even if only to the Midlands.

Air jangled when bombs were falling and exploding. Dim lights reflected on walls as the Food Office shuddered; blackouts trembled against windows. Dust and plaster fell on ration books, our Rembrandt Utility frocks and coiled-up hair, and we, the Food Office girls, giggled excitedly. Nervously too.

I danced inside.

It was smelly and crowded in the Anderson air-raid shelter where we hurried when the siren sounded from the Town Hall. But the eager, jostling bonhomie and crush of strangers clutching gas masks and family trinkets were exhilarating all the same. Above the whispering we could hear fighter planes revving, circling and shaking the earth.

After work I'd stumble home in fog or dark over sandbags and through bomb rubble to Mother's house, hearing Italians singing way over in the internee camp. I'd catch in my lungs the thrill of searchlights and sudden fires.

One would have to be dead not to feel alive. You didn't need a front seat at the Battle of Britain.

Olive and Rachel shared food parcels from America and Northern Rhodesia. I brought in Canadian tea from Uncle Harry (Mother said it tasted like stinging nettles and spat it out into a serviette).

We didn't share nylons. Those without them could stain their legs with onion skins, then draw a line with eyebrow pencil down their calves (though bare legs made no swishing noise when crossed). We all did it in summer. Told to.

'Don't you know there's a war on?'

We did know. Of course we did. We were independent and smart, young and nice looking, even if patched and mended.

I remember the day I shared the Canadian tea because a bomb

fell in a nearby field. I went to see it with other girls from the Food Office. With Muriel and Olive and Rachel and Edna.

Parts of dead cows lay up the sides of the shallow hole it made. A worn shoe in the dirt and some furred wood still smoking. On the edge, boys from the evacuated public school pointed enthusiastically.

'Bostin!' said Rachel who was from Ladywood.

My spirits accelerated. I wanted to be away to London where more than just cows exploded. Where sugar flowed in gutters when the Tate and Lyle warehouse was struck: one could lick the pavements for bliss as the molten sugar hardened. Where a cathedral floated above the Blitz in a magic sky. Where women in square shoulders were just as strong as men. Where rollicking transformations took place, and boys with a teeny bit of gumption were heroes, and pushy girls became ladies. (So I learnt later. How could I know then?)

I'd stay as long as I had to in the Midlands. Saving up to take a course in something, Pitman I suppose, to make me something more. Then get away as soon as ever. In London I'd step out to hear Myra Hess play Mendelssohn at lunchtime concerts in the National Gallery. Aunty Gertie would have approved. Hold to independence, she'd said. Never work in an office.

'Ring out, wild London bells.'

I was vague on details in my single-pleated best skirt doing war-work, but I yearned for a smart flat in Kensington or Chelsea as fiercely as Hardy's Jude for his snarling Christminster – or cousin Clare for county doctors and trunk-loads of admiration. Oh to come from somewhere else, to be going to a place far away. Somewhere where the air was crisp and the talk witty, brittle and allusive. Not even Solihull would do.

You don't forgive a person for messing this up.

You don't forgive your country for fooling you either.

The child's war

Not that a child has one. So coddled. But Maud must want me to create memories. She can't remember anything herself. I'm sure of it: almost sure. I could tell if she knew.

It had to be a girl. Though, out of superstition in that ninth month, I'd said to cousin Clare, 'I incline to a boy.' (In wartime everyone's superstitious: Spitfire pilots look backwards twice at the sun; I once saw an eagle's claw falls from a dead soldier's pocket.)

'I don't know,' Clare said, 'boys are so loud and rough, and they leave you quickly.'

She had two quiet boys whom she sent off to boarding school where Nick had been miserable and been 'made a man of' (not that I could see). I had my girl and felt cheated – as you do when you try fibbing to Fortune.

In the last months I took special care, even abandoning cigarettes that stunt growth, though there were plenty of the cheap sort around and I gagging for a smoke. I didn't bend or lift violently. Nothing would kill it, but it might be deformed and enter the world with a pointy head, floppy limbs or addled mind, and I be left to care for it.

I carried a small flannel in a plastic pouch. Rachel and Olive teased me: 'You planning to bleach your bones?'

'She may look clean but . . .' shouted war posters against syphilis and gonorrhoea. (Ah, yes. 'She' – she with the dirt and disease, contaminating our pure boys.)

I avoided the canteen, hating the sight of streaked plates, spit-coated debris, the residue of what even in those meagre days just couldn't be swallowed. Most months, summer or winter, the girls had colds and their eating clogged with catarrh as they chewed and gulped down bloater-paste sandwiches, semolina pudding and phlegmy tapioca. Even in rain I'd walk up and down over the rubble-filled gaps in the terraces to avoid hearing their fleshy swallowing.

'A shame to see cities blasted,' said Olive, eyeing the cement clinging to my shoes when I returned from struggling through bomb damage.

'There's more than cities hollowed out,' I said.

She looked at me sharpish, then let her eyes swivel down to just below my waist. I moved my hand to show a ring on the ring finger. I could have ripped open my blouse to display the frozen lump of heart. But there was enough drama in the world just then.

What of the thing that kicked inside me, that moved its tape-worm arms? They say it hears music. Does it scream too? When did its brain sever from mine? Did it know – there snugly inside – or not so snugly – what I knew, feel what I felt in the final heavy weeks?

How about those limbless early ones? How about then, Maud?

If it did know and feel, and, if it went on feeding on me and my thoughts and never quite severed itself from what nourished it, did it find it easy to forgive?

Being made – of course I mean, the injustice of being born, created by someone else's will.

How dare we force another person to live?

*

'Contractions are like big period pains,' said the tall, lean doctor. Why wasn't he at the front tending war wounded instead of prancing round among girls? He should have been ashamed.

I was slim but for the great lump draped in Golden-Stripe Utility cotton. Yet, to me, all my body appeared amorphous beside this vain chap with his neat beard and tightly curled, greying hair. Kindly condescending at first in that exasperating mode of educated men, till I said, 'I don't want to breastfeed. The milk oozes on to one's blouse.' (To be provoking is all that's left to women, did he know nothing?) He eyed me scornfully.

A long agony. Elephants' labour can take days. Father's encyclopedia made a cosy picture of cows circling the poor trumpeting mother in the dark night when she and her calf slowly parted. Not so cosy for humans. After twelve hours alone, I didn't care about pointy heads or floppy limbs.

The Black Country midwife came by to tell me to stop bawling. 'Yer can't carry on like that 'ere.'

She saw tears and thought I cried for pain. 'Over soon, duck.'

Twenty-four hours on and its purple, rubbery head squeezed out, slime attached to bits of white, scrubby hair.

'What is it?'

'A babby. Gull.'

'A girl?' I said.

The midwife – was she even a midwife? – dumped the blotched bundle on my chest, rolled up in a dirty green sheet.

'Can you clean it up?'

'Don't y'know there's a war on?' she said – inevitably – as she waddled out. People had to make do, even if they thought themselves la-di-dah.

*

In the ward with other girls wearing their new wedding bands – or curtain rings – some recovering from a dread the baby would be the wrong colour. There were Americans posted in camps nearby with their despised but rather good-looking Negro soldiers.

Rachel briefly stepped out with a white one from Minnesota. When she didn't spread her legs quickly enough – she'd been chatting and smoking – he interrupted, 'Shut the fuck up, bitch,' and marched off.

She snorted when she told the tale. Worse things than vulgar words.

No one was caught out here. Ginger hair can happen to anyone.

We were to get over it quickly: all working girls from offices and munitions factories. The babies were left out on the verandah; the little things made sneezing noises when carried back to the ward. A chilly May.

Relief at the colour of their infants tickled the new mothers. 'British War Relief from the Yanks.' That doubled them up, pulling at stitches. When silenced by Matron, they snuffled into their bedclothes like schoolgirls on cheap cider.

'No such bloody luck,' giggled one, remembering the Yanks joke while gulping down the sugary tea.

'Where's he fighting, m'luv?' said ginger boy's mother.

Months later I met her again. She knew a medium who could contact the dead. She urged on me a leaflet addressed to 'War Widows', given by her sister who'd lost her man in a sub.

'Keep away from me,' I muttered under my breath. 'Don't meddle with my dead.'

I stalked out of the maternity hospital into the street with my wailing bundle. Handed me by the slatternly 'midwife', who expected something from the man collecting his woman, a coin, a bit of chocolate.

But so many husbands were away. As Matron disapprovingly said to us that cold May morning, 'It's a lonely time to bring new life into a bad world.'

As if those girls with curtain rings twisted on their fingers had said to themselves, 'Now is just the moment to be in the family way.'

Mother was tied up with Bertie Shaw whom she, so feckless, had to 'care for'. I'd expected cousin Clare: she'd promised. But her work in the hospital (she hated sick people, even her own mother), I had to understand – no one knew how sorry ... She'd taken off a day already for me and one when Roger came a fortnight ago – she was soppy on the blighter. Roger, of whom we heard no more.

'I'm here at the gate alone.'

I called her 'Maud'. Perhaps I hoped one day the child I'd borne would come into the garden and lie down among lilies, roses, violets and pimpernels. And leave the gate open for her mother.

'She needs another,' Olive said when she stood with me in the Registry for Births and Deaths. (A kind thing, for we weren't relatives or really friends, just workers at the same bench.) 'Another name.'

'Gertrude,' I said.

'No one's called Gertie nowadays,' said Olive. 'She wouldn't thank you.'

Your mother's name?

'No,' I said, but Olive, a stickler for convention despite a wartime flightiness, told the Registrar I wanted it.

Mother was quite pleased when she heard. It was the custom, said Uncle Harry. 'Maud Isobel.' Father sometimes called Mother 'Isabella', especially when she put on her 'Spanish' dress; Clare had 'Aunt Izzy'. When I signed the child on for council school and free milk, I left off the 'Isobel'. Only 'Maud'.

'Come into the garden.'

A pound a week for me, a war widow, seven shillings for the child. Why need a hot dinner with no man coming home to eat it? No call for red meat: an occasional herring, perhaps a piece of haddock.

Better than the Great War, observed Uncle Harry. A magistrate had to keep certifying the child was living for a woman to receive extra. In *that* war, 'ladies' were alarmed that the government proposed *any* pensions for soldiers' widows. Why? Because the 'ladies' would find themselves short of servants. This was said in the newspaper in black and white.

I stood in the office dealing with pensions. The woman in the queue ahead of me broke down. She couldn't bear the shabby begging.

'No point wailing,' remarked someone behind. Even with three boys and a sickly girl to feed with a bit of tripe and pig's trotter, and she so down-at-heel and on the verge with working her skinny fingers to the bone – it simply doesn't do.

In the embarrassed heat of her outburst, the rest of us mostly looked sideways, though the dirty window gave no view.

She brought out a creased photograph of herself and her dead man: two faded sepia lovers posed clasping hands in front of a flowered screen with a sundial.

'There's comfort,' as Welsh Muriel was always saying when

anyone on the benches ended an anecdote with the saving 'you have to laugh' or 'where there's life . . .'

For all her hysteria, the woman got nothing more out of the War Office, though perhaps, like phlegm, it's good to cough up bitterness.

There's thousands worse off than you, scream the walls. If you think Our Decision wrong, try the War Pensions' Appeal Tribunal. All applications acknowledged. Try the Royal British Legion.

If you need more milk, keep a goat in the front garden. Goats aren't rationed.

I held my girl in a curled warm ball. Hazy in contours, full of powdered milk, fragile, twirly ears with a touch of pink. Through my dark lashes I saw white ones covering blue, half-closed eyes. Those pale lashes had been growing in my womb. Not *my* lashes. All those months, growing without my knowledge or permission.

What did I feel? Resentment, anger, bitterness? Just jealousy I think.

Now, while armies fought and flotillas were sunk and atom bombs blasted whole regions, and stones and bricks rained down over cities from Coventry to Tokyo to Dresden, and everyone else was excited and febrile from the movements of fighting and glamorous danger, I was stuck firm 'at home', a limpet to a rock. No dog to shake me off like a flea.

When ashes and debris piled up, and a hollow peace followed England's pyrrhic victory, no soldier with his knapsack of tin cutlery, faded letters and folded photos came to march me out of my prison-house to a sparkling world of London streets. Where sugar and gold flowed down pavements. And people strolled about without encumbrances.

Is this the war you wished to hear about, Maud? Your war. The one I gave you. And you gave me.

Mid-December 1975

Maud said, 'Why don't we eat Christmas dinner in a restaurant? It would save bother.'

'No. Women alone are always given the worst table. We'll stay at home.'

Our 'home'

This pebble-dashed half-house, this 'home' came with the child.

Near term, I needed a place – quickly, for Mother wasn't one for babies.

'I always seem to hold them the wrong way,' she giggled to Uncle Harry.

Out of the question to stay with her. Besides, she'd already agreed to put up three men invalided from the air force. Nice reserved men who wouldn't cry and disturb her at night. Two would fit into the room I once shared with Clare.

I sought to make the 'home' habitable. Didn't I know, even then, it would always play practical jokes on me from inside its walls?

'I wish you were dead,' I once said aloud.

But I went on serving it. On splintering window ledges I put black paint. Surplus to army requirements, of such poor quality it bubbled in the first faint summer sun. Where bubbles burst, old pre-war khaki showed. On stairs and skirting boards, I stripped the peeling paint, chipping it with a little metal chisel, while my mind watched other hands ripping up the boards and burning the wood in a pyre. I leant awkwardly from my swollen ankles over the immense bulge, then with a little more ease when the bulge had gone, leaving only spongy flesh. I never learnt to plaster over old plaster, but, years on, I discovered a liquid that loosened paint.

Yet the effort had been the point: a combat with the house's rusted nails, disintegrating plaster and splintering wood. When tears welled up, I squashed them back with my knuckles. (You must if you want to avoid crumbling. And I did. Only crumble if someone's outside to squash you into human form again.)

When the sitting room needed re-papering, I let Hugh do it, using a restrained, embossed type – now in sunlight the joins are darker than the rest: best keep curtains closed.

Hugh was my longest lodger when every spare bed was demanded in semi and terrace. His six shillings came in handy. He was quiet and didn't take too much hot water for his Sunday bath, so I didn't have to share it.

You don't know what even a quiet man does in the tub.

Long after he'd moved to other digs, carrying away his green cardboard case with its fraying leather straps, he'd come back to do odd jobs, like re-enamelling the bath, and stay for tea. He gave me presents, a silvery bangle and a rose bush in a cardboard box. He admired things about me: my way of speaking and my handwriting – like calligraphy, he said.

He was crumpled into a desk job at the Post Office when he should have been away at war making men stand ramrod straight and bang boots on metalled ground. A pleasant stocky man who cracked his knuckles, jingled coins in his pocket and called himself a 'bloke'.

After two beers or sherries, he'd want to recite 'There's a one-eyed yellow idol to the north of Khatmandu'. He had a voice made rough and raspy by all the shouting he'd done in the army before being invalided out to sit in shame behind the Post Office desk.

He'd ask me to go with him to the pictures. I did once, to see *Scott of the Antarctic*. I didn't go again. Not easy to get anyone to stay with Maud, and I made excuses after the sitting room was papered and the bath enamelled. I had to. Visits from any man would be noticed and pop would go my little pension. You cuckold the state at your peril. It punishes even the shadow of the act.

In any case, by now I'd been too long in female company to accept male sounds, the splash and gurgle in a lavatory or throat. A hand on my thigh. For that's what having a man around means.

Before we were 'demobbed' I'd told Muriel and Olive I'd never impose some chap off the streets on the child.

Muriel shrugged. 'Suit yourself,' she said, laughing. 'It's thin pickings out there and best pick while you can.'

Much later I laid a plain carpet over the cheap boards in the hallway and sitting room and on the stairs (no brass rods on the steps, just glue underneath). I sold part of the three-piece suite (paid for by Uncle Harry in a black-market deal) and bought a wing chair, pale blue, with faint lighter stripes, navy cording, a hint of brocade. On it now, a small cushion Maud embroidered years ago with red, white and blue flowers, the silks left over from her Coronation sampler. Two lamps from a jumble sale to avoid a harsh central light.

Years after the war, when there were Clean Air Acts, we were told to burn expensive smokeless fuel. I blocked off the sitting-room chimney with cream-painted wood; on it three electric bars above a red bulb inside a contoured replica of coals. To the left I placed a fireside companion – in memory.

'Very *mod*ern,' said cousin Clare when I told her. (Stressing the first syllable for irony. No need, I thought, I trapped the tone years back.)

Saves labour and mess, no occasion to 'keep the home fires burning' any more.

Yet I miss coal in the grate, the soot and ashes in hair and nails.

So does Maud. One of her few opinions on the house. She'd watch me as I held the newspaper against the grate with both hands to tease a flame from thin splinters of wood and blocks of papery coal. Excited when a page caught fire and flew away up the chimney to spark its unfinished stories in the winter air.

The chimney's still there, hiding desiccated birds. Some days wind pushes against the wood.

Facing the window, I've hung three Audubon drawings of water birds bought after the war in a WI sale of work.

It's a fine line. Through mean eyes, these birds might be no different from three flying plaster ducks on an anaglypta magnolia wall on a council estate. Had bald Melinda, who came to tea bringing fancy cakes (Maud said they were too sugary), looked through malicious eyes and seen such common ducks instead of Audubon birds? Melinda, whom I met in the park one sunny day and invited in for tea, Melinda who never asked me back.

I wasn't born yesterday, she might have said. I know what I know.

At Feathermore House, a stately home opened twice a year for lower orders to ogle, I saw three plaster ducks on a high ceiling above Chinese wallpaper.

A different class or race of duck?

Near the hatch I've placed my Dudley grandmother's silver-paper picture: a languishing lady in crinoline by a weeping willow, the black silhouette of a gentleman hurrying towards her. Mother didn't want the 'old-fashioned thing' on the wall, not even in the bedroom used by the 'girls'.

One day she brought it over wrapped in newspaper. 'I'm giving you this,' she said. 'You always liked it. I can put something else in the frame when war's over.'

Later I gave it a bluish border and pale wood surround, so it matches the Audubon birds.

Aunty Gertie's *Ophelia* hangs on my bedroom wall. Her black frame's unbecoming, but I've not changed it. I stare at it till my eyes blur into water.

Wide partition doors lead from sitting into dining room. I leave them open to frame the table and six leatherette chairs. Cheap but with an antique patina from much polishing. Partly covered in lace mats, the table's shiny surface mirrors two plated-silver candlesticks and a glazed blue vase. When I had people to tea – Olive or Rachel perhaps – they'd sit on the leatherette chairs and notice the candlesticks and cut rose in the blue vase. Even bald Melinda, just once, admired.

By the partition doors, a white china pot decorated with small blue flowers holding a delicate, poisonous philodendron. Great veined heart-shaped leaves droop from a sturdy stem, catching the sun shimmering through the net curtains. Towards evening they make crazy-paving shadows on the papered wall, framed in a trapezium. Shadow leaves burst as from a single stem, some faint, some clear and dark, lovelier than the real ones. Swags of something mysterious beyond, no harsh tangle just perfect greening flatness, a slow fading on the carpet.

In such moments, the small rooms can seem rich, nothing shrieking or even faintly disturbing, nothing to prick half-closed eyes. A dusky kind of grace.

Just occasionally. As I say, at subduing sepia twilight. Eyes going unfocused, so there's a gap in the world.

Quick, catch the tasteful grey shadows – before they turn to dun.

If the trick fails, all collapses. The glazed china vase tips over to reveal shame at its bottom, the rose decays, the plated-silver candlesticks tarnish, snarl and spot, the curtains mottle and fray. The table with rounded legs, the leatherette chairs, kept like new for some magic never-to-be dinner party, deform and wrinkle, the philodendron grows dusty and mean.

Whose fault is this shabby half-house on the fringe of the world?

Uncle Harry's, Clare's, mine, Maud's?

I must take some blame. I bought it. Uncle Harry signing the papers.

Cheaper than renting in the long run – everyone said so – there was no choice, all renters would buy if they could, declared Uncle Harry, but they aren't so fortunate as to inherit a little money.

I bought 14 Ackroyd Close. A knot that couldn't be undone, a hard route between walls.

You make your bed, or the bed makes you. You pull the feathers over to keep yourself warm or smother yourself.

'Bless this house, O Lord, we pray,' trilled Vera Lynn, 'Bless these walls so firm and stout.'

Christmas 1975

The dinner was ready and hot in the oven, the hen done to a turn, roast potatoes dry, Brussels sprouts firm, apple sauce creamy. Only the gravy was wrong. Not stirred vigorously enough.

'It's all you had to do, Maud,' I said. 'Good thing you don't have a family of your own.'

She went from the kitchen to the dining room, carrying only serviettes. She could have passed them through the hatch, we both knew.

Yes, I was a touch brusque, but why not do things properly? Wash a teapot's inside before it stains; wipe dry a draining board; stir gravy with energy.

She ate little. She's not eaten with relish these last weeks, but her lacklustre picking grows more marked.

'Have some more,' I said.

'No thanks. I'm not terribly hungry.'

Making and eating food are about manners, far more than shaking hands or commenting on the weather in a bus shelter. Is she unaware?

'Dieting, Maud?' She'd adopted the fad in her last year of Grammar. 'I hope we're not starting that nonsense again. It's a bit of colour and shape you need, not shedding pounds.'

'No, really. I had a big helping of sprouts and apple sauce. You saw.'

'Don't you ever get hungry, dear?'

'I think I would if I ate more.'

No answer to that.

On the side of her plate, a half-open gravy lump revealed uncooked flour. I'd have swallowed it, not to let myself down.

I admit, there was chill air cooling our dinner. I was hurt. For, on Christmas Eve, Maud chose to visit Phyllis, a girl who can't care tuppence for her. Why doesn't she wilt under the treachery?

'She asked me.'

'She should be with *his* family.'

'She'll be with them for Boxing Day.'

'Have you no pride, Maud?'

'Don't be silly.' Her words were sharper than her tone. 'She isn't tied to him,' she added.

'A fine beginning for marriage. Giving his name and money to someone who doesn't care to be "tied". I've always thought Phyllis selfish, as you know.'

'She'll go on working. She won't live off him. I don't see why they shouldn't be happy.'

I could tell her. Without scheming, Phyllis will be bored in a trice.

'If there's a child she'll stop soon enough. Or is she too modern for that?'

'She won't give up her job. She can stagger her teaching.'

'I'd have thought even Phyllis would take motherhood seriously.'

Maud blushed before answering, always a sign she knows I know what she's about. 'She has a life too,' she said. 'She'll be a better parent for not sacrificing herself.'

After a pause, I said, 'I've deserved this.'

Is motherhood no 'life', a weak form of unemployment?

If I'd protested, we'd have crescendoed. Maud would have been forced to respond, 'Don't excite yourself. I didn't mean to offend you.' And I would either have replied, 'I know you didn't, dear, and never mind and let's forget it,' or, 'Oh yes you did, and you have, and that's all there is to say.'

In the past I may have uttered unwelcome truths – 'I'm all you've got, Maud,' or, 'I've had little enough joy from you' – I don't set up for niceness. But I have limits: the word 'sacrifice' never passes *my* lips.

A throbbing in my head combined with spasms of indigestion I've started to feel these last wintry months. Maud helped me to a chair, then fetched two aspirins and a glass of water. She held the glass while I put the pills in my mouth.

'You really intend to go?' I said.

'You can manage just this once, can't you?'

'Of course, I'll manage. I've managed all my life.'

'Only tonight,' she pleaded. 'She'll be married soon.'

'Am I so stupid, Maud?'

She didn't reply.

Alone, I switched on the wireless. An opera quiz on the Home Service: a typically cheap way for the BBC to fill time, asking questions for some suave know-alls in London to answer.

'Listen, you out there in the North and Midlands, how sad you can't be like me, Elizabeth Forbes, and have a wealth of cultured information at your classy fingertips.'

'What was the opera with which Mario and Grisi inaugurated the new Royal Opera House in 1858?'

I know, miss, please I know. *The Huguenots* (and that's how you pronounce it, you provincial dimwits).

'What did you talk about, Maud,' I asked when she came in just before midnight.

'School business. Her wedding. Ordinary things.' She reddened as she does so easily; then her hair seems paler, her scalp pinker.

What could they have done? Two spinsters for the last time drinking sherry in Phyllis's egg-cup glasses with colours sunk in the bottom? Did they eat smoked oysters on little biscuits, as they do when Phyllis feels extravagant? Or just fish paste? (She puts the paste on too soon and the crackers grow soggy.)

'Not sherry,' she said, when I caught the alcohol on her breath. 'Phyllis gave me a gin with vermouth. It's a drink Ray introduced her to. I didn't like it.'

'I expect it was valedictory,' I said.

Maud looked away. Not before I'd seen her eyes shining.

Will Phyllis take to the Coventry house those little glasses, her half-full box of biscuits and unopened tins of oysters? Will he enjoy them as Phyllis and Maud did, the lanky sandman who's marrying a spinster? Or will he sit sullenly apart with his gin and vermouth and wonder what he's done and why?

Will she make him run through yellow irises on his pale male legs?

On Boxing Day, I told Maud to expel the prickly, almost berryless holly cluttering the house. She brings it from school, a leftover from someone else's decorations. I let her put it up, but no need for it to stay gathering dust.

The cards went too. The curt printed one from Clare, Nick and the boys, with a picture of their happy family group holding skis against a flecked white background. Such embalmed lies these posing photos tell: families are always successful until they aren't.

One from Phyllis – I saw the envelope. (Maud removed it because the message was written straight on the card – typical Phyllis, ignorant of the fact you need a separate sheet of paper for more than a greeting.)

The other few were limp, tawdry, with pictures like toffee-tin lids, especially Muriel's.

So, we begin the sullen days.

I stayed in bed much of yesterday. Overcast sky, layer upon layer of thick grey cloud shutting in the cul-de-sac.

I got up only to write the thank-you letter to Muriel for her card. I use good Basildon Bond paper. We haven't met in donkey's years. She may have been back to England – or Wales I suppose if she could bear Ebbw Vale. If so, she hasn't told me. No matter, our skimpy friendship wouldn't stand a face-to-face.

'Muriel seems to know an awful lot about the country for someone in New Zealand.'

'She'll have a telly. She'll see our news.'

'I don't think so. England isn't the centre of the world. Not now.'

Maud shrugged.

I intended describing a charity excursion to Feathermore House, but what to tell? People had chatted when the guide recited anecdotes of the Civil War – attentive when she spoke of the absent family tanning themselves on a yacht off the Côte d'Azur. (I imagined this; the guide was tight-lipped about the owners' present whereabouts. For all I knew, they skulked in silk and velvet finery behind the closed baize doors.)

I'd begun the letter, then stopped. Instead I'd turned to this cheap notebook. Now, taking it up again, I resorted to platitudes. 'I do hope you've all had a jolly Christmas down under, Muriel and Ken.'

I asked about their new grandchild.

She'll probably enclose a snap next year. She isn't sensitive.

I look over at Maud's pallid tapered fingers as we wait for New Year at midnight. They lean backwards at the first joint. I noticed this when she held a cigarette just before raising it to her lips. Nothing like that in my family.

Perhaps it's the dim lateness but in the pastel light there seems something refined in her movement, the delicate touch of fingers on a flushed face. I let my eyes settle there, then turn away. (She refuses to use the blue rubber gloves when washing up, not liking the clammy smell afterwards, yet her hands stay smooth.)

I'm hot. Without the electric fire, it's chilly but, when on, it suffocates the room. A musty smell as if cooking old moths and flies – as I suppose it is.

'I feel almost feverish, Maud,' I say near midnight. 'It's not just the fire. Perhaps the start of another headache.' I press my forehead but my hand is warm against it. 'You feel.'

She kneels on one leg by my chair. Skirts are so short now that modesty's fled, but she keeps hers as unfashionably long as possible. A downiness about her shins, as about her cheeks; so she doesn't often need to shave – good since she nicks the skin in her armpits when using the safety razor.

Her movements in her roomy skirts are easy to make, though clumsy to watch. Can legs be cack-handed?

I look in her face. She glances away. Something just beyond

memory stirs, but I can't catch it. Her fingers are hot. Not cool as I'd expected.

'You seem fine,' she says. 'Hardly warm. You're probably just tired. Why not go to bed?'

'I wonder what 1976 will bring, Maud.'

'Much of the same I shouldn't wonder.'

Ding dong, ding dong booms Big Ben at midnight.

'Phyllis will be married,' I say. 'So not the same.'

Early January 1976

In France, girls like Maud are called 'Children of the Nation'; here she's just a 'war orphan'. As for widows, some cultures throw them on the husband's funeral pyre. It solves the problem of the lone woman. But one needs a man's corpse as prop for the drama.

So here we are, a widow with her war orphan.

Is that all I am, all I can dredge up from the rich vocabulary of female detritus? Shall I leave this notebook open at night, pen and ink ready, so a ghostly presence can tiptoe in and write my identity?

Worth a try.

Or maybe Phyllis would creep up during the early hours to scrawl 'witch' over my blank page with her red pencil. I know she calls me that behind my back. Would she take the trouble, now she's almost 'married'?

They burn witches, she'd say, especially in time of war.

But this isn't war now, Phyllis, just a distempered, phoney peace.

My post-war 'life'

Don't you know war's over? Take off your boots and boiler suits, girls, nip in your waist, step on high heels, hobble into glamour. There's a new world out there. Get into it.

Ah yes, the post-war world. Try to keep up.

Take the baby with you.

I did my duty, following Truby King's rules for disciplining infants. (Rachel from the Food Office passed on *Feeding and Care of Baby* since she'd no use for it – then or ever.) Night-time wails mustn't interrupt the rigid schedule of feeding and leaving. That way you breed an obedient child.

Every day I soaked terry-towelling nappies and Harrington squares, whitening them with cheap bleach. The whole house lay in that bucket, the smell so nauseous I retched when facing it at its strongest in early morning, the lodgers still in bed.

Using the entire soap ration, I left no stain on the threadbare stuff. My hands grew flabby and coarse.

'For goodness' sake, Joan,' said Clare, 'buy shaving soap. All the girls do. There's an extra ration of that.'

I wouldn't dare. The shopkeeper would suspect.

I replaced the slightest body odour with a fragrance of talc and vaseline.

'There's waste of vaseline,' said Muriel when she visited after we finished work and I'd picked up Maud from nursery. 'Better mixing it with coal-dust for your lashes. It makes them shiny.'

Muriel didn't fancy babies just then. None of us did. Nobody needed them. I tried to imagine cousin Clare coping with my life.

'Darling, I'd find a rich man,' I heard her interrupt way before I'd begun to capture the tedium.

'You can put babies up for adoption,' said Rachel. 'There's posh women wanting them without the bother. But you have to do it quick before they're too big to be sweet.'

I said, did she have an address? She stared at me, then grimaced and walked off.

I pushed dried egg and rationed butter into the child. Not sickly except in that terrible winter of '47 when she was still tiny, good food was scarce and I skimped on heating. She caught bronchitis and whooping cough, and such a fierce dose of measles it might have carried her off.

Clare looked at me quizzically when I told her.

She'd grow up, I knew that, just as I'd known she'd be born. I remembered the ferocity of the foetus, that darkness moving inside me with its white floating hair and lashes. The child lacked that force, but, tepidly, it still resolved to stay.

Colds were perpetual, noses ran thick and thin liquid. With my nails I scraped the slimed hankies. I washed the white flannel vests with strong harsh soap to kill lice and fleas.

When the grey socks holed, I darned them, positioning my wooden mushroom under the worn part, pricking the thin wool to catch the unravelling spot, then weaving strands until the whole skilful web made the sock even stronger than before. I mended the Fair Isle jumper till it grew hot and unbreathing, as thick and matted as the coat on a Highland cow.

No one can accuse me of not trying. Nothing so threadbare as trying: did I ever tell you that, Maud?

I made a constant effort. I was pricked by 'duty', brought up on it: from chapel and church, from council and high school. I know what duty is and how it works.

Like a virus in the vein.

While I still had my 'little job' – as Uncle Harry called my work in the Food Office, though it took up nine hours of every weekday and Saturday mornings – the child was swaddled into silence in the free nursery. But, with fighting over, women were dismissed and nurseries closed. Mothers and babies were cast off together into their new life.

I tried to keep myself smart. While war lasted, I'd taken sour instruction from Mrs Sew-and-Sew. Then, when it petered out, the New Look came in. I bought a copy of *Vogue*, costing an arm and leg: posh Mrs Exeter spoke from the glossy pages direct to us in our drab kitchenettes. Follow my advice, ladies, and you shabby ones can compensate for the silks, satins and furs you lack. Change the collars, cuffs and lining, and the day dress or evening cape, bought or inherited twenty years ago, becomes as good as new. Play up, play down, make the yellowing of advancing years into mellowing. Never once over the age of fifty wear a coat or mackintosh with a hood.

I cut out her advice, adding it to pieces from other cheaper magazines. I stuck them into a scrapbook using thumb-pressed silver paper to hide the maudlin kittens on the cover. (I don't remember binning the scrapbook, but I must have. What did I think when I compiled it? Good thing one doesn't meet one's early self later in life – I'd have something sharp to say to her if I did. Better pull socks up rather than darn them, for a start.)

I sewed because I had to. Not taking even skimpy pleasure. Mother once had a decent treadle sewing machine, 'lost' in the move along with everything else she had no use for. I used the manual one Aunty Gertie bequeathed me. Turning away at the wheel, I altered clothes, added tucks and pleats, raised waists and lowered shoulders, tightened and let out skirts, moved hems up and down the leg, as instructed year by year. Grimly working with pins clasped between lips.

Nothing fancy despite the scrapbook. Though I did once make a short coat from a yellow blanket.

'What *are* you wearing,' said Mother when I turned up in it on a rare tea-time visit with Uncle Harry, Clare and a neighbour. 'What *do* you look like?' Laughing, mind, not unkind – not so anyone might catch the slap in the words.

Clare winced at the colour. 'Rather dashing,' she said.

'Make do and mend.'

'I mend anything,' sang the Umbrella Man. He sharpened knives too.

So, I ask now: why did I make this effort? What did I learn in all this war and post-war upheaval, when frugality was duty and cutting large corners patriotic?

Well?

What is left when you no longer need to skimp and make 'glamour' by changing cuffs – or bake with dried egg and cook Woolton Pie without meat?

Not a lot of call today for thrift, prudence and frugality as supermarkets open in high streets selling cheap tasteless foreign food. Ever need to make soup with a handful of barley or light a fire with salt-sprinkled coal?

Thought not.

Mother didn't need to either: she was always a pre-war woman. She'd have laughed and said such parsimonious skills were not what make a girl marriageable or a lady respected.

Too right there.

'You should wear higher heels,' Clare told me after the war. 'You look like a WAAF.'

'You've never had it so good,' crowed the old patrician Harold Macmillan who, I wager, never entered a kitchenette to marvel at the little corner fridge or trundled a trolley down a supermarket aisle.

'So good'?

Tawdry throwaway things for throwaway times.

'Waste Littler, Paste Hitler'? Fear of waste's old hat now. Don't 'Squash the Squander Bug'. Be profligate with the world's goods and yourself. Squander, fritter, spend and throw away. We'd all be Lady Dockers if we could, lolling on mink and zebra in our brash Daimlers. No occasion for hoarding. Waste for the benefit of the nation. No need to make tucks and cut down Clarks sandals to let toes grow out. No need ever again to make a coat out of a yellow blanket.

I repeat myself: better to have lost that war and the Empire with it in one calamitous explosion. No reparations, no aftermath. Now dark men with swivelling hips and stout women in tawdry finery have moved into the semis nearest the main road. They nudge pale natives off pavements. We apologise to the air. Sorry, we say. Sorry we're still here. Sorry for All Our Past. For we're now told it wasn't 'Hope and Glory' at all and we never should have done it.

We didn't want them and they don't want us, just what we worked for through so many brutal centuries while they sat and sang in the sun, hungry maybe but warm.

Maud says, 'The Pakistani corner shop keeps open late. The man behind the counter smiles.'

It won't be for long. The smile will fade, the hours lessen.

They'll soon grumble, mark my words. Nothing will be what they hoped, and it'll be our fault they're not prosperous and happy. Their children will demand as much as any soldier swaggering home at war's end to do the hokey-cokey from a conflict that gave him a bounty of expectations – and little else.

What to do then but hobnob with spivs in flashy suits who grew fat on Blitz and bombs?

Many soldiers, even cocky ones, can't turn into civilians again after a war. As I say, better we'd lost. Then demobbed chaps wouldn't have been so cocky or the country so smug.

Same with immigrants. They can't go back to where they were, what they were.

England's the world's great comedy. To know it, you should have sat through the first childish and adolescent acts. Then you'd see, at the end, maturity's been skipped while it strutted around its Empire of 'palm and pine'.

Now in the last act the stage is full of sniggering post-war casualties, miners hoarding coal and sneering as we crawl round in the cold dark to the sound of exulting Germans and hooting French.

Who's the biggest victim? I claim nothing. I've read about those Jews in gas ovens, seen heaps of iced skeletons: no competition once the Pathé pictures obliterated our war. Nothing apocalyptic like that on this wasted shrinking island, no 'black pit'. Simply a world in tatters: the rags and bones of useless effort and spent lives.

Phyllis told Maud that her mother (with two children, mind) has worked all her life as a dental assistant and kept house without

fuss or complaint, though she cries buckets at soppy films. Bot-
tling it in, I shouldn't wonder.

'What's your point here?' I asked Maud. Of course she didn't
answer.

Mid-January 1976

Raising a child

She was slow walking and talking. I compared her with other
children when I took her to the clinic for checking and weighing
so we could get free cod liver oil and blackcurrant purée (you had
to pay for Lend-Lease orange juice). But she was well behaved
and quick when it came to training. Soon everything went into
the chipped enamelled tin pot with its red rim. So eager to do the
right thing she'd move across the floor with it stuck to her little
bottom until she could please with her product; then she stood
up on shaky legs to wait for approval.

Once in her eagerness she spilled her mess on the kitchen
floor. I smacked her on the leg and mopped it up with vinegar
and water. She whimpered for a while but was never so careless
again.

When she went to council school I paid for dinners so she
wouldn't have to stand up in class each Monday to claim free
ones. She'd rather have starved – I knew her well enough by then.

Besides, I hear what children say – and their mothers. 'Poor
child, what chance in life does she have?'

'You'd think the mother . . .'

She wasn't so out of the way. Awkward, not the type of child who did handstands and cartwheels on the lawn in front of company. Nor I. Plenty of girls like that.

I plaited her pale hair that was never unruly, never had pugs after washing in soap. Even years later, when I gave her a Toni home perm to go to university, it lay flat, so fine and light it was – and is.

She didn't cry much. Rarely made the demanding sound that wants and expects someone to comfort or do what's desired, and fast. Perhaps she remembered the day she wailed down the steps from the maternity hospital and knew the sound so awful she must indulge it sparingly.

The day I kept *my* mouth shut.

When she was seven or eight she burnt herself on the stove trying to flip over bacon with a spatula without splattering. She touched the element and seared a patch of pallid skin just above the wrist. She bit her lower lip and her eyes oozed wetness – one can't say she cried.

If I let her go, she clambered over rubble and bomb sites on the edge of the High Street. Often alone but not always, some-times close to a little group of girls carrying skipping ropes and dragging toddlers with droopy drawers.

Once she said, 'Will I have a Jenny or a Joe?' and I said, 'No.' She never questioned my 'No'.

She'd come home, knees scratched, but her frock usually intact, clutching some salvaged thing in mittened fingers.

Yes, we had to throw it away. Dusty, as like as not straight from the hands of the dead.

She was afraid of the dark. She wanted me to leave a lamp on at night on the landing. I told her Mr Churchill would come for her if we did. He rationed electricity in the war: he wouldn't tolerate waste now just because it was peacetime.

Mr Churchill became her bogeyman. She winced when she saw a picture of him with that great cigar in his mouth. Like a monstrous baby sucking a dummy.

One day she carried home a grubby issue of *The Beano*. I jettisoned it, along with the fizzing pink sherbet powder a scruffy boy gave her by the bomb site. She caught mumps: I'm sure it came from that snot-encrusted comic. (Olive said I should have baked it in the oven – best way to disinfect paper.)

Instead of *The Beano*, I bought her *Girl*. If she couldn't go to a posh school, she could at least see another world where children in the upper third got up to fun and games with illicit tuck in dormitories, then went home for hols to nannies, ponies, sailing boats and hardback books, playing in green meadows or town gardens inside smart black railings. (Even my parents' old house once had sturdy railings behind the privet hedge before war stole them.)

Girl had some humour, if not the 'Dennis the Menace' sort; Maud giggled at Lettice Leefe, the Greenest Girl in the School. Mostly it sought to extend female horizons with stories of Belle the Ballet Dancer or the smart air hostess with her 'Kitchen in the Clouds'. Each issue described a 'Famous Woman' through coloured pictures. Mary Slessor, the White Queen of Calabar, Mildred Cable of the Gobi Desert, missionaries in wide-brimmed hats tied under their chins with gauzy scarves, riding camels into heathen sands or bicycles into grateful jungles.

Maud cut out the strips and pasted them in a scrapbook, to please me. Only five or so. The rest of the scrapbook lay blank; nothing after Florence Nightingale and her Lamp.

Did she *enjoy Girl* when she wanted *The Beano*? Difficult to tell if one's bred manners in a child.

The books I chose for her – did she like *them*? *When We Were Very Young* and *A Child's Garden of Verses*. Did she ever become 'Any Reader', told at the close that the child in the other garden far away, the child who has read the poems, is 'but a child of air', so both must grow food for honeyed nostalgia while they can. Come into that Garden, Maud.

Grey Rabbit books too. Maud chewed the end of a plait and listened politely as I read to her, saying, when pressed, she loved Squirrel better than Hare and Rabbit because of her bright colour.

Just as well, for Grey Rabbit would as like as not catch myxomatosis. Classier Peter Rabbit too.

As for squirrels: native red ones were chased out by Yankee greys, bigger and more competitive, breeding over here and spreading the pox. Winning the war in their creaseless uniforms, despite Hare joining the Home Guard.

Squirrel with her pretty red dress was on her way out. Even I didn't see that then – so I couldn't tell Maud, could I?

I prepared her for the world as I knew it. How was I to know it would change – and not for the better?

At the beginning, I imposed patriotism, as Aunty Gertie did on me – though by then surely I saw the country had lost its soul and limbs and was just a bleeding torso for anyone to squat on. I bought her a Victory jigsaw puzzle and a gaudy sampler to sew for the new queen, with crown and petulant lion.

Sweet rationing ended just before the Coronation, so we'd be happy out there on the wet streets watching the gold coach trundle by with the rich young couple inside. (Maud stood in the queue a good hour for a Rolo.)

Huge genial Queen Salote of Tonga refusing an umbrella against the London rain, sitting opposite a small princeling.

Noël Coward's wicked joke:

'Who's that with her?'

'Her lunch.'

Eat up the whole procession, Salote: Queen, coach and all. Wash it down with the rain that always falls on England.

Patriotism never took on Maud; schools no longer encouraged it. She learnt 'I wandered lonely as a cloud' but not 'Oh to be in England now that April's . . .'

Good. Change with change is the way. Patriotism's threadbare, stamp on the past. Empire Day's abolished. Bye-bye Empire. Never did us any good.

Religion too. Half-heartedly, I made her kneel by the bed, put her hands together and recite, 'Now I lay me down to sleep . . .' I told her of Adam and Eve, Mary and Joseph and a few other eccentric parents. You have to know these things.

When Maud was a bit older, Clare said I should start attending church again. She'd taken it up when they moved to their Cotswold 'cottage' from London; it was what one did in the shires. She, Nick and the boys in their holidays went on a Sunday morning before meeting friends for drinks in the George. Good for children to have ritual in their lives.

'That's not ritual, just routine.'

'Oh, for God's sake,' said Clare.

Late January 1976

Is there anything wrong in making your child in your image? How much must you hate yourself if you want it to differ from what you wanted to be?

A secondary modern would have prepared Maud for the world of women's work and disrespect, but maybe in grammar school she'd change, grow confident and soar up, dragging me with her, clean out of Ackroyd Close.

Go into the garden, Maud. Pick flowers. Give your mother the bouquet she surely deserves.

I helped her pass the 11-plus. I made her listen to the Saturday play on the Home Service: the sound of unusual words and proper vowels improves the mind, like sun strengthening bones by stealth. Out shopping, I forced her to calculate change and the cost of individual items sold in bulk.

Not that I ever quite believed that education – someone else's and in a tarnished world – would truly rescue me from a humdrum life. If I occasionally indulged the pathetic dream, Phyllis could be depended on to be its spoiler.

Name tags

Grammar school was expensive: I had to buy a brown velour hat and blazer from Daniels & Sons, and two pairs of navy bloomers for gym. Other items were second-hand. I sewed Cash's name tags in everything, but left the gymslip with 'Frances Johnson' on another label. A careless act.

In a way I was as careless with myself. I always had an alien tag showing despite decent appearance and a child at the Grammar. One day a Mrs Patterson spied the tag.

She was a stout woman about my age with wide, incurious face, eyes like fried eggs in an iron frying pan. She used her accent – call it BBC, though I suspected Birmingham born – without any blanketing diffidence.

Mrs Patterson caught me outside a classy teashop when I gave her Charitable Organisation sixpence for some wretched cause. Starving Koreans, I think. Or mince pies for Irish orphans.

My stomach churned when, after a little commonplace chit-chat – I indulged in it then – she invited me to a 'gathering'.

'That would be delightful,' I said. Why wouldn't I? In brown, waisted coat with black astrakhan collar and tan suede shoes, I was dressed as one should be to say such words.

I went because I said I would: delight had nothing to do with it.

General talk, forced conviviality, nothing worth being in a room for. A niece called Madeleine was mentioned. 'Something wrong with the poor girl,' said a thin bristly woman. 'She has nervous breakdowns, you know, moody.'

Nothing that some sock-pulling-up wouldn't stop in its tracks, I thought.

'She's such a lovely girl with so many chances.'

A teaspoon clanged in a teacup.

'They say now it's to do with hormones,' said a woman with a cream-bun face, thick jam piped in for mouth, bulging fish-eyes.

'They say that about fat people,' said Mrs Patterson with more acidity than her matching garments and comfortable bulk led one to expect. 'Nobody believes in self-control any more.'

'When I was young . . .' I began but was interrupted.

'Were we ever?' said some fuchsia lips in a laughter-shaking voice.

I glanced perhaps sharply, 'What do you mean?'

'I don't think our generation was ever young. We had the war.'

I said something. No idea what. Mrs Patterson gave me a look.

Oh, that war! Don't you know . . . ? Special bit of ham for you Mrs Carruthers, but not for you, Mrs Uh or is it Miss? Oh! what a lovely war!

Yet it was not I who finished the talk by saying, 'Yes, there was some spirit then. You couldn't afford to be depressed. No time.'

It was glass-coated Mrs Patterson.

'Girls are so unhealthily self-absorbed nowadays,' said painted lips, clicking teeth.

'So true,' said cream-bun face.

At the end, though I'd suggested inventive schemes for collecting money, Mrs Patterson and the others left together without me, their feathered hats a moving tepee out of the room. Talking as if I were sitting on the moon in a high chair, my feet in dead dust.

What had I done? Had I been a hard-cheese grater rubbing everything I touched the wrong way? Had they seen a flaw? The wrong sort of face, an eye of suspicion, a judgemental wariness? My look and looking both amiss?

An obscene name tag left showing.

I stacked the used tumblers and carried them from the table to the sink for the charlady to wash. As I descended the stairs, I saw a loose cord hanging from one of the badly hemmed curtains. Someone might slip on it. They might.

*

You throw out a shoot. Out stretch the world's secateurs. Held in lobster hands.

Why this obsession – my writing proves no less – with bleached-faced Mrs Patterson, eyes and emotions as cold and rough as grouting between old bricks in winter?

Might as well be honest in a cheap, lined notebook. Why write if not to humour what lives in one's head – the green imp, a sort of blindfold devil churning up the waste from scratchy moments with its long spiteful nose?

'That's a tremendous idea,' I'd said to a proposal I'd made and someone else repeated in more self-assured tone.

'There's no j in "tremendous".' Mrs Patterson smiled and chuckled. 'Why do you say it like that, my dear?'

Why? Because I always have. Because Father and Mother said it like that. That's why.

And I answered with an imploring look, when I should have been aloof, disregarding the snakes behind the fried-egg eyes.

I excel in being humiliated, I might have said proudly. I take umbrage in my handbag wherever I go.

'Why are you so ridiculously self-centred?' cousin Clare used to laugh. 'Do you think the world turns on you?'

Ah yes. How tedious! It turns on everyone.

I'm left with a query: when did we stop wearing hats? And why? Those little hats with poison-tipped feathers.

There's only one sort of 'education' that matters in England. Why else do parents skimp on carpets, clothes and Sunday joints to pour all their pleasure into fees for Eton and Harrow and Cheltenham Ladies'? Tell me that.

'Do you want your son to sound like a navvy, your daughter like a common trollop? Of course you don't.'

That U and non-U rigmarole was a toffs' joke. Maud's generation shouldn't care about the pre-war poppycock of napkins or serviettes, vegetables or greens, pudding or dessert. Yet to speak so no one despises you on the first vowel: there's a trick to have up your sleeve and in your mouth. You don't have to write in a shabby notebook if you can speak, squash and squelch with a single sound. Everyone knows it.

On the page 'epitome' is quiet and demure: ravenous only when said aloud. Belvoir, St John, Ralph, Beaulieu, Cholmondeley: no chatting for you, Mrs Uh, with those sorts of people from those addresses.

You can write them, any old time; just don't open your vulgar mouth. If you do, be sure to dole out the smelling salts.

Maud is 'educated'

A year after she went to the Grammar, I bought her a narrow green-and-blue-patterned divan with cushions, so she could enjoy sitting in her room to read or study: a place of her own that didn't look bedroomy by day.

'You might have a few friends here,' I'd said. 'You could play Monopoly or draughts or do homework together.'

But the divan is never a couch. The cover, faded though no direct sun reaches it, isn't pulled firmly over; the extra cushions aren't scattered, just stacked like a child's blocks against the wall.

She's free to buy herself a bigger bed. There's space for it and she has the money.

'The narrow one takes smaller sheets and saves on laundry,' she says when I suggest it.

'You really could make yourself more comfortable.'

On a shelf a few French books from university days, not arranged in any order I can see: poetry of Victor Hugo, novels – *Adolphe, Thérèse Raquin* – and worn Proust volumes (don't say his name!).

Things are put away in a fitted wardrobe, I've always insisted on that; I never have to pick up a hanger or hankie from the floor. But the place doesn't feel neat, just austere.

So little speaks the occupant that, if one day she didn't come home and I prepared it for a lodger again, it would hardly look different. Yet one item screams out: on the window-sill, a small pale-blue pot with yellow irises painted on the side.

She went on a ten-days' holiday with Phyllis to France. (It was supposed to be longer, but my cold was developing into pneumonia and I needed someone in the house. As usual, Phyllis harrumphed, implying I'd maliciously curtailed their fun. 'You'd only believe it if you saw the undertaker,' I remarked.) Maud brought back a Camembert cheese, two small black mugs embossed with skewed sunflowers, and that pale-blue pot. It might have held perfume, though iris perfume isn't common.

Did Phyllis and Maud exchange scents while away? I smelt nothing when I put it to my nose.

Phyllis mentions irises more than once, waiting for me to ask. So often she hints about yellow flowery fields and Maud running loose-haired through them, then pretends surprise if I give in and raise a querying eyebrow.

Maud cavorting through a field of yellow irises! As if she would.

In any case, irises should be purple.

I encouraged her to go to university, though it meant more un-earning years. She lived with me of course, her small bedroom being comfier than stark dormitories choc-a-bloc with strange girls.

'Not worth paying to be away from home,' I told her.

Perhaps, after this further time, she'd be equipped to wrest riches from the world or pair with someone who'd deliver them. Though, by now, I could have expected it only in moments of sour levity.

She studied French! The choice bewildered me. Prattling French suits the coy seventeen-year-old. How can adults purse and pout their mouths for a language that resembles cheap-tune, smoochy music? And those silly r's. What do you do with French out in the world? In England?

Sell onions on a string from a bicycle in Kent, wearing a beret and striped jumper. Or teach.

'I was only good at French,' said Maud.

I supposed she might talk more in a tongue that said less and wasn't hers.

Years later, while dusting her bedroom, I found a couple of printed cards inside the Victor Hugo. One was an invitation for drinks, the other was to a party and had 'Bring Bird and Bottle' written in ink at the top. It couldn't have been hers.

Was Maud ever a 'Bird'? Did anyone 'bring' her with a bottle? Why would she have – and keep – the invitation?

For a while, at training college, she spoke of a boy called Clark. Nothing came of it. By then she'd met Phyllis, who felt the need to let me know, 'in passing', how Maud had for a while 'stepped out with' a short, shy boy from Shropshire looking more like a girl. He failed his teaching practice.

When she finished college and returned to the local Grammar, I said, 'Maybe now we might buy or rent a house somewhere away.' Maud agreed but her salary never came to enough.

'This one's roomy and convenient,' she says, her job close. 'The park isn't far. A good place to walk. I like the lime trees sliding down to the lake and those willows laced with mistletoe. You pointed them out one day when I was a child.'

I remember I had. She'd said, 'Christmas in the trees.'

In the past, yes, but those trees have grown old now. Hags with straggling hair, staggering to keep their feet firm.

Does she think she had a happy childhood? That would be insane.

Could she *like* this house? Would she collapse like a snail without its shell if I pushed her outside?

Once or twice I began talking to her about a future. She was unresponsive. Are her horizons so hopeless?

'Diffidence compliments others,' I'd say. 'Don't allow people you despise to make inroads. You should be ashamed to feel inferior, with your education.'

Her face would look blank, even sullen.

Is she shy because I've done something? (People blame mothers for what a child becomes. Even Myra Hindley: ask what Nellie Hindley did to her?) Had I ever shown indifference or pique with a distant look remembered for ever, but not by me? Was she chastised with a thin belt and shut alone for hours in a bedroom with a bursting bladder? (That last didn't happen to Maud – though I don't know for sure, time being so warped and fraying.) Something else?

I *do* think her eyes may be poor because I didn't stop her twitching the curtains when she had the measles. The weak eyes may blame me.

Or is it something I am, not something I did? Might I be infecting and re-infecting her like Typhoid Mary in Aberystwyth after the war, blithely unaware she was killing her customers with her polluted ice creams.

My fastidiousness?

Possibly.

At university middle-class girls imitated common accents, put on funny voices. So Maud told me.

'Why?'

She shrugged. 'It's a fashion.'

'A morbid one,' I said. Like wearing old scruffy pullovers and flat shoes when you have cashmere and high heels stashed in the wardrobe.

'What class are you, Maud? How do you think you speak?' (I couldn't make her – or me – talk poshly but she could be correct, avoid 'Me and So-and-so went . . .' or a j in tremendous.)

'I don't really know. I've never thought.'

I dare say not.

'When did you change your accent?' I asked Phyllis, provoked when she started saying 'yeah', suggesting that not just this word but all about her was assumed – and acceptable. Theatrical even.

'I've always spoken like this,' she said and sniggered.

My right hand twitched, yearning to flatten this middle-class, post-war child of the Welfare State. Her kind slouch round in dirty, unmended clothes, copying vulgar vowels and glottal stops, aping some imagined working class keener to grab colour tellies than sell the *Daily Worker* by the factory gate. When they know from the cradle that saucers for champagne have given way to flutes, tumblers and glasses are not interchangeable.

Phyllis went on a 'Ban the Bomb' march to Aldermaston. She was at the back with 'BAGGAGE' written on her bosom. Maud giggled; Phyllis is well endowed like me. 'You should come along,' she said to Maud. 'It'd look better on you.'

I was silent beyond a mutter. Neither knew the power and glory of bombs. Secretly craving a war they'd missed. We're all *conchies* now, all have White Feathers.

Ban the past, Phyllis. The future will never be as real. You'll never know what we know.

Later she travelled the common way: thinking 'back' and 'baggage' weren't the place for a girl – or 'woman' as she'd begun calling herself. I once spied *The Female Eunuch* by Maud's schoolbooks on the dining table – from Phyllis, her initials on the title page. Left for me to dip in, rumple, ravage?

I know more about sex than I once did, ignorance being thought the best guarantee of virginity in my day. Young women with the 'pill' now demand shrill 'orgasms'. Yes, yes, it's happened to me from time to time, a certain gooeyness in the knickers, an odd slithery, inadvertent tingling, then a little detonation. Even if with full orchestra and organs bellowing, with better whistling and louder ringing of bells than I've ever heard, it remains what it is: like any other demanding bodily need and satisfaction.

A body can do most things by itself. I presume Maud knows that. (You do, don't you, Maud?)

Lick menstrual blood off a penis, says *Ms* Greer? Isn't blood of one sort always there, its oxygen? Perhaps Miss Phyllis doesn't yet know. Why force such stuff on my daughter?

I know her type. Put yourself first, love yourself, have *more*.

Of what exactly?

Equality, to be sure. 'I am a woman, hear me roar.'

Roar away, dears. Equality, with the trappings of sex. Delicious! Then see if your roaring frightens off the sticky tangle of men and the men inside you. Women's Lib indeed! I know what that means. It means 'Like Men'. We want what you have: your guns and bombs, your boots, berets, nonchalance, money, authority, bad behaviour and stomping privilege.

But, girls, there's a snag: men have these things because women do the world's work of cooking, cleaning, sewing, tending and mopping up after pain and injured pride. With or without complaint.

Who's to do all that, then?

I know, miss. Don't tell.

'Other People.'

'I've dusted your Proust books,' I once said to Maud.

'It's pronounced Proost,' she said without hesitating.

I slapped her face.

Education indeed! What you grow up with is what you are. Unless you fake the rest of your life. Like immigrants should do.

February 1976

Phyllis invited me to the wedding. She knew I wouldn't come. She'd already cast me as the bad fairy, excluded and powerlessly cursing the feast.

It will be in some dreary Leicester suburb, probably industrial, too far to putter in the dwarf car. Besides, it's the slack part of the year when no one likes travelling. Maud couldn't have wished to go, she hates formal events.

'For my parents,' Phyllis assured us, that new smug grin stretching her mouth.

Twaddle! She'd set her heart on it.

She'd never wear a ring, she also said. But she will.

Then she'll be off to the groom's Victorian terrace house in a poor Coventry district, abandoning her Anglia for his four-door Cortina. Bored Maud to tears about how she'll transform the long scrubby garden with ornamental patterns of white stones and shiny evergreen leaves; an urn on a concreted plinth at the dark end by the yew-tree hedge to direct the eye. (Phyllis has ideas, I'll say that for her, she's handy with a spade.)

Will she take to Coventry her Mateus Rosé lamp and butterfly-wing settee – or put them where they belong: on the rubbish heap? Will she abandon school, loll in the afternoons with a Milk Tray and *Woman's Own*; winding white or blue wool in a deckchair? Though she's old for babies. Perhaps she'll just continue to unravel the old life and leave it at that.

'I'd as soon have settled down with Maud,' she said. To me. To the back of my head.

Maud slipped out in the morning before I was up. I'd intended making her a warming bowl of porridge. She'd rather get herself off alone, she said. I didn't argue.

'Open a tin of peaches for lunch,' she said the night before. 'There's some evaporated milk left in the jug to pour over them.'

'Don't trouble about me.'

I didn't open the peaches. I dislike tinned fruit despite their being such a treat in wartime. Slimy and wrinkly – like oiled old-age flesh.

I missed Maud a little, even for so small a thing as making tea in the late afternoon after school. I put the cups, saucers and plates (the delicate blue, white and gold-rimmed Prince Albert set) ready for her on a tray in the kitchen, avoiding the cup with the glued handle. All she has to do is warm the pot, spoon in tea leaves and pour on boiling water, stir, let it stand to brew, then fit on the padded cosy. Not much but, without her, tea tasted grey.

It's not *any* company I want. Once the local vicar knocked on the front door expecting to be invited in. I was polite but kept him standing on the step till he fingered his dog collar and went off – whistling. Not a very clerical sound, I thought as I shut the door behind him.

A winter sun shone on the wedding. The photos would come out despite the unpromising season.

I questioned Maud, but it was like pulling teeth.

Phyllis's off-white dress? Beyond lace and ruffles, she lacked words. Too far away to notice the groom's hired suit (legs in rented trousers wrinkle round the ankles). Yet she appeared in some photos – bride and groom called her over – so she must have seen more.

Phyllis smiled at her as she walked down the aisle – that much I learnt. The mother cried uncontrollably. She must almost have despaired at getting her ugly daughter off her hands: relief would have made her blub. Her wedding present was a turquoise cotton percale bedroom set adorned with yellow roses, marked 'Easy Care'. So she knows Phyllis's slovenly ways – and vulgar taste.

Different cuts of meat, rice and potato salads for the wedding breakfast; only the sesame-covered rolls were warmed. Not very sustaining on a January day.

I probed further. Then she admitted Ray spoke to her: he hoped they'd be seeing a lot of her. 'They' indeed!

By now Maud was flushed. 'Just tired,' she said. She'd been to bed later than usual. She was biting her lip. It gleamed with blood.

Doubtless it was unsettling. Phyllis so tactless.

'You'd have been better staying at home. You could have sent a telegram and given your casserole dish later. Her brother only sent a telegram.'

'Graham lives in America.'

In the evening Maud was morose, so I watched television with her. A nature programme comparing coloured fish from sunny waters with bleached fish of the deep where no sun reaches, phosphorescent fish, dead in light. People fiddle with colour televisions, making the newsreader into a red clown or green vampire. Grainy thickness of a single tone is more dramatic. Think of those piles of Jews in the camps – always in black and white. Not so good for fish though: they swam in different hues of grey.

We refrained from turning them off. When I have the urge to quit talk on the wireless, I inwardly apologise. People are unmannerly with this habit of flicking a switch at the first tickle of boredom.

Grace Kelly marrying Prince Rainier was our first time with television. Maud was thirteen. No one had heard of Monaco and never did again. Not a very gripping spectacle: a prince with a pretty show girl is common enough. We learnt that presents included a Rolls-Royce and a hatchet of bone and gold. The rich guests left so much jewellery lying around that all the world's thieves were drawn in like a magnet.

Pageantry paid off: Princess Grace was pregnant. Such easy reward for luxury and pampering. 'Wham, bam, thank you, ma'am,' as the American GIs said in the war: polite boys when not frustrated. No doubt medical male fingers had probed her down there, delicately as they must for the privileged.

Too delicately for Queen Soraya: perhaps abashed by her beauty, they stayed close to the surface of that splendid body, afraid to compromise modesty by intrusive pokes. The bully-ing Shah blamed her; so, twenty-five and childless, she was exchanged for a more productive womb – like Grace's. Soraya too had a grand wedding and gorgeous presents: mink coats and a desk set with black diamonds from Joseph Stalin.

Barren or fertile, such close states, the smallest difference in flesh and thrust.

'I wish to cry like Soraya.' Is she really worth crying about all over the world? Who kept Stalin's desk when she was ejected from the kingdom in luxury with no encumbrances?

Maud fidgeted, then got up to ask me if I wanted a cup of Oval-tine, knowing I didn't.

'What's bothering you, Maud?' I asked as she left to fill the hot-water bottles.

'Just a bit tired from yesterday. It's hard getting back after time off.'

'Is anything wrong at work?'

'No,' she said. 'Why should there be?'

'I've no idea. Gracious!'

She didn't reply.

'I didn't mean to be difficult,' she said at last.

'Phyllis is married,' I said. 'No need to worry about her again.'

Marriage is the end of the plot. Only fools imagine a life after.

Early March 1976

Maud's mood hasn't lightened. At the weekend I suggested we bundle up and drive into the countryside for a walk. She didn't respond.

'I'd have thought you'd be used to driving by now.'

She'd passed the test first try but was too timid to go far. 'You should use the car more, Maud, or the thing will rust away.'

I hadn't been consulted about this purchase which was intended to make such a difference, for, so the theory went, we could visit a pub, a river, a friend. Go to the ends of the earth. As if anything on wheels could conquer our walls. Unless a pantechnicon mounted a frontal assault.

Phyllis's idea, compensating for the treachery she was about to serve, though Maud didn't see it. Slapping my face in the choice: a small, loud-yellow box. Both of them know I hate yellow.

'A good vehicle for young people,' I said when I saw it. 'At my time of life, I'd have preferred something more dignified than a Mini. A rolling goldfish bowl.'

'It's square, Mrs Kite,' said Phyllis, who'd found the car in a used-car lot by her flat.

'Would you like to learn to drive?' Maud asked. 'You wouldn't have to depend on the bus then. You hate waiting in the cold.'

'A bit late for me I think.'

'You'd get accustomed to traffic if you faced it more often,' I said now.

'I do enough.'

'If one surrenders to timidity, it wins. Remember how frightened you were when you began teaching. With time you overcame your terror.'

Maud was silent too long. Then she swivelled her eyes, 'I still find it unnerving.'

'But you do it. That's the point. It would be the same with the car.'

She let the talk lapse, as usual now.

'We could go to the woods we visited ages ago with Phyllis. Remember? Near the reservoir.'

For an instant she pretended not to recall. 'We'll go if you want.'

'Maud, my dear, haven't you a mind of your own? I propose going out for your sake more than mine.'

'I'd like to go,' she said. 'Let's go now.'

She didn't even drag a comb through her hair – it needs another Toni perm but she'll never agree – just slouched on her duffle coat and her unbecoming headscarf. I rubbed Pond's cold cream into my skin; the slightest chill chaps one's cheeks and nose. When I came downstairs she was looking at the road map.

'I'll navigate,' I said.

She was reluctant to move.

'Let's be going, shall we?'

We got into the toy car, heads nearly touching its tinny roof. Maud backed out timidly. I feared she'd scrape the low wall in the sudden lunge that had to come, but I guarded my tongue. At the end of the cul-de-sac where it joins the main road she seemed unsure of the way. 'To the right,' I said.

'I know.'

She stalled at the first traffic lights. Her lip trembled as the car behind hooted.

'Start it,' I said. 'Do please go on.'

Her knuckles were frost white on the steering wheel.

Later the car behind overtook us. The driver stuck out his head and shouted, 'Stupid cow.'

Maud found a spot to park. I couldn't alight without stepping in mud.

'Come through my door.'

'No thank you, Maud. I don't care to heave myself over the gears.'

She offered to move the car to a drier place. 'It'll be harder to manoeuvre into,' she said.

'Don't bother if it's so much trouble.'

She backed out with little tentative starts, then fitted snugly into the new space. She was too close to another car on her side but she struggled out. One advantage to being a beanpole.

It was fresh, not cold, the ground moist. I tried conversing, then gave up. We trudged on in silence following signposts.

All of a sudden she spoke about school, tumbling out her words. I only half listened.

'Helen's so free with the children,' she was saying. 'She lets the girls go at their own pace and rewards them. I said it needs a definite personality to make this work. No, just goodwill and patience, she said. It's her first job after bringing up three boys. Strange to be so idealistic. Miss Janes is as strict as ever she was in my time. Never has to raise her voice, just dictates and demands rote-learning. The girls cry and beg to drop her classes, but she gets excellent Latin results with the ones left.'

'And you?' I said as Maud jerked to a pause.

'Me? I don't like teaching.'

'You chose it.'

'Did I?'

'Well I don't know who did.' I stopped walking to face her. She wouldn't turn towards me. 'I didn't push you into it. Don't try to blame me.'

She walked on. I hurried to catch up.

'I'm not blaming you.'

'Then what can you mean?'

'I didn't feel I had a choice.'

I looked at her sideways as we walked. She kept her eyes on the ground. I almost tripped on an exposed tree root.

'But there *was* a choice. I always hoped you'd be a solicitor. You'd have met a nice sort of person then and had a very different life. I tried to persuade you. You must remember, Maud.'

'I know you did, but it wasn't really a choice. I wasn't good at much else besides French. School recommended teacher-training.'

'If you're as spineless as that, I'd say you deserve what you've got,' I said.

'Perhaps so.'

I was losing patience. 'There's not much you can do about it now short of finding someone to marry.'

I hear myself. I know about choice! Only those trite sayings would do. 'What can't be helped . . .' as Aunty Gertie said, rather too often.

It can't be the same for Maud. It IS different I could have screamed aloud, then and there on that country footpath. It is NOT the same, Maud, whatever I said – or let you think. *You* had a choice and you chose wrongly.

She held the ends of her drab scarf to her chin, looking up at the sky once or twice, wrinkling her pale expanse of forehead.

Was she fretting because she'd been called a 'stupid cow'? Surely not. Such abuse from a man in a car was common enough. Women are always trespassers on the male road.

Was she thinking of that 'choice'? If so, why now?

The scene reasserted itself. The reservoir wasn't full even after a winter. I thought there'd been quite a lot of rain, but evidently not. Indeed, these last weeks must have been drier than usual.

No longer looking directly at the ground, Maud stubbed her toe on a small stone.

'Would you see more if you wore your spectacles?'

'I get dents on the sides of my nose.'

'They'd disappear if you wore them more often. You wouldn't need to peer.'

We lapsed into silence.

A slight mist in the air, the result of a heavy dew, enough to lend perspective to trees and lengthen the short views along the path. Twigs made black-edged panes against the darker wood. Drops of water clung to them, swelling, then falling with a thick plop on to the matting of old leaves. A blackish bird – wrong beak for a blackbird – was following us. Landing on a branch, it shook off watery beads and rustled as it hopped to the drier ground.

I like an early spring when it could be December or March. Everything's tasteful: greys, fawns, beiges and browns, like autumn in a *Golden Treasury* poem. No raw buddings or shoots of thin sickly green and white – they're present but hidden under a tough skin of earth. But here today there was a sense of stirring and shifting. Fooled by premature warmth, shoots were pushing up too boldly. It'll come to nothing when temperatures tumble.

We walked for more than three quarters of an hour.

'Perhaps we should turn back,' said Maud, her voice thickened by silence.

'We can continue a little. It's pleasant here.'

'I was thinking of your indigestion. You say it gets worse with exercise.'

We'd slowed to exchange these few words. Just then a dog, a sort of overgrown boxer with inquisitive ears and wrinkled, astonished face, bounced up and sniffed at us. Maud gave a start and stepped out of the way. I glanced behind.

'Henry,' shouted a male voice. 'Henry!'

Round the bend in the path came a man, his wife and three children, out as a family for a Sunday walk in smart matching leisurewear.

We stood to one side. They made no swerve in overtaking us. We were invisible. Maud looked down, fiddling with a wooden peg on her duffle coat, her one foot caught in the muddy leaves where she'd stepped.

I too lowered my eyes, just for a moment, then looked up to catch a smile I felt must come. Having stared briefly, the children loped on ahead like outriders.

As the couple passed, I smiled 'Good afternoon.' Like Maud I had thickness in my voice, but I was audible.

The woman paused in a tale to her man and moved her mouth. Only slightly, as if fearing it might bleed. Then they went on.

That smile not returned. How dare they? Such vanity. Rancour bubbled up in my gorge, 'Very well, thank you,' I muttered aloud.

We turned to head back. The mist had thinned further and the scraggy wood on either side seemed denser and flatter, a chill now noticeable. The wind, puny though it was, must have caught the path and funnelled against us. I felt tired and pressed the palms of my hands to my chest.

'We'll go more slowly,' Maud said, urging me on to one of the flat sides of the path, while she stumbled along on the central grass ridge. We passed a sagging wooden bench with no urge to sit down.

'Lean on me,' she said.

I took her arm, letting go some weight.

Maud drove home more deftly than when we came, although like me she was lowered in spirits. A little middle-class indifference scratches more than an insult from a coarse driver.

The yellow car slid into the tight space between house and waste patch, grazing nothing.

'That was nice,' I said. Why not? I've given up expecting a circus to come round the corner.

That evening she was again solicitous, her morning moodiness diminished, though you'd not know it from her words. She buttered some hot scones and I ate one before it went clammy.

I didn't see her eat, but she must have done. If she hasn't, what am I to do? One can't inhabit another's mouth, clatter the teeth and swish the tongue.

I let Maud make dinner. She was a long time about it.

I went to bed early. Before going to her own room, she turned my light off and, as she left, leant down and kissed my forehead. A cool kiss, softer than her thin lips promised.

I don't care for flamboyance between family members. I keep a dignified distance, intimacy so easily degenerates. When, like all children, Maud seemed uneasy at embracing after absence, I never insisted. I made her touch her cheek to Clare's in greeting, but only when she was young. I never kissed Clare's boys – anticipating their distaste. Nor Maud for that matter.

Just before she sat the 11-plus, she grew over-fond. She'd dash home, try to hug me, climb into the wing chair if I were reading, then sit still, squashing me. 'You must be having an awful time in school,' I'd say.

In the mornings before I'd taught her to make tea, she'd creep into my bed in her winceyette pyjamas and snuggle beside me, fingering the lacy edge of my nightie. 'I need more sleep. For goodness' sake go and read in your room.' Most of the time she wouldn't obey, even if I turned from her. She'd run her hands along the top of my back – I was a little fuller then – crumpling the flimsy stuff in her fingers, then rubbing her face against it. All long ago. Yet an echo here.

I've fossilised the moment. Maud has watched me moving my pen.

'Do you think I'm writing about "Aunty Clare", Maud?'

She doesn't bother to catch my gaze. 'Yes,' she says.

I let my pen drop on to the page, then repress a snort. My feeling lingers in my face. Finally, she looks at me and blushes. I pick up the pen.

'You don't know anything, Maud,' I say.

'Well tell me then.'

'No,' I say. 'Nobody can do that. What you put into words is a lie. Words set down their suitcase in your head and you have to accept it whether yours or another's, however shabby.'

'That's just a metaphor,' she whispers, showing off that education I paid for.

'Aunty' Clare

One year in May, perhaps twenty years back, Maud and I went with 'Aunty' Clare and her family on a holiday to Wales. It was the boys' half-term, a time cheaper and less crowded than the summer. Clare wanted to keep the main break for Nick and the family; we were meant to know ourselves a burden, Maud and I, though they were never out of pocket by us.

We travelled independently, they by car – Nick still had the black Rover – we on a train changing twice, once at some junction without a ladies' waiting room. As usual it was cold, and we hadn't brought quite enough to wear, holding to some silly hope of a balmy late spring. Harder on a train than in a private car to carry along clothes for every turn of weather.

A pub offering rooms, though Clare called it a country hotel before we booked, cosy in the evenings, morning-afterish at other times. Indoors was warmish, mainly from the thick smoky air of open log fires. (Funny how we rejoiced to abandon dirty grates, then welcomed them as décor.)

Maud and I had to share a double bed in a room over the bar – we'd been promised twins – but we must put up with what we were given. Used to that: a war widow with an only child. So much fresh air by day that, after a first restless night, we slept easily enough. We learned to stay still in the bed, each by an edge with a pillow at our backs to keep out draft.

The second morning after breakfast we walked to the waterfall. Clare's idea. She'd seen pictures of a wispy tenuous skein of water in a guidebook. She thought it would be a 'breeze' to hike there.

I hadn't liked the scramble uphill, passing wobbly trees brittle from old moss. The toes of my shoes pinched. They'd been cheap but looked smart in the shop.

'Do for walking anywhere,' said the young assistant, who'd never been three yards from the tarmac on Norton High Street.

I feared I'd sprain my ankle.

Stouter, less elegant and far dearer than mine, Clare's brogues were meant for crags and droppings. Condescendingly, Nick helped me when I was trapped in mud or stringy grass. At times he was even attentive to Maud. She had on her Wellington boots. She hadn't learnt the knack of clenching her toes so socks didn't work down and bunch under her soles; she made blisters on her heels, but she didn't seem to mind. 'Oh gumboots! What a good idea,' said Clare when she saw the wellies.

We struggled up the diseased, scabby hillside, with sheep droppings so numerous that thistles and ferns could only just push through. Wind pulled at hair and congealed the face: any smile cracked the surface.

In Maud it put some colour. Not as thin as now, her downy cheeks could become almost ruddy in boisterous weather. Like mine, her hair was blown about, but on the young a natural disorder isn't unpleasing – though she did remind me of a sheep tangled in its own wet wool.

We took ham-and-cheese sandwiches from the inn to have a picnic despite a chill wind. I don't remember who carried the food, perhaps Nick in his knapsack, or the boys. (I can hardly visualise those boys now, wrapped up in themselves, vaguely polite as expensively educated children usually are, sending identical bread-and-butter notes for Christmas socks and diaries, but never showing real friendliness. They didn't care for Maud, though not actively annoying her. To them she was nobody's sister, neither child nor adult.)

We came down the hill into a narrow valley of wet slippery stones and muddy trees. The heel of my shoe quickly attracted a mix of earth and dung. The valley was too narrow a place, too enclosed, too full of sodden branches for comfortable walking. Then the waterfall appeared, sparkling, leaping and dancing. No coiled 'wild cataract', but something more than the wispy affair Clare had pointed to in the guidebook. Each spurt fell as an intricate silky cascade.

'Come on, it's here. Oh, do come quickly,' cried Clare. 'It's quite spectacular.'

'It's beautiful,' I said after a pause, 'well worth the effort.'

She glanced at me. 'Yes, it was a bit of a scramble.' She laughed and bounced off, her laughter hanging like a grey cloud in the dank, noisy place.

Without her, I went to the falls at the point where water frayed at the edge. I took off my dirtied shoe and balanced precariously on one foot while I wiped the heel with a chunk of partly dead grass, then held it under the water. Even from this thinner part, the spray was vibrant and alive. It sprang on to my face, hitting with fine needles.

Suddenly beside me, Maud took my arm to steady me.

'Thank you, Maud,' I said wishing Clare had seen it. But, like a child, she was away clambering over rocks and mossy hummocks at the side of the waterfall, following Nick and her boys.

My shoe cleaned, we stood together for a while looking at the tumbling water. Maud was nearly my height.

'Are you cold?' I asked.

'A bit.'

'Do you want to go back?'

'No, I'll follow them.'

'You'll never manage to clamber up. It's quite dangerous, much higher than it seems from here.'

'Aunty Clare went.'

'Yes, she did. But she's not quite at the top yet.'

'The boys and Uncle Nick are, though.'

'Oh boys!' I smiled and pressed her hand. 'Why don't we go to the other side on this level and see the falls from there?'

'I don't mind.'

She was tired. The train journey had been long and the first night so interrupted.

She followed me. We studied the water from the left and right.

I wasn't blind to what she was wanting. But I knew what she didn't: how out of place she'd be up there without me, among Clare and her family. Making her sheep's eyes at an uncle who was more woman than man and wouldn't notice if the poor girl evaporated in front of his eyes.

'Look, it's so lovely and sheltered here. I'm not even cold. It'll be brisk enough going back, so we'd better enjoy ourselves now.'

'We'll have to,' she said, almost rudely.

I was irritated by the change of mood, so blatantly expressed, when a squat horse, incongruously on us in that dank place, brought its velvet bony head close to my back. I exclaimed at her for not warning me. The beast had a captive, cynical eye. I forget the rider.

The final 'Aunty' Clare Christmas in the Cotswold 'country cottage'. Though the place was far from rural smells and sights, scruffy hedgerows, dray horses and sluttish gypsy camps, centuries back the dark rooms had held peasants, so the cottage has 'character'. Bathrooms, under-floor heating, recessed lighting all tacked on, a pigsty in the garden transformed to a bunker for shop-bought logs.

An incongruous magnolia with fleshy flowers peeps over the roof. 'Here when we came,' said Clare. 'We haven't the heart to chop it.'

We sat together in the low-beamed room. Slightly too grand furniture from Clare's childhood house, in store after Uncle Harry died and Aunt Laura went into a 'home': a red buttoned Chesterfield and ornately carved Indian cedar chest. On one end a painted wicker basket filled with shiny darning mushroom, bobbins and old silver hatpins; on the other a grey glass vase with fresh, peachy-white flowers – in winter!

No boys: they appeared only for the mandatory part of family festivities like Christmas dinner. As ever, social duty fell on me, Maud making no effort, though old enough by now.

Avoid politics: need not guess whether Nick votes for a toff from the grouse moor or a Huddersfield football supporter. A champagne socialist with his Home Counties drawl and effeminate clothes. (I've nothing to say on politics that should be heard.) So, after they'd companionably run down their many friends whom I didn't know from Adam and Eve, I'd no choice but to try polite chat on books.

Way back when we shared a room at Mother's, I'd tried to talk to Clare about Tennyson and Keats, thinking she'd know something more from that private education. I'd wanted to discuss Hardy's *Jude* and its morbid pictures of human miserableness.

I can still hear her snort, 'For God's sake, Joan. We're not schoolchildren. We've finished with all that.'

My eye now caught a pile of hardbacks beside the fireplace: on garden design, parish churches, pebble polishing, medieval glass and bosses, no doubt presents from 'country' people entertained to cocktails or dinner. Stacked according to colour! (I have a sense of the absurd, but best not indulge it. Aunty Gertie had a weakness that way: just once I caught her shutting down a glance at Father strutting off in his new bowler hat with a rolled-up newspaper under his arm.)

I was reduced to new popular novels. I mentioned a couple which, according to Mrs Jenkins in the library, discerning people were reading: *On the Beach*, *The Leopard*.

Neither Clare nor Nick had heard of them. Glued to the colour television, watching *Crossroads*, hands round a 'G&T'.

'Too busy to read much,' said Nick. Clare smiled a wifely smile; the pair purred a little. Seems they – or actually just Nick – had read some crime thing by Agatha Christie called *The Clocks*. Clare remarked how much she enjoyed the new colour Sunday supplements, such interesting travellers' tales and tips on fashion. A long silence followed.

Clare broke it by remarking on her cousin Betty's boy. University-educated though only Leeds (Nick went to Oxford). On the dole despite having use of arms and legs.

I was hardly listening, knowing nothing of Betty, her boy or any of them from that side of the family.

Nick rumbled agreement in his soft drawl. I noted the white cardigan draped over a shoulder like a girl, the casual indoor shoes with no socks.

Her elbow on Nick's thigh on the settee, knuckles pushing against her cheek, Clare continued, 'It's not just youths, everybody should work for what they have. You can't expect the country to keep you. It's just robbery.'

They? You? I heard that.

Silent as usual, Maud was slyly regarding the folds of Nick's cardigan. Clare caught my eye, smiled coldly and looked away. Her pampered feet in thick colourful Mexican socks were tucked up under her. A kittenish child, she even wore the sort of bolero Maud had when she was six. Maud's was angora, this was a kind of faux fur, girly and expensive. (Clare keeps two stuffed furry animals in her bedroom: a striped badger and a brown owl with yellow eyes. I can't be doing with that sort of childishness in a grown woman.)

'Stick it on the wall, Mrs Riley,

Enough's enough for any old bit of fluff.'

An unfortunate lyric to spring to mind; doing nothing to cool my rising heat. Two can pull out swords, even though one pretends to be a pettish child wielding a toy.

'You've rarely done a day's work in your life,' I said. 'What would you know?'

Clare glanced at Nick.

'Unused to wine,' he muttered and shrugged the white cardigan.

'That's no excuse,' said Clare unfolding her legs. 'You come here every Christmas and we try to be hospitable.'

Nick sat up a little straighter and gazed towards the window with its made-to-measure Liberty curtains.

'Try,' I said, exhaling fast. 'Do stop trying, Clare. My daughter and I can cook our own turkey in future, thank you.'

Does she think us scavengers on her plenty?

Maud was biting her nails, then sucking the side of her thumb.

'Haven't you a tongue in your head, Maud? You're old enough to respond when your mother's insulted.'

She looked up briefly, then rested her eyes on Nick's soft tan shoes.

'You're your own worst enemy, you know,' Clare said as I packed our few things. She'd come to stand in the doorway, nursing a mug of tea in both hands.

I admit to being a little out of humour with myself. 'Cutting off your nose,' as Mother always said, dancing out her clichés. But being in humour with oneself never much helps: it's always a betrayal of what one really feels, what one should feel.

Nick ran us to the nearby station at Chipping Something in their new maroon Wolseley. He tried to make peace. We this, we that, his mouth and left hand gesturing.

'I can forgive you, not her.' My fingers smudged the shiny wooden dashboard above the glove compartment. I was glad to be making a mark.

'No, we're together,' he said. His lips pursed primly, like a woman's.

'I see that.'

We drove on in silence.

Maud said nothing. She'd always had a puppy love for Nick, handsome in his effete way. She followed him with her eyes as if he were a shooting star. He rarely bothered to speak to her.

She must miss 'Aunty' Clare and 'Uncle' Nick. Otherwise she wouldn't have suggested the topic. I'd not thought of that. They don't care a straw for her.

Late March 1976

My day in 14 Ackroyd Close

If you write your life, tell your truth. Why else do it? The dreary with the dramatic. The dreary IS the drama.

Just before she started teacher-training, Maud said, 'You might like to go out to work.'

A remark with the ring of Phyllis.

I've no qualifications. What would I do? Did she want her mother selling turnips on a market stall or cleaning public lavatories?

So: here's my day. Can you laugh with your mouth closed? Is it a ha-ha laugh when you do?

We have the *Telegraph* delivered till April. When the subscription offer lapses, we'll stop keeping up with 'the world': no more Lon Nol and Viet Cong, cosmonauts and oily Arabs, Ulster and who killed whom; no more Cod War against mighty Iceland.

While Maud prepares breakfast for us both – a recent habit – she looks through the paper. When finished, she folds it to suggest it's pristine. But, if I give the gist of an item, I see she knows already.

Once I tested her. 'You've read it of course.'

'Yes.'

'While making the toast?'

She coloured. 'Chou Enlai's death was in yesterday's paper too.'

Safe there. We use each day's *Telegraph* to wrap our wet rubbish.

At Feathermore House, the butler ironed *The Times* before presenting it to His Lordship.

Father used to read passages out loud to Mother when he'd moved from the *Daily Mail* to the *Morning Post* under the Harrisons' influence. Vague as a high cloud in summer, Mother never protested – and never listened.

Could he have credited her interest in politics and foreign affairs, even her comprehension?

Possibly, for, by then, she'd perfected that elusive look of the simply bored.

To continue to the meat of the day. I fill my chubby Parker pen from the pot of dark ink.

For breakfast I have two well-done pieces of toast, one under a poached or scrambled egg or beside the boiled one, the other with marmalade spread into each corner – thick-cut marmalade ladled from a tin into an empty Cooper's Oxford jar. (The cheap *tastes* the same as the costly.) Occasionally we share a grapefruit, using the special knife to ease round segments, then grapefruit spoons to pull them free. Fruit's expensive this time of year, often shrivelled too.

When she's finished, Maud slips upstairs to make our beds. Bending too far forward makes me dizzy now. When I check, I find my dark-blue candlewick bedspread is never quite smooth.

She bustles round before setting off for school, squashing her pencils – ends corrugated with teethmarks – into a brown transparent plastic case, packing the pencil case, textbooks and corrected exercise books into an old leather satchel.

A couple of Christmases back, I bought her a smart over-the-shoulder canvas bag in navy blue with a wide white strap and buckle. She thanked me and never used it.

'The leather one suits you, Maud,' Phyllis said, knowing my canvas one a gift. Always sly, Phyllis, so no one can groan aloud.

Going and returning, Maud looks tired. She shrugs off my concern.

'One must make an effort, else one fades to nothing,' I say.

But she's an adult. I'll dwindle into a nag if I persist.

On Tuesdays she leaves money for the milkman in a brown envelope on the step beside the washed bottles. We don't speak to him. He's not the lame old man I registered with during rationing who poured milk into our metal jug. Just a shaggy boy. He and other youths hang round the lamp-post outside the Wimpy Bar like derelict ivy.

'Have a good day,' I say.

'I'll try.'

I wave to Maud, except when weather's raw; then she lets herself out and quickly closes the door to prevent draught.

Sometimes I watch her through the net curtain as she walks along the pavement past the waste patch – no bomb site, just proof the pre-war builders of the Close were poor at geometry. I step aside when I glimpse next-door wife peering in on her way to the shops with her plastic Mickey-Mouse bag.

Beasts in cages keep themselves to themselves.

I used to exchange a greeting with this Ivy Something

(peroxide marigold hair, mutton dressed . . .). She'd say, 'Good morning, Mrs Uh,' or 'Mrs K,' in her overlaid Irish. To her other neighbour I heard her calling me 'snooty'.

'She might as well been talking Paki,' she sniggered, gesturing her head towards the Pakistanis in the rundown houses at the street end of the Close.

Occasionally Maud talks to her, never to the scrawny husband. He puts his hands in his coat pockets and looks to the horizon when he sees either of us.

A hairy son comes some weekends. His motorbike squats on its haunches, showing off way too much metalwork. Then, like an incontinent bug, it leaks oil where daffodils and narcissi once grew. When it roars off, it leaves brown, greasy stains on the concrete. I can't boast, but I've tried with the small front garden. When no longer urged to 'Dig for Victory', I put in bulbs. They rotted. Hugh said they'd gone in upside down. Happen they had. On sale, so most likely old. Now a few forget-me-nots furtively spread beside Hugh's rose bush.

Once Maud's left for work, I dress carefully and organise my face. I apply black pencil under and upward from the edge of my eyes, then brush grey-green shadow on the lids. Powder and lipstick but never too much. Nothing blatant. Make-up is courtesy, not coquetry. (Just sometimes I catch the eyes in the mirror and glare, then polish the glass with my sleeve.)

So easy to grow slovenly, to find oneself some afternoon slouching from the house bare-legged with feet pushed into down-at-heel fur slippers, hair still stretched round pink rollers, buying sliced bread from the Co-op.

I spit at her, that shadow of everywoman.

On alternate mornings, I rinse out my nightie and hang it on the wooden bathroom rail. Were we rich, I'd sleep in fine clean sheets and cotton shift every night of the year, knowing they'd be pristine when bundled up to be washed by other hands.

In winter and sometimes in summer, we take bed linen to the laundry. An extravagance I've insisted on since Maud brought home an income. I hated the smell of damp sheets steaming for hours in front of the electric fire. You can't avoid the tell-tale singeing from such mean living.

Once dressed, made up, and alone, I go into the kitchen to make my second cup of tea. I have it in Prince Albert china in the sitting room, holding the vessel in the palm of my left hand. I feel the warmth and exquisite thinness of the membrane between liquid and flesh: so fragile the thing, yet with all my strength I can't crush it.

Today before drinking my tea I feel a sudden vexation, for I spy in the corner of the kitchen counter the small marmalade jar in which I saved farthings and ha'pennies.

'Do you call that money, you nincompoop?' I hear Our Masters say.

I do, despite your brain-washing.

Ordered without a by-your-leave to drop a thousand years of pennies, crowns and guineas, then pop to the shops with new coins as if they were exactly like old pennies, forgetting there was ever such a thing as a farthing with its tiny bronze robin.

One thing in wartime for Lord Woolton to make us cook magic jam from carrots, or that old ham Churchill to demand we accept retreats as naval victories. But now? We're told to use an old name for what's strange, a new one for what's old hat, to think something we don't, forget something we know.

'Just do what we say, shut up and spend your new so-called "pence".'

It doesn't stop there. I switch on the wireless. Some good music on the Third Programme – sent out, remember, for the 'refinement of society'. But an edict has come: I must call it Radio 3.

The Home and Light Programmes are rechristened too. No pretence of 'refinement' on those stations.

Music While You Work? Housework we mean, dears, not war or paid work, housework done in black-satin bullet bra, high heels and frilly blouse, just in case *he* comes home early and catches you with the sweeper.

Housewives' Choice. Such magnificent choice.

The wireless changed my life, said Mrs Crump of Slough.

'What's on the table, Mabel?'

'Whoopee.'

'Give her the money, Barney.'

To go on. Five days a week I run the sweeper over the sitting-room carpet, not needing 'music' while I work. I live in this room. Unlike so many housewives who make their home in their kitchens by the stove, kettle, ashtray and tin of biscuits, hoping that one day just possibly their 'choice' might be played on their grease-splattered transistor wirelesses.

On Wednesdays I use the Hoover, vacuuming stairs and bedrooms as well as the sitting room. I make straight lines in the pile, like tidy grass on a municipal lawn. (Maud hoovers haphazardly.) I sweep the kitchen floor. I dust window sills and the tops of the television, wireless, gramophone and grandfather clock, sometimes picture frames, wet then dry dust. I flick the cloth over the mock-flame below the electric bars.

Twice a week, I polish the dining- and side-tables and run a duster over all the chairs. Once a month or so I climb the step-ladder to wipe along the picture rail, fingering the cheap dust as it settles on the rag. I rearrange the kitchen shelves, cleaning them before replacing each item.

With my bedroom I'm extra fastidious. I tidy the drawers of white and beige knickers and camisoles, taking a small pleasure in the way the ageing lavender sachets still explode into my nose. Though she'd rather I didn't, I dust Maud's room. I don't rummage in her drawers.

Mid-morning, I have a break and make myself a cup of real coffee. A more pungent smell than instant and it takes longer to prepare, needing bits of paper and funnels and all the clearing up. I like taking trouble where mind's uninvolved, the process intricate.

For lunch I have a Welsh rarebit or just Cheddar cheese and water biscuits with an apple – a Cox's Orange Pippin or Worcester Pearmain, not the sweet foreign varieties they sell in 'supermarkets' with shiny plastic skins in vivid red or green. If the morning's been tiring, I open a tin of tomato soup or mulligatawny. I don't live out of tins.

Then I read for a while. Only biographies now. From them I've learnt that Lady Mary Wortley Montagu rejoiced in being a woman because she wouldn't have to marry one; that Vita Sackville-West dismissed people like me as 'bedint', using her bloody, jewelled vowels to convey her scorn. Expecting us to put coal in the bath, knowing no better.

Entitled upper-crust ladies with cushioned miseries or fabulous luck: not a lot to say to me. No biographies of Mrs Uh in her sitting room with her spectacles on the bridge of her dripping nose or by her geyser in her semi-detached kitchenette.

Yet, these stuck-up ones can't stop me knowing them. Even if Miss Sackville-West came to my front door, knocked, then walked right through me out the back. I'd recognise *her* and she wouldn't like that.

When I tired of posh Englishwomen, Mrs Jenkins steered me towards the Russian shelf. Russians are like us, she implied, snobbily hungry for old tsars in their cold, sullen towns.

Ivan the Terrible frying supplicants, an empress so indolent she could hardly move, freezing a dwarf out of sheer boredom. Gruesome details if one thought of them, but books aren't for thinking. They're to wash over one or, better, let one wallow in a sky-blue, buoyant swimming pool of words.

Mrs Jenkins's shelves are neat, with volumes aligned and pulled to the front. She doesn't care for people disturbing them. Maybe she recommends works so she can prepare ahead for their absence. Rarely if ever borrowed, the large Russian biographies are clean. Though she checks when I hand them back, she knows they'll be pristine from me, no dog-eared corners or traces of jam and crumbs between pages.

We exchange books with a few courtesies and thin quick smiles, as if the transaction of checking out, handing over and receiving, is indelicate. The volumes are neither gifts nor instructions, I'm neither buyer nor patron. Like collecting cheap NHS pills over the counter in Boots, something faintly shameful about not needing to pay a proper price, a kind of state largesse of print. Words on Welfare, a dole of books.

'You're lucky you can borrow from the library,' a crumpled widow at the Pensions Office once said to me. 'You're a rate-payer. They just let me sit there in the warm.'

*

Later in the afternoon I have a rest. Not an under-the-sheets-and-skirt-off sort of rest, just a gentle relaxing in the wing chair or on the settee, eyes shut, mind wandering, not dozing.

(Now would be the point to remonstrate, stiffen sinews, be 'master of my fate'.

'Get a grip,' I might say if there'd been anyone to listen and embarrass. But no one's present beyond my censorious mind, and that, in this absurd, quiet time, is softening.)

Sometimes before Maud comes home I shut the velvet curtains when it's not dark, not even twilight. Then, with no lamppost screaming across the window, I may dream this house away.

I may, for example, imagine a mellow beauty, the sort one feels when a bulb is dim with dust or shines through diffusing parchment at the right angle; when one's sat still for a long time, and sight's grown hazy and blurred. A fissure opens so that light flows in along a honeyed stream. Nothing at those rare moments of unison to pursue or track or seek.

The wing chair fits round me. Feet resting on the tapestry stool, eyes closed, adrift in 'drowsy numbness', perhaps with Brahms or Dvořák seeping into my ears, I let go.

(Of what? I ask now I'm writing. The mind squatting in my head with its arms folded? Or the embarrassingly soppy –and sloppy – body? Both so incontinent.)

The coarse, tacky contours of this half-house dissolve into spectral scenes. No ill-made props and pretty, smirking faces: my own auditorium for my own soliloquies, curtained in silvery lashes, I as playwright, actress, scene painter and theatre manager.

Once, I tried fancying my pale arm like a gold fin lying along a man's dress suit, touching the old sad romantic dream. It failed to take, though copied (I think) from that *Blue Angel* I wasn't supposed to understand.

Instead, my mind saunters quite away from men and my body. I become a floating jellyfish in a warm, dim Voysey-lined aquarium. Only then do faceless people with pale mauve-gloved hands tiptoe in, ghostly, flapping like lost birds.

An upright figure, soldier-like but doused in perfume and flowers (not really a man with those hips, just an adjunct, more Lola Lola than Professor Rath), an elegant older woman of pink and green, with 'dainty, dainty waist', the clean gloss of grey satin, a glimmer of pearls in her pale, pale hair, a faint almost unpleasing smell. The pair trip round my chair, then seem still though dizzily moving, centre of a whirligig dance, hair swishing through gleaming, flame-shimmering air. No pushing or prodding that witches' circle.

Did Phyllis really call me a witch one dark November afternoon? I think she did, whispering it, hissing it as I was leaving behind Maud. Did she think I waited my moment to cast spells? Or was the word 'bitch'? Could be either, her mind so commonplace.

The elegant lady, tall and fair in her pearly skin, is attentive to me though my body's dissolved. Ready to pull close some swathes of wavy stuff or light another candle, this one shiny grey like the sun swaddled in cloud, setting its red-yellow flame dancing to silvery, kaleidoscopic flicker. She can grow smooth piano music behind a silken wall, tinkled by her long white elastic fingers that play effortlessly and for ever a song that never needed words.

As those bright, untarnished dahlia eyes come close and flash a mauve odorous insolence, such pleasurable pain pit-pats and shoots through the dissolved me while the long-fingered hand smooths the silky petticoated thighs.

'And I would be the necklace ...

Upon her balmy bosom.'

Are they ghosts of ghosts by now? Ageing infants astride the horns of Elfland?

Eat the colours, swallow the silvery crimson and sepia, dove-grey, mauve and rose-pink. What churns then, in the stomach and loins?

Go on. I know an addict when I feel one. I enchant myself muttering what should be hidden, but life's too short to lay down better habits.

Crude, adolescent, infantile, you think?

Of course.

Sometimes music conjures them from Some Enchanted Programme. Best not seek a source, just accept the magic gauze of words and sound.

Yet, might something shimmer along from a white gown and puffed sleeves, admiring eyes of two brothers? A snaky cousin caressing silk thighs?

Doubtful. The scene was set by then – though, as I say, time goes back as well as forward.

A downy bed, small, sharp, so-sexy teeth in the nipple of a white breast sinking into the pulp of an orange-yellow plum, juice welling over an unformed face, touching rubbery gums – sweet juice making a roaring in the ear of the world?

Surely not. That would be ridiculous!

One thing's clear: nothing to do with 'unconquerable' and

captained souls. More's the pity. Father, why didn't you pin 'Invictus' on to my forehead and glue down the edges, instead of leaving me to the women, to careless Mother and cunning Aunty Gertie with the 'purple riot' in her *Agnes' Eve*: her limping hare, her tiger-moth's 'deep-damasked wings', the cool jellies, creamy curd and 'lucent syrops', her strange, damp, alluring smell, so ascetic and sensual.

('When does Madeline eat the food?' I once asked, as she recited for the umpteenth time in her apple-doused accent. She couldn't have scoffed it on St Agnes' Eve – it'd be sacrilege. Now, though I never knew the answer, after so many years, at least I know the taste of those crimson words.)

Did Gertie insert this faerie poem into my deep parts?

Could be.

The moment's always on the verge of tumbling, the softened mind never securely relaxed. Images quicken, run riot, and dissolve. To sit or lie in mellow light with music, ears fringed against discordant sounds, and feel an instant of mind-emptying absurdity in the middle of this dismal dwelling is to know it's gone, poof! in an instant.

Then the blue chair merges into a street of purple-patterned curtains. Every house and every body becomes a palace of velvet spies, with my eyes.

Humbug from start to finish.

Sometimes I fear I'll wake up in the silky woman's dahlia dream and be rejected with teasing strokes.

Or perhaps, under anaesthetic or too old and demented to keep a slack mouth shut in the nursing home where I'm parked like feeble, unwithering Aunt Laura, I'll humiliate myself by letting this faery dust blow out and be tossed about in the air. Then

Mother will come back from the grave and stand by my sick bed, giggling and covering her mouth with her youthful hand and painted claws.

Nap over, I prepare for Maud's coming. She arrives at a quarter to five or, if she grabs some shopping, it's more like twenty past. I have the kettle on. I plan the dinner, often we make it together. She has a good wrist for chopping.

Over the meal we chat a little, avoiding tension. Then, afterwards, I pass the dishes through the hatch and Maud starts washing up while I dry. We don't waste hot water – the immersion heater's expensive – so we boil a saucepan.

Once again I say, 'I wish you'd wear the rubber gloves.' But she won't.

Sometimes we listen to the wireless. Or I read while she embroiders a tray cloth in chain stems and lazy-daisy flowers or marks exercise books. Occasionally we'll watch television. Then she may go out for a short walk beyond the cul-de-sac and round the block or even down to the square by the park. It closes early, so she can only look through the railings.

'Don't stay out and catch cold,' I warn.

Silly walking without a dog. What does she see as she tramps through the twilight?

Before bed we either have a cup of instant coffee in the sitting room or a milky drink like Horlicks or Ovaltine. Maud makes it and brings it to my chair. Her attention pleases me. She's at her most relaxing.

She fills the hot-water bottles and places mine inside my nightie. Sometimes she fills it too early and it's tepid before I get in. Nothing to the midnight iciness of that stone bottle Megan

139

gave me in the very coldest times, when Mother and Father had a coal fire in their bedroom grate.

If it's especially chilly in the house, we undress downstairs by the electric fire, one after the other, not immodestly. Or we take the portable one into the bedroom, mine, then hers. It's costly to keep it on for long.

I have extra bottles of prescription sleeping pills, mainly Mogadon, given by a careless chemist who misread the doctor's handwriting. I'm sensitive to them, so I cut them in half with the curved nail scissors, not wanting the chemical dust on my Florentine pair. Sadly, pills work for only a few hours, then leave one both confused and alert. No matter. By then they'll have given respite. And one can always take another portion or two.

Maud switches out my light on her way to the bathroom to clean her teeth.

My dissolving life

What exactly has fed my day here? Why have I exaggerated?

Because it diverts me to see my world in black and white or all-over grey? My world as it has been: for a time, for the time being, for my being time. After all there's no other.

Writing to press my face in the ordure of my ordinariness? So I make the lifelong little snobberies and embarrassments (I know, becoming quainter with each passing month) cut the page like a kitchen knife silently slashing youthful skin which can no more heal than the old and wrinkled.

More to the point: why have I written of a life's that's passing – as if it were still my present? For, truly, I'm not so energetically fastidious as I once was. Nothing in this rotting house is any longer quite pristine. Dust is accumulating where it used never to linger, along the picture rail and across the false coals – one smells it when switching on the bars.

Some think carelessness makes a house unkempt and comfortable, no fear of smudge and scratch. This could have been such a house if I'd let it, a home for sexy slovens and self-regarding sluts; it had the makings. I anticipated and scrubbed away such indolent notions. But now?

Does Maud ever wonder what would happen if some day I stopped tidying, dusting, polishing and sweeping altogether, stopped keeping myself smart and making up my face? Would the house collapse with us like naked broken dolls inside – shattered, bleeding china limbs strewn over the rubble? The wing chair a heap of dead flies.

Was something always apprehensive about my spotlessness? Only servants should make a house as clean as I keep – or kept – this one. But there's never been a servant. You make and clean your own dirt in my house, our house. As everyone should.

If Maud read my writing, what would she feel? This half-house is her skin. Its pebble-dashing has given her no rash that I can see. Or, if it has, she'll have learnt to soothe it in Phyllis's tawdry flat on my lonely weekends and evenings.

Would Phyllis have scratched it for her? With her clumsy nails.

Who's to do that for me? Best keep your skin clear with your own sweat and unguents.

Hold fast to independence.

*

In the war, blackout was meant to shut out *all* light. If your window had a chink, the warden would rap your door. Later we learnt all this tacking and pinning, this gluing and spoiling of good window frames, was no use at all except to teach Obedience. More people died from road accidents on dark streets than in bombed houses with a sliver of light round the window.

Testing us, you see: give up your iron pans and railings – no matter, they're used for nothing much; we'll watch to see if you grieve for your wrought iron and ruined sashes. If you do, we'll know you're unpatriotic.

In the last months of the war came 'dim-out'. Were German bombers so exhausted by the Baby Blitz their eyes had grown weak? Intending Birmingham, they dropped bombs on Nuneaton. I should have fixed a green light to my chimney stack and invited over the weary Luftwaffe.

Now there's just the IRA. Might they too lose their way one night? If they can kill the Birmingham drinkers in the Mulberry Bush and the Tavern in the Town, why ignore the housewives of Ackroyd Close?

I could send Hugh Callaghan and Paddy Hill an invitation with directions. Take out no.14, like a rotten tooth, please. (The Irish appreciate courtesy.) Maud would forgive, she's not resentful. She'd be content to go with me.

Or the H-bomb which they say must detonate soon might work its mushroomy magic: it could rise above Norton, for surely we're midway between Russia and America, and there are accidents. Then there'd be one magnificent immolation, *our* holocaust.

But nothing will happen. No Luftwaffe or IRA, no bomb or earthquake is big enough to swallow all the scarred Midlands of England – the part that's neither North nor South, East nor West, just what's left when proud excluding bits of the country's great bottom, Kent and Cornwall, sail off; no hurricanes fierce enough to blow down the semi-detached and terraced boxes of Norton, the last crumbling back-to-backs and hideous new blocks of concrete flats scabbing the squat hills and swamps where no one should have built and no one wants to live; no floods deep enough to wash us and our gritty nastiness away; no river to break its cemented banks, no conflagration to burn to ashes; nothing whatever to wipe all the stain and filth quite off the face of the earth – and me with it. Nothing to make us feral along with the downtrodden beasts and beetles, nothing to cleanse the old world's fabric before the man-cancer devours it all.

My, my! I suspected what writing might do but didn't dream it would work so fast. A pity I gave up smoking, or my lurch from home-making and make-believe into this ferocity would demand a fag. I'd enjoy the calming ritual of opening a new packet, fingering, lighting and taking the first and only real puff. Or, better, tidying tobacco into folds of paper, then licking. More there for the hungry mouth to do. Still, such lacerating pleasure in giving up.

Maud said – and it was out of character: 'Perhaps you ask too much of life.'

Not so. I don't ask Life anything at all. Life and I have had nothing to say to each other this long while.

April 1976

Maud's feeling tension, I know it but don't interrogate.

All these years tormented by the sly nastiness of girls. She can't be well thought of, though no one's complained. Perhaps they have and she hasn't told me. She holds things close to her chest.

She must keep some order, but what happens outside the front rows? Do the girls laugh at her, tease her, mock her even? Do they call her 'the beetroot' – she blushes so vividly? Do they draw rude pictures on her blackboard and giggle when she sees them? Launch pencils and paper daggers at each other when her back's turned? Or to her face? Perhaps some saucy child puts a foot out to trip her when she walks between desks to correct French spelling.

Have they ever assaulted her? One reads of such things in the newspaper. A sharpened pencil in her side or an elbow stuck in her mouth and the great girls laughing at her as she falls. Her eyes would water with thin tears.

She'd never tell me. She'd keep it all inside her pinched body.

This last weekend she brought me breakfast in bed. The boiled egg was watery. Too late to pop it back. The toast was right, though, still hot and crisp, the marmalade spooned on to the side of the plate. I propped the pillow against the padded wooden headboard and leaned against it. I felt a crumb of hard toast caught in a tooth.

A gap in my lower back, so I eased down a little. I was warm and soft, the bed a little cloying. I drank the tea from an odd angle and spilt a drop. It ran smoothly down my neck, tingling through the skin, reaching the cleavage that, glancing down, I saw was too white – like those sunless fish in the depths of the sea.

Wrapped in her green felt dressing-gown with its girdle of twisted green and white cord, Maud sat at the foot of my bed rifling through a copy of an old *Telegraph* I'd left upstairs. She had tea only. She'd eat later she said.

When I'd finished, I felt a twinge of pain in my chest and arm. I must have sat awkwardly without realising. Maud took the tray and placed it on my dressing table, pushing aside the frosted-green brush and her small framed Polyfoto taken on a seaside holiday. She slightly tipped the loose glass top so that brush and photo teetered on the edge. I said nothing.

'Why don't you stay there? Nothing to be up for.'

'No, I must get on,' I said. 'I can't laze in bed.'

'I'll help you then.'

She came over with my fawn suede slippers and, as I slowly swung my feet out of the bed towards the floor, she knelt down and put them on, one foot, then the other, brushing her fingers against my flesh. Quite in silence. I felt almost dizzy, close to tears.

'I must have sat up too quickly,' I said.

Maud suggests I make an appointment with the doctor for my chesty pains. I see no purpose. Just indigestion.

When Mother and Father were alive, the doctor came to our house. Father paid him there and then. We called him our *Family* Doctor. *Mother's* Doctor I'd say: he held her hand just below the place one presses to take a pulse. He did this even when it was I who was supposed to be ill: he feared the strain of it on her constitution, he said.

145

'An old woman's disease,' said the NHS Indian when he saw the tiny blisters on an angry skin just above my navel when I had shingles. I was thirty-seven. (He knew that. Your birth date is your identity in the NHS.)

I don't need a doctor: I don't need men's sharp nails probing me. I know my own body and what's inside. It's Maud who should see about herself. Pallid beyond normal. Something not right but I can't put a finger on it.

Last night as I finished listening to Clifford Curzon playing the Mendelssohn Piano Sonata in E on the wireless (not liking it so much as his *Songs Without Words*), I noticed she'd taken out her books to mark. She should do this in recess or a spare period in schooltime.

'Did you have a nice day, Maud?'

She looked up uncertainly. 'All right,' she said. 'It was a reasonable lunch.'

'Are the girls in the top form up to last year? You thought them inferior in the beginning, didn't you?'

She put down her red pencil and rubbed her eyes. 'They turn out much the same in the end.'

'Do you have any you especially like, who might go on to try for Modern Languages at Oxford?'

She'd taken up her red pencil again and looked at me uncomprehending for a moment. Then her eyes returned to the book. 'No, no, I don't think so. I suppose it's not right to have favourites. The others would resent it.'

Her pencil slashed a word as she spoke. She didn't look up again.

I recalled the jerky outpouring at the reservoir. Must I depend on her timing?

'Are you getting more effective as a teacher?'

She raised her head and sighed. 'What did you say?'

'I asked whether you felt your teaching was improving, Maud.'

'I don't know. I don't feel any. I do the same thing over and over. The girls are more difficult I think. I can't judge really. It's not easy to say, is it?'

'I wouldn't know.'

Her halting speech disturbed me. I sought only common chat in the silence after music.

She went on marking, though her hand was less steady as it hovered over a book. The side of her left eye twitched. She rubbed it with her forefinger. The twitch grew more pronounced.

'Why don't you put on your spectacles. You're straining your eyes.'

'I'm all right.' She turned a page in the exercise book.

'I can see you're not. Shall I get them for you?'

For a moment her expression was almost sour, then she coloured. 'No. I think they're in my satchel.'

She stood up awkwardly, dropping her pencil, along with the book she was marking. The others were stacked in a precarious, untidy pile on the arm of the chair. When she returned, she'd have to slither in below them to prevent them falling in a disordered heap. An instant's thought would have avoided this.

With her spectacles on, she looked older, more strained, although the frames hid the little tapering lines fanning from her eyes. Her high bony forehead was accentuated, not softened as I'd once expected, its worry lines deepened by the harsh parallel of the dark tortoiseshell. Not cheap frames, not wire and plastic NHS ones that cut into the tender back of ears, but perhaps, after all, not chosen with proper care.

Who's to do that if not Maud? Jealous Phyllis perhaps? Marring the face she envied and as good as slapped.

She'd picked up the pencil and was busy marking again, taking, I noticed, longer over each page. A Chopin Étude was playing. Does she like the music I like, the words I like? *Really* like?

Through the kitchen hatch I once caught snatches of *Semprini Serenade*: 'Old ones, new ones, loved ones, neglected ones.' When I turned on the wireless later, its dial was awry. A booming voice congratulated the best Mum and Dad in the world on their twenty-five years of happy marriage. (Grown men in posh houses call their mothers 'Mummy'!) The unexpected sounds pelted me like icy gravel.

'It's better like that, isn't it?' I said, looking at her bespectacled face.

She glanced at me, as if dazed. 'Yes, thank you.'

'Are you all right, Maud?'

'Yes, of course.' She put down her pencil and rubbed her eyes again, pushing her spectacles off her nose, stretching the white empty space of her brow.

'It'll be worse for rubbing. Why don't you use some Optrex?'

She sat in silence, rubbing and screwing up her mouth.

'You don't look well. You aren't eating properly. You *are* dieting, aren't you?'

No answer.

'Why on earth can't you say something?'

'What did you say?'

'Really, Maud! I asked if you were dieting.'

She looked at me. Almost transparent. 'No. It'd be silly at my age. I'm not as hungry as I was.'

We'd not had our milky drink yet, so she got up to warm it, again leaving her pile of books untidily on her chair.

'They're nearly falling off; one's already on the floor,' I said when she returned. 'Why not stack them neatly? It takes no more effort.'

She bent down to pick up the exercise book. As she did, she pressed one hand to her forehead.

'What's the matter? Are you ill?'

'It's nothing.' She stood up. 'I felt a bit faint, that's all.'

'It's not nothing,' I said. 'You shouldn't have such feelings. You should see a doctor.'

She went out to fetch the cups of warmed milky coffee. She'd put a biscuit on my saucer, not on hers.

'I had one in the kitchen,' she said.

'You should make an appointment.'

Aunty Gertie would have taken Maud on to her lap and reached out for her Huntley and Palmers tin of ginger-nut biscuits to feed her one. Like a baby.

I think uneasily of Aunty Gertie. Maud here, as she is, so different in outline. The one so bulky, the other so thin.

Phyllis used to feed Maud vegetables from her allotment, grime still sticking to them. Rarely carrots or peas to shell and smell fresh in the kitchen; sometimes leathery runner beans left too long on the plant and way beyond juiciness; tomatoes good only for green tomato chutney since they'd never ripen in a month of sunny Sundays; small tart onions with earth in their layers; and failed cabbages with coarse outsides and soft decaying centres.

Mostly, I remember the marrows – sleek, grained and big in those years when slugs didn't cut them off before their fat, watery prime. They were sugary, insipid things. You must be ingenious to make a marrow tasty, stuffing it with spiced mince or mixed breadcrumbs and mousetrap cheese. The jellyfish of plants. (During rationing we cut it into pieces, soaked them in pineapple juice, then pretended the pieces *were* pineapple. The marrow had a purpose then.)

Why write now of Phyllis and her encroaching marrows and tough beans? Phyllis digging in the earth with a charm bracelet jangling from her plump, dirty wrist.

And Maud eating up her vegetables.

That food won't be going in Maud's pure body again.

May 1976

Maud's birthday

On the Welsh holiday in 1957 or maybe '58, when we returned from the waterfall Clare constructed a birthday party for Maud. Sometimes in past years she'd forgotten the date, as now – she said she hadn't but that was a lie. She gave Maud money instead of a proper present, no card. I produced a lace-making kit with instructions and an anthology of quotations. I'd wrapped them in blue tissue paper before leaving home.

That day there was no high tea and the dining room was closed. So we were in the dull, comfortable sitting room, full of easy chairs, a settee, and a square central table: they called it a 'lounge' as if we were sailing on an ocean liner. No one else there except an old lady in the corner sitting upright to read *Country Life*, never once rustling the pages; perhaps she contemplated the

'Girl in Pearls' and imagined being a young debutante.

Maud turned crimson when we sang 'Happy Birthday'.

'No, please,' she begged.

But Nick, who'd forgotten the occasion altogether and probably felt guilty at not wanting us there, insisted. He forced himself and the boys to sing. He kept smiling at Maud. Clare mouthed the words.

The old fruit cake must have been stored in the back kitchen behind baking tins and china rolling pins. So dry the knife crashed into the plate once past the rubbery top. We all had to have a piece.

'Not much for me,' said Clare. 'It'll soon be supper-time.'

We each swallowed some, the boys taking seconds because genuinely hungry: they'd have eaten cardboard. Maud managed to prod down a slice though I saw it stuck a little in her throat.

After the song and the cake, we sat in the warmth near the smoking fire. Nick and the boys were at the table, flicking through magazines on cars and trains. The boys kicked their feet against the legs of chairs in protest at being confined. They were still hungry, with an hour to go till supper. Clare and I chatted as women always must. Maud was awkward but looked not unattractive in the quiet glow of the fire. I moved next to her on the settee. It was to avoid the fire's concentrated heat. I told Clare so.

Words are wily: there was always an undertow. Was Maud staring at anything? I can't recall. Besides, her eyes are hooded and look obliquely.

In past years I've baked a birthday cake, but not this time. I laid out the bought sponge, feeling no shame. It had been an effort to get it, the bakery being farther away than the High Street. To reach it I'd had to go through the underpass with its disgusting graffiti and obscene drawings.

I'd also made a few cucumber sandwiches. I removed their crusts and cut them into triangles, then placed them on a doily.

When Maud returned from school we sat down to eat. I let her be mother with the teapot. She offered me the plate of sandwiches, taking only one for herself. 'Saving room for the cake,' she said. Though she ate the slenderest slice.

But she did eat it. I watched with hawk eyes. If she's planning to disappear, she'll need to do it in private.

'You like sponge,' I said.

Her mouth gave a quick smile, then fell back. 'You've tired yourself going out,' she murmured as she carried a second cup of tea to my chair.

'I had to go,' I said. 'It's only once a year.'

I brought out her presents nicely wrapped in special paper. I was forced to take the whole roll of gold and silver striped stuff, though exclaiming to the unmoved shop assistant. It was, I thought, worth the extravagance.

As usual, I gave her two things. A solution that made bubbles when squeezed out under hot running water; I hoped she'd enjoy it though we're still careful to have shallow baths. A cream scarf slashed with crimson to bring out the colour in her face – or add some.

'You shouldn't have bothered,' she said, as I always say, and as Mother laughingly said when Father brought home his extravagant, silly gifts at Christmas, on her birthday and sometimes randomly. With Maud, it seems more than ritual courtesy.

'I should,' I said. 'Your birthday's quiet enough as it is.'

'I like it quite well.'

Does she really? Last year, the day after her usual birthday tea with Phyllis, she and I went to a pub by the river. As ever, we sat in silence lulled by a clinking of glasses and cutlery. A man passed us from the rattling outside lavatory. There was a small wet spot beside his zip, which hadn't been pulled right up. Two tipsy middle-aged women, each holding a rose on a long stem, did little dance steps, clutching each other's arms as they lurched happily by.

'I think we should go,' I said.

'Oh, why? It's so pleasant to sit in the sun like this.'

'I'm glad you're enjoying it, Maud,' I said.

'Aren't you?'

Of course not. Neither of us was.

Or so I thought. Perhaps I was wrong. Was she content sitting in silence among drunken, chattering fools? On her birthday?

With her own mother?

She *seemed* cheerful enough, her mind blank or sailing away over the water in a ship of fools.

Does she enjoy eating a mean sponge cake almost in silence in a shabby house? Celebrating a birthday that marks another wasted year? Now? A cake *bought* by her mother and carried home in a shopping bag? Does she want the cake, the cucumber sandwiches and gifts? She didn't look especially grateful.

Can she take pleasure in a piecemeal life?

Phyllis always did something for her birthday. What's happening? Has there even been a present? Where's the card?

When Maud was sixteen, I gave her a charm bracelet. I paid more than I usually do for things: the bracelet was under glass in the shop, where they keep the dearer items. It had four dangling charms: an enamel bird, a plated silver fish with tiny open fins and gills, a filigreed diamond and a green shamrock. I told her we'd add other charms as time went by, but we never did. Over the next years I assumed she treasured the bracelet, even if she didn't wear it.

Then, when Maud and I were having Sunday tea and scones with Phyllis, I discovered she'd given *her* the bracelet. Phyllis mentioned it to make sure I knew: *five* charms, she said.

Maud had added the fifth: a tiny silver hazelnut. Phyllis once said her name had to do with the hazel or almond.

You could have cut the silence in that room, but I wasn't the one to do it.

If I gave the bracelet to Maud, she should be free to give it away again. Yet it wasn't like the unwanted gifts Mother kept under the bed to pass on to someone she didn't much care for: china ear-ring boxes, scarves and silver trinkets from Masonic ladies' nights, not like those. Maud must have valued the bracelet once, even if it dangled too freely on her thin wrist.

I avoid thinking what went into the little addition, the effort of finding and choosing and buying the special charm, then the giving.

Phyllis knew what she'd done in blurting it out.

Not the first or last time she's aimed to rile me. 'Do you remember,' she'd say when I was there like a ghost at the feast, 'the time we had the special birthday tea with cream slices on green plates? We pretended we were sisters.'

A sorry pretence I'd have said if I hadn't bitten my lip. Sisters indeed! Nothing like: Maud so delicate and indistinct, so pliant and pliable. Phyllis so thick, stiff and ungainly. With her coarse hair and ugly lines about the mouth, light years distant.

And always those absurd irises on the tip of her cunning tongue.

We didn't speak of the bracelet and its charms. Maud saw what I felt, looks were enough. We went our separate ways after tea.

'The gods themselves cannot recall their gifts.'

When she married her sandman, did Phyllis wrench the bracelet from her thick wrist and chuck it back to Maud?

If so, when? At the wedding? Over the warmed rolls? Or before, at a little private ceremony? Gave back the hazelnut that hung between them.

Or do you still have it, Phyllis? I rather think you do. Have you ever tried to crack that hard, intimate nut between your fat fingers?

I do know the bracelet isn't in Maud's dressing table. Needing to dust, I noticed one drawer improperly shut. A grey silk scarf in cellophane touched the rim making the drawer bulge. To close it I had to pull it open. As I say, I don't rummage in her things. A pile of little gifts squashed together: brooches, eau de Cologne, silk flowers, some still in wrapping paper. Phyllis's name all over them. Small expensive things, so they fitted that drawer. But there was no bracelet.

How could the vicious woman abandon my Maud?

Early June 1976

Though tired myself, I proposed a meal out at the weekend. I registered Maud's indifference, so added, 'If we don't like it, we might still enjoy anticipating.' She made no comment. 'The weather's strangely warm and dry.'

We chose a place she'd heard recommended by married Helen in school. Not a scotch-egg-and-Branston-pickle café but not classy. 'Good atmosphere, not too pricey,' she'd said, assuming we weren't well off.

By the time we arrived, Maud had taken on a bit of colour, probably from the effort of driving down an almost empty road. She lolloped along from the car park in her full checked skirt and khaki blouse. I wore my old dark blue costume in seersucker, with pale brown, almost tan shoes that toned with the blue. Though hatless, I looked reasonably smart. As we walked towards the restaurant, the sun shone so brightly it yellowed the trees against the sky.

It didn't suit. We knew at once. I'd half expected it: I'd not met Mrs Helen but I had a dim view of her from opinions Maud occasionally quoted. Despite Mogadon, I'd had a disturbed night and couldn't muster the energy to march straight out.

A low-timbered room with shadowy corners, candles in bowls on tables, lit to make small flames in daytime; near the entrance a banquette of purple velvet with little bare patches where one must wait to be seated if there were a queue.

None today for we'd arrived early. Yet the few tables for two were already taken and we were put in a place laid for four. The waitress was surly, preferring proper couples. Men tip more than women, they say. Of course. Women are poorer.

'Full, isn't it?' I said.

The waitress snorted. 'It'll be a lot busier later. This is nothing.' She flounced off.

Maud sat down, sticking out her thin elbows from the table in teacherly pose. She was infuriatingly ill at ease, bits of her moving involuntarily. When after much pressing she spoke, her voice croaked or slid upwards. The dimness made her hair look heavier and thicker, wisps shining with back lighting.

Like Marlene Dietrich in *The Blue Angel*. She has the legs too.

'Does Helen eat here often?'

'I don't know. I don't talk to her much.'

'Strange you achieved this recommendation.'

She didn't answer.

'We should look at the menu.' I'd glanced at it: 'quiche' was the only properly priced item. (When did a savoury custard with bacon bits become a 'quiche'?) 'What do you want?'

'I don't know, what are *you* having?'

'Does it depend on me?'

'No.'

'I'll have the quiche with potatoes. It'll probably arrive quickly.'

'I'll have that too.'

'I thought so.'

No one came by except a young man for the drinks order. I was bending down to take a handkerchief from my bag, so he addressed Maud. She shook her head and he left. When I looked up, I said, 'I'd have liked some wine. One can get it by the glass.'

Maud was settling herself from the encounter. 'Do you want to call the man back?'

'No, you'll have to. You're facing that way.'

She bit her lip and clutched the knuckle of her long middle finger with the thumb and index finger of the other hand, a common gesture with her. 'I can't,' she said.

'Why? Do you expect me to twist round when you're facing his direction?'

'I can't.'

'You could try.'

'I really couldn't.'

'Just raise your hand or signal to him in some way when you catch his eye.'

'No really, I can't.' She paused, red-faced. 'I could go up to him,' she said at last.

'Good heavens, no,' I said. 'It's his business to come here. We pay him.'

'I can't.'

How many times have those words dribbled from her lips?

She was twisting her fingers so uncontrollably I glanced round. Everyone was talking or eating. No one observed us. Why should they?

'You're unbelievably annoying, Maud. What a mouse! How ever do you cope in school?'

'Badly,' she said, unsmiling.

'I do wish you had more about you.'

The waitress came over, we thought for our orders, but it was to seat a young couple at our table. The girl didn't disguise her dismay at sharing; the boy said, 'I'm sorry. Do you mind if we sit here?'

A boy taking out a pretty girl for lunch, of no significance to us or the world, yet I summed them up, even while wondering why I bothered. Naturally they paid no such attention to Maud and me – or Maud to them. I alone was spectator at the hum-drum theatre.

Might as well be a prompter ghost or recording angel; I never fail in vigilance.

The young man, red-haired with ruddy face and gold eye-lashes, wore a pale-grey woven jacket with a pinkish shirt, grey silk cravat and enamelled cufflinks. He could have been a youth of any time this last half century, pre- or post-war, exuding not vanity exactly but a careless well-being. Fingers thick and coarse, not from work but from clutching a wet ball or rowing on a river in drizzle. When he laughed, which he did whenever he spoke, the gummy mouth frothed, leaving at its edge a slight debris of suds. A bit of a rattle I judged him; an upper-middle-class but not county voice: son of a well-to-do doctor or wealthy busi-nessman? He'd be a loser in life if not so well nurtured. He sat knees spread wide in his chair, as men do.

She was just as easy to place, with her Carnaby Street face of mascara and heavy glittery eye-shadow, dark hair topped with a knowing fringe, cut at different levels. Slacks and a green polo-necked ribbed jumper, short leather waistcoat with tassels, and homemade-looking pendant of twisted metal. She'd tied a fringed scarf jauntily like a ribbon round her trousered hips, as if making her loins into a gift for the onlooker. Small mouth and little rat teeth, across which she swirled a pink tongue. One could see she didn't come from much, but she was cannier than her chap and would soon be in control. She gazed out bored, a malevolent tinge distorting her cheaply pretty features.

'Will you have some wine?' said the boy.

'Don't mind,' said the girl, Wolverhampton in the trailing vowels.

'If we have the steak we could have a newish Beaujolais. The Moulin-à-vent is good. What do you think?' (Whatever did he think she'd think?)

'Choose what you like, Tony. Just so long as it works.' She giggled.

I heard and saw all this because Maud and I sat in silence.

'No, we haven't been here before,' I said to the boy's query. 'The service is rather slow.'

'Yes it is.' He laughed a sudsy laugh, then with his great hand beckoned the wine waiter and gave his order.

He was planning to cross the Sahara to Timbuctu in an American jeep he told the girl. She made an amusing dig about sand and flat tyres which he failed to catch.

Finally ordered and delivered, the quiche tasted adequate, though not quite set, the under-pastry too moist.

Like an indulged two-year-old, Maud ate the centre, leaving the brown side crust and even the base. She held the knife and fork tightly, as weak hands hold garden implements.

I watched her pick at her food. For a while I refrained from remark; then I said, 'Maud dear, I hope that's not all you're going to eat.'

She gave me her pained look. 'I've had enough.'

'Not very appetising, eh?' put in the young man. 'You should have had the steak. Excellent, isn't it, Carol?'

'It's good,' she said. 'A bit of an effort on the edges, but OK.'

With only a trickle left in the bottle, they were growing chummy. The stupidity of her beau no longer troubled the girl. She scoffed and pouted, then sat back preening. The pouts reminded me of cousin Clare practising faces in front of Mother's bathroom mirror.

The young man stared at Maud's pastry leavings. 'You know, it may be very gross of me to suggest, but I've got an awfully large piece of meat here. If you'd like a bite, I could slip it over to you discreetly.' A full-bodied laugh followed. The girl sniggered.

A spasm crossed Maud's face. She blushed, sweat leapt on to her forehead making beads of crimson blood. Her knife quivered in her hand. The offer seemed not just tactless, not merely humiliating or embarrassing, but abhorrent. She looked at the man's plate as if it displayed undercooked rat.

The girl noticed and sniggered again. The youth remained unaware. Silence lengthened. I couldn't speak for her.

'No,' she said at last. 'No really, I couldn't take it.'

'Oh do,' he urged. He even started to cut off a piece of the spongy meat.

'No really, I've had enough. I never eat much. Please.' Her tone was so imploring that even this ox of a man caught it.

'As you wish,' he said, offended. 'Perhaps you're dieting. Women do a lot of that.'

The girl looked at the thin, ageing face and grunted.

Abruptly, Maud spoke. 'Excuse me.' Her voice was high and strained.

She got up, dropping her knife on the floor. She didn't stay to retrieve it. Her soiled serviette lay exposed on the chair.

I tried to plaster over the moment with social chat, but no one was listening. I shot a look round for Maud and saw she'd dashed the wrong way. Floundering in the dark end of the restaurant.

At last, seeing her haunted or bewildered face and fearing perhaps she'd be sick in her section, a waitress accosted her. Maud spoke too low or used the wrong word. (What do you call the lavatory nowadays? The Toilet, the Facilities, the Bathroom, the WC, the Cloakroom, the Ladies, the Loo, the last so affected and public school. Americans say the Little Girls' Room or the John or the Crapper, so I've read.) The waitress looked irritated, then understood.

Maud set off again across the cluttered interlocking rooms.

She passed our table without a glance, her face mashed and vulnerable.

The red-haired young man looked pityingly at me. She was ill or weird. He squashed his huge hand on to his girl's saucy one, covering a coy little heart-shaped ring. He'd been attentive to her glass and they were on the second bottle. She left her hand in his public grasp.

'Your friend looks ill.'

'She's my daughter.'

I was exasperated with all of them. My head ached with the pressure of other people behaving wrongly. Maud hadn't over-turned a table of condiments and tumblers or tripped up a snooty barman with a tray of wine bottles. Her pathetic, mal-adroit display hadn't been disastrous, just faintly comic.

Our waitress came by and, with a flourish, retrieved the dropped knife. I meant to say something like 'I think I'll go to see how she is,' or 'She's been unwell,' anything at all of a social sort. But I didn't. I felt what I was, an insignificant elderly woman with an imbecile daughter.

An image flashed before me: of Maud in the now empty chair. Why should I pursue the poor pale thing? It was her private mis-ery, something with which I should have nothing to do.

Or everything.

My hands grew wet like Maud's brow, sweat in lines and creases. I shared her trapped and rising panic.

We are a pair.

I see it as I write now: she with her diminished appetite, almost a sickness, and I with my sudden aches and indigestions. Oh yes, like Mother used to claim she had. But no resemblance: I never press my hand just below my bosom or put a red claw to my mouth to mute a burp. Whatever's in me, I swallow, all of it. Whatever tries to come up and out won't. Not from *my* body.

Perhaps Maud is swallowing herself too and has no room for any other food – not even underdone quiche or Phyllis's marrow from the abandoned allotment.

Eventually she came back. The young people were thrusting slender silver spoons into peppermint parfaits in long thin glasses, overflowing down frosted sides. The boy was still speaking to the world, now about cars and their different capacities for expeditions, while his fingers moved rhythmically over his girl's hand.

I'd forced on Maud a small vanilla ice from the dessert menu which the waitress stuck in front of my face. She didn't want anything, but I was afraid she'd faint. Sugar would help; as a girl she loved sucking sugar cubes.

'Let's have coffee at home,' I said.

At once she began getting up.

'We'll get the bill first.'

When it came, it was too much.

'What's the matter with it?' demanded the waitress.

'We seem to have been charged extra, but I haven't checked it yet.'

Her waiting manners, if ever possessed, had long since evaporated. 'That's what you ate,' she said, 'count it if you want.'

The fault was the new VAT; also the ice cream was a preposterous price. 'It's all right,' I said.

The waitress whisked the money away. Maud fidgeted. We were silent until she returned with our change. I left a tip in the saucer. So awkward for women alone. The waitress stared rudely at it as she passed to another table.

'For goodness' sake, let's go,' I said to Maud. I too should have visited the Ladies' Powder Room – apparently that's what they call it here – but didn't. As I say, I hold myself in.

I detest public lavatories: squatting so awkwardly in that raised defecatory position to avoid contact, as one does. Now here in this pretentious restaurant, my unfulfilled desire dragged up another scene. One of those humiliating moments wedged in my head like a dead fly caught in a dirty, lidless marmalade jar.

Moments that drive out the present, I'll say that for them.

Once, and not so many years ago neither, the cover over the seat in a public convenience near Rackham's was down and I didn't notice.

As I felt the unexpected warmth steaming up between my buttocks and along my thighs, I experienced the kind of horror that smashes one's face into a thousand hot jagged pieces.

I managed almost – but not quite – to cut off the stream. The dreadful liquid had splashed on to my hitched-up wool frock and crinkled knickers, and run on to the floor, a yellow stream trickling under the door and on to a stone-flagged floor. Where nothing seeps in.

Only a roll of unabsorbent, institutional toilet paper in the cubicle. I tried mopping up what I could and soon exhausted the roll. I took out my handkerchief and the small flannel I always carry in a pouch in my clasp bag. Sopping wet at once. Moisture oozing now from every pore, sweat staining my brassiere, waves of heat breaking over torso and down limbs.

I couldn't reach under the door with the sodden paper and

flannel, though I was almost on my knees. I wanted to crawl out and wipe the shaming flagstones with everything I had – blue chiffon scarf, even white blouse, my whole shaming body. It would have done no good.

On the lavatory door, as I stood up, the pile of sodden paper, flannel and handkerchief in both hands, I read words scrawled in red chalk: 'A Woman needs a Man like a Fish needs a Bicycle.' Below it in pink lipstick someone had drawn the outline of a smiling fish riding a bike.

At least my three-quarters coat was dry: I'd hung it on a hook to one side. I put it on now, covering the worst. I had to stay in that cubicle until sure no one was outside to connect me and my piddle-soaked skirt to the tell-tale trickle. Over and over I read the inane messages on the door, dabbing the cubicle floor at intervals with the sodden heap of paper and cloth. Aching to flush it all away, but fearing it would get stuck round the bend and make *everything* well up out of the bowl, not just my but other people's foulness.

I lifted the lavatory lid, put in half the sodden paper, then pulled the chain. The wad expanded in the bowl. I stuffed the rest into my coat pocket along with the handkerchief. The flannel went back into the little pouch, now so wet and bulky my bag would hardly close.

The clogged lavatory could take care of itself.

I listened for a sound of doors opening, feet stepping closer, skidding on my effluent. I waited until I thought I heard silence, the din between my ears making it hard to judge. Then I wrapped my coat tighter, the wet paper and handkerchief bulging its pocket.

I came out.

At once I saw the woman by the main door. A woman about my age, gaunt, with greying unkempt hair and tanned wrinkled face, teeth protruding against a bottom lip. A type I could place immediately, a hiking wife – there was a knapsack on her back – who did craft in women's groups with raffia or stained glass. She must have had silent crepe-soled shoes on her solid, stolid, no-nonsense feet. Or did she creep in on rounded tiptoe?

On tippy toes, as Clare used to say to Mother in her little-girl voice when she was already full grown.

The woman would have seen, must have known, yet she smiled. She was about to speak. I couldn't bear it. I looked away, then rushed from the room with the sodden wodge straining against my coat lining.

I detested the smile. Had this woman failed to see the wet mess? Would she slip on it as she moved towards an empty cubicle? Or, worse, had she seen it and so knew everything of me and what I had done – and felt pity?

Like the red-haired, frothing boy.

To whom is this pity directed?

I boarded the train from Birmingham with my damp clutch bag in one hand, the other pulling my coat tightly to me, the wetness in the pocket now working through the thin lining and wool frock, prickling my skin.

Fearing to leave a shaming wetness on the fabric seat, I stood by the door. Then I saw the woman. She was sitting nearby, still smiling but not to me.

With better temperament, one might have gone home, pulled up a chair, sat down at the kitchen table with a cup of tea and digestive biscuit, then roared with laughter at the thought of this incident. At my own expense of course.

Not with a friend I think. Would Maud have told Phyllis, or Phyllis Maud? I can't hear them giggle.

Possibly with a sister? Too intimate for a daughter?

I assume so. Perhaps the roar of laughter would always need to have been in private.

I never shared it with Maud, but writing this after her little embarrassment at the restaurant is a kind of sharing, without the risk.

Can humiliation ever be funny? It might be. Funny ha-ha. On the page, that is, in blue-black ink. I can if I wish smudge it a little.

Mid-June 1976

Removable parts

Phyllis's sobbing mother is a dental assistant. Standing by her man in a crisp white uniform, she hands him little sharp silvery instruments with which to prod warm, wet, sensitive private places. Such proxy power she feels as the body below the mouth squirms and hands clench nails into shouting flesh.

The husband made enough money to send his children to a private school, but he doesn't hold a candle to the dentist drilling and pricking those bleeding caverns. Phyllis will know and resent this.

Ivan the Terrible was born with two teeth: using one he could devour his enemies, with the other his family. In 1953, the Soviet Ministry of Culture inspected his corpse: they noted that the main teeth appeared only when the Terrible was in his fifties.

Their irruption would have tormented him. (It's no excuse for a vicious life.)

Two of my teeth are false, stuck on a plate. One an eye-tooth. An 'I'-tooth. A 'Me'-tooth, upfront. 'What you see is what you get,' the Yanks say. Nothing personal.

When the first tooth decayed, Muriel said, 'Why don't you have them all out? I did. You get a nice even white set top and bottom. Like a film star.'

Clickety-clack: she banged her rows of teeth together, then followed with a skeletal grin. (How's she faring on New Zealand mutton with her elderly pair of fake choppers?)

'No,' I said, 'I don't fancy the pain' – or the look, I might have added.

It happened not long after Maud was born. A tooth fractured and rotted, the brown decayed part falling off one morning as my tongue wiggled it. I showed a jagged gap like a dwarf portcullis until a dentist was free to fix it.

'Don't you know . . . ?'

In the dentist's chair to have the rest of the rotten tooth extracted. 'We'll stop if we hear a doodlebug,' chuckled the old man.

Strapped down and masked, I was away over the waves, my head becoming – as it so often did without help of ether – an exploding white and sugary mass, long oozing soft insects slithering over it.

No ether and wide awake when the dentist used his treadle drill to 'tidy up around', as he put it. His hands were gnarled with arthritis, more than Aunty Gertie's.

'You have to look after teeth,' he said, wagging a deformed finger, 'then they'll look after you.'

When war ended, another tooth decayed. Perhaps 'battledress refill' corroded human enamel. A further false one was soldered on to the plate like a fender to a farm cart. NHS economy. That time the ether was more suffocating and smelly, the sugar head crawled over by rubbery worms.

I thought I'd never tolerate the plastic and metal plate in my mouth. Then I did, accepting it like a wily, tipsy uncle you can't turn out of the house, however irritating.

Plate-people are a fellowship. We twist the gadgetry round with our tongues for thrill: when forced to speak, we must make the quick click back. In private darkness we set by the bedside (or washbasin if shameless) a mug of fizzing Steradent, waiting while its bubbles wash away the odour and filth we've made chewing and chatting all day.

The rich don't have plastic and metal plates. They used to yank living teeth out of poor people's mouths and pop them into their own rotten, privileged gums.

Maud has good teeth. I note it when she eats cream; it forms straight lines down from the gums. I can rightly say I made those teeth with more than their share of rationed milk and butter – perhaps I crushed my own weak ones in their creating. They're a little too big for her mouth: if her grave is opened, they'll look like alien monsters settled in her skull.

A crumb of toast lodges beneath my plate.

'I'll fetch a toothpick from the kitchen,' Maud says. We keep some in the chicken eggcup, a little softened from damp – we rarely use them except to push gristle down the drain.

'Open your mouth,' she says. She prods inside with her long fingers.

Have Phyllis and Maud looked into each other's mouths,

169

moved sweetmeats from one to the other like birds, squirmed tongues?

Of course not. Maud would never. How have I let such sickening intimacy invade my mind?

Yet the weak have to make demands. Remember Aunt Laura serviced throughout her supine life.

The days are stuffy, air thickening. A threatening warmth penetrates clothes and skin. Normally I keep shoes on when resting downstairs – unshod feet look so unfinished – but, with toenails growing crooked and insistent, pressing the flesh inside my shoes, I had an impulse to ease them off.

I mentioned my discomfort to Maud. 'Especially the left foot,' I added. 'One can feel light-headed bending down.'

She offered, as I wanted her to. And yet, like the toothpick on the gum, it teeters on the edge.

I've done it for Maud, of course: held her tiny feet on my lap to trim the nails. On fingers I rounded ends with scissors, then filed off harsh points.

When she grew older she attacked her nails, biting and gnawing them until they bled and revealed the fleshy dome above the nail, white from her sucking. I smacked her to make her stop, but it did no good.

She ceased in her own time, then relapsed when she started teaching. Gradually, after the first fraught months, she relented. The abused nails grew back strong, though she cut them too short, often with the large kitchen scissors. She could ask to borrow my curving pair. Or, if she found them difficult to use, even my best Florentine ones (I've kept them so carefully in their white felt case ever since, as a girl, I put them among my blouses to prevent their being damaged or mislaid). I've told her this over and over, but she cares so little how she looks. Three snips to each nail over the rubbish bin.

In the last weeks she's cared even less. Perversely, the nails have grown longer and stronger. They'd be elegant if she'd shape them. I polish and buff mine, yet they've become wrinkled, with deep grooved lines and white spots. Like the slice of an old tree infected with fungus.

We waited until I was ready for bed. I sat in the wing chair, legs propped on the tapestry stool, curtains closed, light dim. Maud perched on the stool and took the Florentine scissors from their felt case. My left foot on her lap, she held each toe in turn to cut the nail. My breath tightened. I pressed my hand against the skin of my chest.

My ankles and lower calves are flabby, a little repellent perhaps though not totally unpleasing – if one squints through hooded eyes. How indecent those words for body parts! Toes, legs, calves, ankles, thighs, buttocks, the visceral comestibles liver and kidneys, all so intimate, beyond common obscenities. Like flesh, words can be spotted and stained with age and disease.

What sort of memory will we have created with this breathless snipping? Dirty, clean, shabby, painfully sweet? Only dirty memories stick fast to the sides of the mind, the gritty adhesive oozing from that green imp's nose to ensure they're always available. Perhaps fading a little, they are revived by the feel of fluff in the nose from a feathered hat, a horse looking aslant, actors preening, an old threepenny bit balanced on a flat side, a rough nail. Anything prickly and intense. But others may linger inconspicuously: will I add to these the long fingers pressing my flesh?

*

As I stop writing, I spy something on the carpet by the chair. It's a toenail.

Maud put the clippings on to a flannel ready to shake into the rubbish bin. She picked up a few that had leapt away from the scissors. But here one sits. From its size, it must have been of the big toe, the 'I'-toe. She'd cut at the right one twice, awkwardly so it was jagged.

I flinch at the sight of this nail and its razor edge. Then I am struck by a wild notion: to pick it up and stick it on the paper in this notebook. Between words.

Things speak louder than words.

Late June 1976

Has Maud pricking memories? Memories that can't be squashed by blinking, thinking, reading, eating, agitating, twitching, sniffing, scratching in painful places.

'La la la,' we used to say in school, our fingers plugging our ears and our eyes rolling upwards. Does Maud ever need to say, 'La la la'? Is she deranged by memories? Ones I don't share?

She should know by now that people are two-legged hyenas, that behind the eyes lurk submerged crocodiles. Or have I kept the secret from her? Maybe I've been too vigilant.

At Clare's London house, a grapefruit stuck with toothpicks of tinned pineapple and cheddar cheese, like a hedgehog. I'd admired it to be polite.

Clare said, 'Oh God yes, oh dear. Pansy brought it.' She

snorted and put a maraschino cherry into lips of the same fat red colour.

'Pooh-Bah,' I said.

'Come again?'

Then Maud dropped a glass full of orange squash. It broke and liquid spread over the small woven rug on the basement-kitchen floor. It was careless, splintered glass is dangerous. I struck her lightly. Clare clucked and Nick stared at Maud. For I remember he'd come into the room, never looking at me, of course.

Clare said, 'Oh goodness, never mind, it can all go to the cleaners.'

Maud just stood there, her hand frozen at the instant of dropping that glass. Her face stricken.

Does this memory prick her? Will that scurry to the 'Powder Room' in Helen's restaurant?

When she arrived home breathless, a bit disordered, what had happened in the street or elsewhere? In university or college or further back? Phyllis's flat? What there? What mauling of mind or body has she had to endure when I've not been by?

Well, she can't match my discomforts – or my few comforts. You can't 'share' everything, Maud. It's not for her my 'best friend' sneered across the classroom. She never sat between Mother and Father in a chilly chapel, nor with scarred arms in a cooling bath on a scullery floor. Nor worried about geese walking by to market on their tarred feet or a thin moulting marmoset on the barrel organ pulled on top of a baby's pram or an uncherished dog called nothing but Spaniel. She didn't meet Cedric the station horse clip-clopping by on great shaggy hooves. You'll never be at Aunty Clare's Variety Performance or Aunty Gertie's calamitous funeral. You didn't know the bustle and bother and self-importance of a *Boy's Own* war that put inches on people unless it slashed them to midgets. We don't all sit in stalls at the same farce, Maud.

Am I repeating a commonplace: that my memories aren't stored in Maud's brain or any other body part? Nor hers in mine, though that's more certain: I didn't spend nine months in her, eating up her substance.

I've known Maud from a cluster of cells, a small defiant raspberry insisting – as she never quite did again – on being here. From an infant to a child to an adolescent to this. I've been with her at almost every twist and turn. I've watched her grow, seen her move, heard her babble, then whisper, understood her mistakes of speaking and gesturing, her hesitations and faltering, the few successes of all this progress and progression of years. I'm ahead of her. I know the route. And the carrier: this pebble-dashed semi-detached three-bedroomed (one no more than a box room) prison in a cul-de-sac. What can she imagine out there beyond these walls, a few French books with French manners – and me?

And Phyllis, who knows nothing.

What's in her head? If I offered a new debased shilling instead of an old penny for the thoughts, I'd not succeed with that mental tangle.

She's more educated than I was allowed to be. Or Father or Mother and her horde of siblings. Or the thousand years of all of us before, never pushing our heads above the parapet of place and time and history; making our crosses in parish registers only so we could pay our dues and deserve the workhouse when time came.

What would Mother and Father have made of their only

grandchild who knows French? What would Maud make of them?

I look at her now, quiet, reserved, retiring, wasting away. With her opportunities, I'd have made some splash in the river as I entered life. But she has no idea how she should exist, has nothing to live up to and for. What can she grow into? How can she drink life 'to the lees'? Will she want to, and did she ever?

It's a fair question, even an urgent one.

I admit I peered in her schoolbag.

Lodged in a textbook I found a brochure for 'Transformation Training'. Phyllis did the 'course' last year, months before she announced her engagement, as I now learn.

'You don't have to play the role assigned,' its title page declares.

Hmmm.

Despite some scruples, irritation propelled me to speak. Maud murmured a protest. For a moment she looked me levelly in the eye. I held her gaze.

'What did you expect? You wouldn't leave *Playboy* or *Oz* around would you?'

She reddened. 'It was in my satchel,' she muttered, turning away.

'What's that you say?'

Phyllis – and indeed Mrs Helen (apparently, they're acquainted) – propose the fad for Maud. For *my* Maud! A suitably subterranean way to undermine me, to make Maud as vicious as themselves.

'You wouldn't want to do this,' I said. 'You'd hate it. Three weekends of expensive rubbish in a stuffy hotel ballroom.'

175

She continued looking away, gnawing a lip.

'They're not allowed to visit the lavatory during the training.' I read this in a newspaper last year before I knew the cult would reach our house. 'Have you heard that, Maud? Did Phyllis tell you it's called "no-pee therapy"?'

'Yes. Other people manage it.'

'Other people may have cast-iron bladders.'

'Helen says it's to break down defences, so they can be properly rebuilt.' After a pause Maud added, 'Phyllis says the same.'

Phyllis says. Simon says. Try that in wartime. Not the best recipe for victory.

Let me say it directly. Are control and character neither here nor there now? All must hang out on washing lines across the dirt-strewn street, sluttish underclothes and stained linen smelling the breeze. Is privacy no virtue, reticence, reserve, recoil, humility, withdrawal, abstinence? May one not be unobtrusive without censure? Can't one keep oneself to oneself without being prodded and trodden on? Is it obligatory to smile and be sanguine? Must one reverence community and comradeship? May one not find them fraudulent?

Does 'the world' fear one might just step outside one day and thumb a nose at its values, its pompous priggish fads and fashions? Knowing that not everything can be helped, not every self transformed.

I stir my mind with these fine prickly questions: perhaps this 'world' might regard me as a misfit. But may not the world be at fault being afraid to say No? No to colour when black and white will do, no to a rechristened Light Programme, no to licking blood off penises, no to playing new games, no to buying and spending, no to joining in, no to being a good sport, no to suffering the nonchalance of other people's half-baked notions.

No. Ravishingly no.

'I won't go then?' said Maud.

'I really wouldn't.'

I won this contest. 'Transformation' indeed! Trepanation more like and with a blunt drill. But Phyllis won't give up. She's been playing and manipulating Maud so long, subtly squirming her sharp little knife through the timorous skin towards the tender, unsuspecting heart. Prepared always to be amazed if challenged. 'Something I did? Surely not.' She's made my Maud an instrument for her own pleasure. Striking, grabbing and withdrawing, so that the nerves have rattled off their once smooth tracks and now jangle piteously. Agitated, her victim cries out as Phyllis drags her knife below the skin to and from the heart, smiling. How she triumphs over there in dismal Coventry, gloating as Maud tries pathetically to retune and balance herself.

Maud's about to bring in tea on a tray with a Battenberg cake. She won't eat much.

You can never be too rich or too thin, said Wallis Simpson, who really was too thin and too rich inside her glitzy Schiaparelli frocks. Maud is ignorant of riches and she walks a different slender path.

'It's good to stay slim,' I used to tell her. 'Fat is slovenly.'

She chose the cake for its paleness. Light yellow and pink squares surrounded by creamy marzipan, pastel colours of ladies' underwear in Marks & Spencer's. Scarcely eating, she cherishes every insubstantial morsel, its colour and texture.

Songs Without Words playing on a scratched record serves as doily to this frivolous confection. The music dies as the scratching on the vinyl grows intense. The imperfect sound is painful except in descending moments; then it accelerates the mood. Waiting to pour and sip her tea, Maud will be oblivious to the aching notes. 'Do start, dear,' I'll say, expecting that instant when the trilling turns into the melody of Spring. I want her occupied.

When she was a child I made her sit with her plate of spinach or tapioca until she'd finished every spoonful. If she insisted on leaving something, I served it again for the next meal, and smacked her roundly if she persisted. Megan did the same to me. It avoids creating a finicky adult. But now, she's decomposing her fleshly world, recoiling even from salmon paste, Battenberg cake and thinly sliced cucumber on white bread. Does she want to disappear?

She's taller than I am: I can't force-feed her with tube and wheel. She must eat or not as she pleases. I won't and can't rape her mouth.

Has Maud a deep-down unhappiness that has nothing to do with ordinary food, ignores it altogether? Has she suffered from something quite inedible or definitively unappetising? Something on that butterfly settee that, withdrawn, goes on poisoning her body? An evil macaroon of the sort Phyllis used to serve, doused in bilious clotted cream?

What is she about, stooping to talk to me, showing her withering thinness? Consommé and perhaps a plain biscuit, and here's the result.

'Maud, my dear, why ever?' I've said so often.

'It's your imagination,' she says. 'I'm just not as hungry as usual. Perhaps I have a cold coming on.'

'You'll soon be too thin. As it is, you've hardly any shape. You'll be a drainpipe. You should eat more potatoes – they build one up.'

She responds as usual, 'I eat a good lunch in school.'

Is she starving herself or is some fiend eating her substance? Is Phyllis hexing her from pure spite to nourish that new life over there in Coventry?

Or is Maud just bored with it all?

I'd understand that. Eating, digesting, excreting, over and over. Babies sometimes look bored when they've hardly started the grind.

Now I think better of it, why should she make the effort to eat what she doesn't want? She's free and fluid, no need to take up more space than she wishes, filling skin with sickly marzipan.

I'll stop writing now and Maud will pour my tea, bring the cup to me as she's done over and over, then place it on the side table.

My hand still aches from pushing my plump pen. I see with distaste its age spots and scribbling veins beside the blue shade of the lamp. I squash my right hand with the left. Now the left looks living and the right dead. I can kill any limb at will.

Phyllis would never notice, would Maud?

Her delicate wasting fingers will cut the cake into little sections for me and put the fork towards my hand. (The 'vixen' Wallis Simpson never ate cake as richly delicate as this.) My head will be heavy against the striped chair and my feet, so weighted, will dawdle on the footstool where sometimes Maud now sits.

'Have another morsel with your tea, do,' I'll say, knowing she won't.

Early July 1976

This is England in an English summer. We're accustomed to a fugitive, milky sun, the sort that's furred round its edges, gliding mistily past a silhouetted pine. How to explain the unnatural, seaside-postcard blueness, this suffocating blanket of sky? You need rain to make sunshine worthwhile: it's tedious otherwise. Grey skies are deeper and more vacant than blue; no planes cut across them, they display no human bric-a-brac.

Like a menacingly patient army, sun patters against our windows. In the early morning it forces a shaft of light on to the settee in the sitting room where Maud failed fully to close the curtains. We used to open them last thing at night, but habits change.

On the wireless a voice exclaims, 'What a scorcher, ladies.'

Not refined Patricia Hughes: she knows full well the sun is all it takes to collapse standards. But other announcers can't resist treating the medium as a chummy next-door neighbour, sitting by the microphone tieless or bare-legged.

Platoons of white ladybirds crawl across the kitchen counter. They carry our icing sugar on their backs. It stops them flying and will kill them. But, before they die, what sweet bliss! (Learning in that moment the closeness of pain and joy – profound knowledge for a tiny ladybird brain.) They travel from uncleaned cupboards: now I've stopped baking, I've grown careless, old packets of sugar and flour are damp and leaky.

I don't squash the ladybirds, not even through kitchen gloves. The bodies would cause more mess than their scuttling feet. Sugar and guts combining into glue.

Southend Pier's gone up in smoke. Brighton next? Blackpool? Scarborough? All that protrudes from the ragged sides of weary England.

People let themselves go slack and indolent in heat. How much easier to be fastidious when air bites you! A bite declares edges and keeps the carapace intact.

Until the grave, when we silently spill over and out. That of course.

Through the front window I see wives lounging on squat walls or in striped deckchairs on cement patches. Untidy straw hats on their heads, tight pink tops stretched over lazy breasts, legs bare and peeling. They drink pop from plastic mugs and let transistors bang out rhythms so empty it's no wonder they must smoke and cackle against the din. Pet dogs pant saliva on to thick matted hair. Decked in the same violent clothes as the mothers, toddlers get sticky knickers from melting tarmac on the road.

Far hotter in India, Uncle Harry would have said had he lived to see this summer. Even if you think the air's boiled, left to evaporate, then diluted, so that breathing its thinness becomes arduous – even then, compared with the steaming tropic places he spoke about time and time again, it's nothing but a little warmth blown from a single cosmic electric bar.

Is India so special, now that any Tom, Dick or Harry in uniform could have dropped his trousers in it during 'our' war? As for me, I've not been in the tropics.

And Uncle Harry is dead.

Clare popped round to tell me long before we had a telephone. Radiated to death apparently, the ultimate heat.

'Like Hiroshima?' I said.

'Not quite.'

'Funny idea burning a person to a crisp to get rid of a tumour.'

She looked coolly at me. Fair enough. But she didn't show much sympathy when Father died. Or Mother, for that matter. Not that I'd wanted it.

'Only Aunt Laura left and she in a nursing home. Poignant since she's been ill all our lives. Maybe nerves are more resilient than livers and hearts.'

'You have a strange sense of humour, Joan,' said Clare.

'Mother and you used to say I hadn't a funny bone in my body.'

Poor Uncle Harry, dead before he could visit the Cotswold 'cottage', drink G & T with an Oxford-educated son-in-law at the George. What a waste!

Truth be told, it was hotter here in England in 1955. But people made less fuss two decades back.

Remember that year? The year Maud's bogeyman, Winston Churchill, resigned from government at eighty, seeing at last through the haze of whisky or brandy or whatever ancient rich men drink that the post-war world was not at all his world, and that his antique verbal heroics were as out of date as W.E. Henley's 'unconquerable' captain's. That year Maud took and passed the 11-plus – with my help. That year when there'd been a great freeze, not just a bit of wind over the fens.

Yes, things were way more dramatic then. They hanged Ruth Ellis for shooting her lover. Which she'd every right to do – more than right, he was a beast. And Princess Margaret gave up her dashing Peter Townsend because she wanted to stay an HRH and keep her gluttonous life.

1955 was quite a year.

Feeling clammy, I suspected symptoms of a cold. Maud made a tepid drink for me to have with the aspirins. She stroked my hair once – quite absent-mindedly.

'Would you like me to read to you?'

'Why, Maud,' I exclaimed. 'What a kind thought!'

A headache was fading with the pills, but the echo lingered. I lay back in the chair, my eyes flickeringly closed, an agitating purple darkness behind the lids. Maud read in a corner of my head, a halo round her hair. She looked like an upright, glistening Ophelia come out of her pond.

Has Maud ever noticed the resemblance? At night if I glance into her bedroom by the dim hall light, her face is gentle and rounded like Ophelia's; when she wakes, it blotches and flushes. In sleep, her breathing is regular and refined; by day, it grows uneven and hitched as it leaves her mouth. She never sees herself sleeping.

Aunty Gertie said *Ophelia* was the painted version of *Songs Without Words*. I spy the girl now as her artist saw her, lapped by sweet water, no picnic rubbish crowding the river bank where she lies; just flowers, the lovelier for being brushed into delicacy. Water flows in and out of the open mouth, always pure, passing through the drowned body with nothing hindering it, nothing that anyone could be squeamish about. So clean a death: no, life rather, for there's no sense in this great picture that Ophelia's any more dead than her painter. Or than I am.

As I look at her, the face, her face, my face slips under the water. Bubbles rise and pop in the air as limbs float serenely down.

Now I'm in the frame I see much more. On the right a green imp scrambles up the bank and away from the supine body. Lying there, bloodless, under and over the water, she's free of him; she lolls in her liquid bed with no fear of being pricked into spasms and jerks – if she ever was. The point is she's comfortable.

As I might be inside that quiet water.

No, I could never be so thin and pale, *I* could never be Ophelia.

But Maud? She's no need to purify her body into such clarity. She's already so delicate, so very slender. My Ophelia.

This writing, this memory, this scratching with jagged nails in the graves of one's head, is not for the faint-hearted. Not everyone welcomes the dead coming up from deep water.

She's reading to me a biography of Grigory Rasputin. It appeals to neither of us. Though her voice isn't mellifluous, her accent neither common nor posh, her tone is pleasing. Words fall creamily over my face and body. Occasionally I spy her through my lashes. A little flushed, the top edge of one eyelid twitching now and then; the shaded light subtly powdering her complexion. She gives 'repose': that's the word for a soft quietness, different from rest. Re-pose: quieted moving.

I let my mind wander. Foolish to stop her because the words lack interest. If silent, Maud would be self-conscious. Once, just after I've glimpsed her face through my eyelashes, I think to stretch out a hand, to place it on her knee, fingering the checked skirt that hangs loose from her lap. Setting it aside to touch the skin that barely covers those fragile white bones.

What route of desire does she travel in this heat? 'Come into the garden.' Did she ever unlatch the gate and see the black bat fly?

I think not. As I say, I didn't leave the *Golden Treasury* open for her at the right page.

Good: she's far too educated to get stuck in a poem.

I lean back in the chair, quite still, feet up, a numbness invading the back of my knees from stretching my legs out too long. Maud leaves off reading to go into the kitchen. On the Third Programme a series of Elizabethan songs with lute accompaniment; I hear the syncopated music, not the words.

She's clattering on the counter. With that noise, she could be preparing a rack of lamb with three kinds of vegetables when, as like as not, it's half a cauliflower with melted cheese or a bit of tinned fish bought from the Pakistanis in the corner shop, then emptied out on a bed of limp lettuce. Or rissoles, put under the grill. Crumbly fruit cake in a packet for dessert, if that.

Half the time, only I eat this dull stuff.

She re-enters the room with a small tray of mousetrap cheese on toast and a few tomato quarters sprinkled with granulated sugar. She spreads out a serviette like a tablecloth on my lap and places the tray on it.

'Feeling better?' she asks.

'Much the same,' I say.

She brings her own tray in then, same food but smaller portions, the cheese more melted so that it covers and hides the white bread.

I'm detached and silent. I expect to eat slowly. She rushes down her meagre portion, fearing the cheese will cool and harden. One overhanging piece beats her. She prods it aside.

'Do you want anything else?'

She speaks from habit. I know she's bought nothing for dessert.

'I'll make some coffee and biscuits then.'

She places her own tray on the side table, her fork squashing the uneaten cheese to hide it. She knows I know what she's done.

Then she comes over and leans down to take my tray. My arms lie along the arms of the chair, the fingers of one hand dangling. On my plate, knife and fork are left awry – it costs me something to do this against the grain – a few crumbs on the serviette.

As she lifts the tray, I don't seek her eyes but feel she's looking at me and blushing, perhaps from the effort of leaning down. She places my tray on top of hers on the side table. I should tell her it may fall from that precarious place, but I stay silent. She collects the serviette. I make no move to help her. My breath tightens. I must be careful, for chest pains flare up so easily. She rolls up the cloth with the crumbs inside and takes it from my lap. She steps backwards twice, slowly.

In the High Street some weeks ago I waited in a queue at the Post Office for the woman behind the glass to finish examining her nails and change the sign from 'Position Closed' to 'Position Open'.

In front of me stood a girl, a young woman really, a common sort with black-rimmed eyes like a panda and blanked-out mouth, skirt up to her bottom. She looked round once to check for someone but, not finding him or her, she turned idly back towards the front of the queue.

I moved up close to her and was disturbed by a musky, musty scent. An allure I presume, something interacting with her animal smell. What was it supposed to be if not inviting? And for whom? Her hair was tripping out in thick tousled chestnut skeins. I came closer but still behind her. I raised my hand and fingered her hair once, just once, the impulse of a moment.

My fingers sprang back as the girl jerked round. The face jarred. 'There was a small insect caught in your hair,' I said.

She looked at me coldly. My heart flipped over and froze. I made a little public noise to indicate I'd forgotten something and left the queue.

What was the letter I wanted to post?

Best stay in.

Every morning Maud gets herself ready for work. She puts the strap of her school satchel over her right shoulder, hoists up her load of books, and goes out, too often without a word beyond 'Bye' thrown to the air.

She's cheerless. Occasionally, when I ask obliquely, she declares she's 'pleased enough', but lifelessly, with a half-smile that never reaches her eyes. She forgets to put on the lipstick I used to make her wear; even that odious orange-pink colour Phyllis chose is better than nothing. People must think her a ghost creeping along the street.

'School's not going well.'

'How's that?' I say. 'You prepare enough. You work away at all hours.'

'No, it's not that. I've trouble with the girls. The new head-mistress doesn't like me.'

'Everyone has bad spells. Why take it so to heart?'

She comes over and picks up my cup from the chair arm, taking it into the kitchen to wash later. As she returns to the room, she says, 'The government's threatening cuts to selective schools. If we get a small allocation next month, someone will have to go. I think it'll be me.'

'Grammar,' I say. '"I". But never mind. Anyway, I doubt it. You've been there a long time. That must count for something.'

'Not as long as the senior teachers like Miss Janes, and I'm not as popular as the newer ones.'

'What about the married women like Helen? They ought to go first. It's selfish of them to take the place of people who need to work.'

'They're popular,' she says again, fingering an embroidered tray-cloth started an age back and hardly changed over the months. Is she a Penelope unravelling her crinolined ladies and hollyhocks by night while I sleep?

'Has anyone said anything to you?'

'Nothing really, not as such, but they've hinted. No one will know for a week or so.'

'Oh, hints! You're probably wrong. If they took you in the first place, why should they want to be rid of you now after so many years?'

She doesn't answer. She lays down her embroidery and goes over to pull down the front window in the bay. It's been opened slightly to let in air. What entered had been hot and dense.

'It's getting noisy with children playing outside on the waste patch,' she says as she sits down again. She doesn't take up the tray-cloth.

'What has the new headmistress got against you?'

She was silent.

'You may well be mistaken. If you aren't, why not pull yourself together and try to be what they want? Phyllis got a new job easily enough. With that man's help of course. Not a good school like yours though.'

She isn't listening, just looking at me in her weird, weary way. She's silent. Truly, it's hard to bear.

'Get the book now,' I say. 'I'd like some reading.'

She rises, colour seeping back into her face, drained even by this little talk. She fetches the book.

When it's finished, it won't be replaced. It would be too much for me to visit the library. Besides, there was something queer in Mrs Jenkins' expression when I was in last time and she handed over the pristine *Rasputin*. Perhaps she's ill.

'Do you want your music,' Maud asks.

'My' music?

'Put on the Brahms sonata on the second record, the F minor one.'

The volume is too low. I tell her to turn it higher.

No demur.

She brings over a dining-room chair and settles herself to read against the sound, holding the book up, not resting it on her lap – I'd always told her the importance of posture. One should be dignified sitting or standing. She looks like a four-years child with a slate in a dame school.

*

Heat enters our rooms as if already drunk. It invades furnishings, fitted carpets and velvet curtains. Then it knocks and roughs up living flesh, destroying boundaries, swelling tongues and gums, and rattling teeth. Predatory and cannibalistic, it chews and ingests – but so slowly we can't fathom what's happening while it happens. Nor can we halt it. A nebulous unease runs about my chest, slithering in from the rude air. Sometimes it reaches the stump of the belly. My heart flips over as if a dying eel were nudging it.

The heat pushes one further and further towards stillness, the kind that, if it moves at all, is slithering, soothing and subtle, like being eaten while dissolving. Oh, the luxurious slipping from that 'unconquerable soul'. At last. Slow decay, flickering off, sleeping for centuries. 'So sad, so strange.'

No catheters and drips and tubes, no explosion of guts or snapping of heart or nuclear burning or dirty diphtheria. Just fading with Tennyson's casement growing a 'glimmering square'. Floating along with his sad idle kings in velvet pantaloons and curly slippers in a glowing *Golden Treasury* world.

Every day Maud and I grow more sparing with effort. Together we slip and slide down the category of Things.

Here's the list of our economies: Crimplene, Biro, Fish Fingers, Bri-nylon. What a catalogue of disintegrating standards!

Of these sorry items, I shopped for only the one, a Crimplene skirt not from Rackham's but from a dowdy shop on the High Street with dead wasps in a corner of its window display. The stuff was concocted in a factory in Crimple Valley where no cows munch or sheep stumble through bracken.

Good as armour – 'the kind of woman who wears Crimplene',

they say, or 'her look makes me think I'm wearing Crimplene'. Well, I am that woman.

The fountain pen died with the Biro; so did the pot of blue-black ink and stained finger ridges. The duel of writing with a rapier nib is over. 'Adieu to you all.'

Biros in the staffroom were only red and black, Maud said; so she purchased one in light blue for me.

RAF crews used them during the war. Quite right: martial men must conform, Biros allow no eccentricity of pressure. They tell no story beyond words.

'They worked well at high altitudes,' Maud added. (Who told Maud of the RAF? Am I discussed at school? Phyllis? Surely not now, though her brother did National Service. No matter.)

Then the post-war, pre-chewed Fish Finger. The very food for a decaying widow and her spinster daughter in a pebble-dashed semi; so handy for the new little fridge pushed into the corner of the kitchenette because its whiteness grimed everything else. Remember: 'You've never had it so good.' Proof: You'll never have to cope with another million-boned fresh herring, ladies.

The fish finger, battered and breaded, slides down with nary a chew or hitch. A crone with not a peg in her mouth could thrust this fusion down her gullet. No herring, probably no cod or haddock, just minced, reformed, lobotomised 'fish'.

Now we come to the grand finale: Bri-nylon.

Maud and I used to change our bed linen each week; then she'd drop used sheets at the laundry on her way to work. I said she should take the car but she never did. The bundle was heavy, too little energy reaching her stick-like arms and legs. If she won't eat she must take the consequences I once thought. But, in truth, it couldn't go on.

The advertisement declared Bri-nylon could be washed at home, dried, aired over a clothes horse, then popped back on the beds in a trice, needing no ironing.

'Labour-saving,' said the smiling young lady with the Mary Quant hairdo: she held up a sheet with long painted nails – to show how little effort washing took. See, no nails broken, no hands puffed and wrinkled by hot water. All without rubber gloves.

The new 'bed linen' arrived in a package of shiny cellophane. Glued sides, impossible to open without kitchen scissors. As I shook out the flimsy stuff, it snagged my breath. How absurd to be deceived by a girl with lacquered hair and red nails, touting material from a grim northern factory that, failing with cotton, sourly turned to synthetics!

Maud's proprietorial about the sheets for she'd spied them on a page in *Woman's Own*. I watched now as she ran them through her pale fingers. Lurid pink, clammy, yet with a slithery, deceptive dryness.

'The heat makes them seem damp,' she said. 'The colour will fade with washing.'

The sheets spread like liquid over the beds, no creases, almost no substance. (They make knickers from the stuff. Best not imagine.) They were as hostile to us as we to them: being in bed was like lying on an oily raft. We fought against slithering off – nothing but the mattress edge to grip. Once I did slide off, falling on to Muriel's sheepskin.

When the moon comes up and curtains are left open, the world's no longer silvery, nor even bluish, just enveloped in the sheen of chemical sheets. If I'd lain on those sheets in my Crimplene skirt I'd have sparked a fire.

For Crimplene clothes and Bri-nylon 'linen', we've installed a spin dryer, a strange machine that wobbles as it works. It spins its entrails round in an uproar attacking wet washing, then shunts itself across the floor from beside the fridge. I hear the chirpy machine revving up and hopping round the kitchen.

'Heeeere we go!' it screeches. It oscillates from ear to ear as it pounds the linoleum.

Something mean about it, something that goes with kitchenettes, fish fingers, Crimplene and Bri-nylon, and not quite enough room for proper living. When it jerks away from the plastic bowl placed under its spout, it messes the floor. Yet – how can one put it? – there's a quality in its noise and antics that almost invites one to address it on a hot morning, talk to it, maybe tell it more than its tininess deserves.

As it stops, for example, decelerating gradually from its frenetic whirling, one might say, 'Perhaps I too could wind down.'

Then it might reply in its vulgar lingo, 'Not bloody likely.' And one might be heartened?

Just a fancy.

I hate shabbiness. I hate Crimplene. I hate Bri-nylon. I admit this to the spin dryer, which sneers because it knows it's of the same common class and background. But it sneers jovially, slipping away from its mess on the floor.

'Really,' I say, 'you'll have to wear a nappy if this goes on.'

Through the party wall I hear the pit-pat of Wimbledon from the television, left switched on with no one watching. 'Ribbon developments' and 'party walls'. Such wheedling metaphors.

'Advantage Borg.'

Upstairs

On the stairs as I climb slowly up to bed with Maud's help, again I crunch ladybirds. Dead or alive? Why have their frames not collapsed into mush or powder? How can they still have structure?

Why do they want to live here? On our stairs and in our drawers, with our sugar shackling their wings.

I hear a dripping tap. Maud won't telephone a plumber and there's no one to mend it for us. Usually I see to what goes wrong. Or we just manage. Not everything that's broken must be fixed.

The tap is distant and perhaps it drips only in my mind. If it exists, its noise will cease when rationed water is shut off. We're the Welfare State's responsibility: will it send round carts with sodden sponges on metal poles to thrust through windows, wetting the parched lips of its dehydrated people?

She's unfastening the clasp of my brassiere, difficult for me now there are twinges in my upper arms.

'Thank you, Maud,' I say.

Her knuckles are warm where they graze my back.

Then she helps me on with the nightie. As she fiddles with the draw ribbons, I smile to show I appreciate the attention. She keeps her head bent, intent on her task like a child trying to knit with thick blunt needles.

'It's good of you, Maud.'

Flushed, she replies, 'It's so little.'

Before she helps me on to the bed, I accidentally knock down the book she brought up to read to me the night before. She stoops to pick it up, not quickly but with a nerviness in her movements that makes her seem too eager. Placing it back on the side table, she touches my hand, resting for a moment her elegant, naked fingers on mine. So flimsy, so insubstantial and white one would expect any pressure on them to sting or stain.

I can't easily sleep. Maud must stroke my head, running her fingers through and through hair not washed or permed now as much as it should be. I repeat, standards slip in heat.

Only with such stroking in the long, dwindling light before it's properly dark can I ease myself into a kind of stillness. Midnight comes too soon – bringing along its undressed, shifty moon. Then the silvery custards topped with crimson petals, the orange plum jelly frosted in a web of woven gossamer sugar, shimmer against my lips, go round and round my tongue, into the throat, then down and down.

Dearie me! Such ridiculous images to live so long, to have gained so little subtlety. Yet, the elegant lady is still and mostly solid gold and her cradling breast shadowed by glowing petals is snowy below its amber juice; she shines scratched and drunk in her gauzy knickers, with those purple dahlia eyes that awaken the fireflies.

See, I can still work it up, but, to be honest, it doesn't any longer quite serve. It tends to flop listlessly if given half a chance. Soon it may be curtained off for ever within its peeling pink and green abandoned theatre. It was always a pretty mediocre play.

I embarrass myself. Quick, pop back into my head and shelter yourself from derision, be safe. (The spin dryer would have something to say if it wandered up here instead of clattering around in front of the fridge. 'Jesus fucking Christ,' it might exclaim.)

The St Agnes' Eve lovers run off and leave the melting jelly mess to the old beldame to clear up. Maud, you'd never do this, would you? Never flee from a house which was all for you?

'Maud,' I say, 'come closer.' My Madeline. There's no Porphyro with his tempting little biscuits and oysters. You know that. It was all faery moonshine.

Fatigued by stroking my head, even so lightly, Maud loses her rhythm and stops. She tiptoes from the bedroom and, with a flick of a forefinger, puts off the landing light. If I must get up in the night, as so often now, I sometimes have to call her. Then she switches on the lamp by my bed and helps me out. I've grown so stiff. Stiff but covered in flesh that's hard and flabby by turns, like a decayed oak tree whose rot creeps up from gangrenous roots.

Perhaps I was corseted too long in the old days and flesh grew lazy.

Is anything more loathsome than fatted thighs and buttocks?

Ah yes: teeth in a plastic bedside mug.

July – it must be

I should look at the kitchen calendar, but its blank pages say nothing to me.

'Write of Aunty Clare,' Maud said last year when she brought home the notebooks. She meant the holiday in Wales, those Christmases in the Cotswolds. But there was a Clare long before 'Aunty Clare', Clare in wartime, Clare at war, cuckoo Clare.

Coming of Cousin Clare

When Father was alive, Mother existed in him. His love made her more and less than what she was. As Aunty Gertie's doting must have done when she'd been the darling of a family depleted by deaths (left with only one none-too-clever boy and too many plain girls).

A doorknob was too stiff for her to turn, a chair too heavy to move, Spaniel mustn't pull its mistress, so delicate she was. (Poor Spaniel, dead after four agitated months, dropping hairs from its distempered body, Megan kicking it to make it stop. 'Sit,' Mother ordered as its paralysed legs splayed out behind it.)

Then, not long after Aunty Gertie, Father died. A messy, exploding death, nothing holding inside, heavy unconscious breathing, and a final startling cry of 'Sally'.

'Perhaps some floozy he met in the war,' said Uncle Harry with uncharacteristic coarseness.

He was carried to the church in a yew coffin with brass handles: six pallbearers including Uncle Harry and the Masons, Mr Harrison and Mr Thompson.

For the funeral, Mother wore a costume in a sombre shade of mauve, on the lapel a brooch of china violets I hadn't seen before. She dabbed at her eyes with the corner of a lacy handkerchief.

How would she cope without Father? She came from country people, robust in mind and body, but she was fragile, lacking their mental and physical fibre. And no sister Gertie to do for her.

She did cope. Well-managed dependence always attracts.

Though we had to move to a smaller house, she didn't seem to mind and soon she was walking out as the merriest widow in town.

'Nothing improper,' she said gaily, though she saw less and less of the Masonic wives with whom she'd once held 'little teas' with the best china.

War brought good dining and dancing with Colonel Brampton, stylish in his army uniform, and Bertie Shaw, 'old friend of Jack's'. She was supposedly in the Birmingham WVS but giving little service beyond making cups of tea in a mobile canteen unit near the park. 'Met Bertie there again, bombed out of his grand house, poor dear.'

As evacuee, Cousin Clare might seem an added burden. But not so. Neighbouring women brought round homemade pies, their men repaired burst pipes after frost – though, to be sure, they hurried home after they'd finished or round would come suspicious wives. A pretty, helpless widow, you know, and an alluring, nubile niece.

Slender at the waist as I am, Clare had small breasts, thick bulging thighs and too shapely calves, though ankles came in trimly enough. She lured men with her overstated make-up, bright lipstick, then pancake powder and rose rouge, then whitened lips and eye blacking – she thought this last looked French: like Juliette Gréco. Sucking in her cheeks, she made a dimple and an impression of bones in an otherwise amorphous face. Not quite a beauty, but with the mannerisms. When you think you're a beauty, you're one till your dying day, face and figure and mind.

We hardly felt rationing. Mother and Clare would chat up tradesmen and out would come hidden eggs and butter. Especially from the grocer's boy who was sweet on Mother though she was older than both his own worn-down parents. From the shop we had cheese in broken bits and scraps – crumbles of

Caerphilly and Red Leicester. So much milk poured into our big metal jug that Clare washed her face in the stuff. 'It refines the complexion,' she told Mother.

The grocer turned a blind eye on the boy. He too gave more to pretty ladies than ugly crones, even if registered customers with saved-up coupons. He could hardly berate the lad for doing the same. He might have profiteered and didn't, so no one blamed him.

Besides, he had his own darlings at home: three hungry motherless daughters, the eldest the sort that makes one want to throw all the tin trays and yellow dusters on the ground before her so she'd walk on them and make syncopated music with her white feet. This was said by the lyrical publican in the village when he'd had a pint or two and was automatically wiping his trays and counters with his yellow rag. The grocer was a weedy little man, and the stout butcher with his leathery guts joked he'd spent all his strength in getting his great girls, then feeding them most of the town's ration of butter. The butcher had time for cracking jokes since he'd precious little meat to give out for coupons.

The grocer's eldest daughter married an American bandmaster and went to California. There she divorced him and married someone older and richer.

'Astute girl,' said Clare when she heard. She thought beauty ought to deliver luxury and shouted Hosanna! when it did.

Young Joe married one of Maria's sisters and had three children. Young Joe of the dry, longing kiss in *The White Horse Inn*.

'My heart is broken, but what care I?'

Clare had to share my bedroom; the other was kept for lodgers who came and went. Two narrow iron beds, only one made up when I was alone. It was covered in a shiny reddish-brown satin spread, an ample double one meant for a far bigger bed; every morning, after I'd tucked in sheets and blankets and placed the eiderdown squarely on top, I had to fold the bed-spread in two, then stretch it over the entire bed in double thickness. It was slippery and, if one weren't deft, it slithered on to the floor, lying there like a guilty puddle. This happened even when Megan made the bed in the old house. She'd say she'd done it proper and, if 'the wench' couldn't keep it tidy, that was her lookout. Dogs and children were always a nuisance indoors.

When Clare came to occupy the second bed, Mother cut my bedspread in two; Clare and I hemmed the cut sides. Half the width, it was easier to manoeuvre. The only good thing from her coming.

How her presence freed Mother. Still a child in years, Clare appealed to what Mother had too long repressed. Easy, for she'd been grown-up since the age of eight. On her second day with us she spoke knowingly of cold cream, tits and calamine lotion. The language, the attitudes, so vulgar.

After living with Father who had some standards, Mother must have known this. I felt uneasy. But, whatever she knew, Mother was home at last. Once she began a sentence, 'Your dear Father wouldn't . . .' only to break off spluttering with laughter as she caught her niece's eye.

Clare was demonstrative – it came from having her own father as lover, Aunt Laura abdicating the role on the onset of migraines. She'd embrace Mother before leaving even for a weekend, then kiss her on the cheek when returning. Mother lapped up this sort of display.

'You could do with taking a leaf out of Clare's book,' she said, having heard me mutter 'smarmy'.

The pair were always fiddling with bits of their bodies. Plucking out hairs from eyebrows, rubbing in cream between fingers or smoothing it along their legs, holding their painted toenails in the air as they caressed their own calves, Mother sitting on an Indian pouf, Clare on cushions. Once I saw them dressing up their heads in beads, coloured feathers, bits of pretty material and pearl buttons Mother kept in her button box for something or other, singing together, 'When the red, red robin comes bob, bob, bobbin' along.'

Mother showed Clare how to shine and strengthen her nails with olive oil bought in a little yellow bottle from the chemist for unwaxing ears. She sprinkled the oil on to cotton wool and rubbed the nails. (Phyllis cooks with it instead of lard, Maud says.) Then they'd put on crimson varnish, got from heaven knows where. I saw the two of them at it, smoking, giggling and painting their talons.

Father wouldn't have enjoyed the bright red nails on his widow. He wanted people to look nice but not artificial. A woman should be a woman. Probably he gave Mother credit for being 'natural' even when decked out in the finery he delighted to buy her, the silky blue, red and black kimono she used as dressing-gown, the grey Delphos-style crêpe-de-Chine robe with the small orange flowers.

'Look at your Mother,' he'd say. 'Such a trim figure, such shapely legs.'

He probably thought she smelt naturally of La Belle Saison or Bouquet de Faunes.

'What an unnatural girl you are,' Mother said to me after

her triumphant night in *The Gondoliers* and my failure to be winsome and winning. 'It really is a trial having a child like you.'

Clare and Mother listened to the same popular dance music, their bodies attuned to banal rhythms, their minds to soppy, needy sentiments. 'One for my baby.' Together they read romances. At the end of the war, after she'd moved out, Clare sent Mother *Forever Amber*, a sexy novel that was 'all the rage'; hardly the sort of gift a niece gives an aunt.

Whispering loudly in her ear, Clare'd tell her 'Aunt Izzy' how some child in uniform squeezed her hand or gave her a bold admiring stare from the corridor of a lurching train. 'I must look my best tonight if I'm to make a conquest,' she'd say, or, after first meeting, 'He's not husband material. Fine in uniform but can't see him in civvies. To hunt again.'

She moved to show us her best 'profile', her most winning side of soft waves.

'Don't be such a crosspatch,' Mother said catching my would-be ironic smile. 'Everyone has a best side.'

She was as much a flirtatious child as cousin Clare. Cruel, stupid Maria was shrewd enough to see it right away.

Clare went out unchaperoned. Mother even helped her get ready for her risqué excursions. She'd tart herself up in the tightest skirts and best high-heeled shoes in shiny black or nutmeg brown and green.

'The other frock is more becoming. It suits your colouring,' Mother'd say. Then Clare would change, chuckling all the while. The pair would make little clawing feminine gestures in the air or against their breasts to illustrate ruffles, soft gatherings, ruched shoulders, and hanging collars that drew attention to the neck and cleavage.

Clare had expensive pre-war clothes: Uncle Harry had more money than Father and spent little of it on wilting Aunt Laura, who always wore the same white blouses with a cameo brooch at her throat tied by a purple velvet ribbon.

Once, after she'd stepped out on the arm of a young man who'd called for her with his friend – all right if there were two chaps, Mother giggled – I tried on the discarded red and black frock with the embroidered belt lying crumpled over the second bed. In the dark at first, fearful she'd return or Mother'd come in.

When I switched on the light, I expected an image of some-body like Clare in our wardrobe mirror, with parts of me added. Like a Face-in-the-Hole Board on a seaside pier.

I smeared on her red lipstick to see if it made a difference, *the* difference.

But I almost knew by then it wasn't just a frock and cosmetics. What Clare and Mother wore was always fancy dress, put on for an audience. They understood how to look at themselves through clapping eyes.

My first party with Clare, who was such a 'romp'. Mother insisted I go with her, to take 'a leaf out of her book' I suppose. Or was I to act the chaperone she should have been. For surely by now her niece in backless oyster-satin frock was puncturing what even Mother would regard as the desired veneer of decorum.

I stood alone in the low light, my feet vibrating with the bare uneven floorboards. In my stubby fingers I clutched a drink of something strong and brutal. (When Clare had alcohol inside her, she put her hand beneath her breast to feel her galloping heart, while turning sparkling eyes on nothing in particular. After a couple of sips, I simply felt dizzy.)

A half-drunk soldier came up to me, tried to talk, then groped. 'Frigid,' he said at last – a word I heard for the first time. Everyone else was loose and amenable apparently. That was the meaning of a war. Didn't I know . . . ?

No, I didn't. I knew less than nothing.

Clare used to come by cider in a square bottle. Got from 'some fellow in the NAAFI'.

One night she arrived home late, Mother not noticing such naughty hours though Clare was always noisy. She shook me where I lay in bed. I'd not been asleep, but my eyes were closed.

'I'm parched,' she said. 'Want some cider? Got gallons.' Her breath fouled the room.

I turned away. 'No, I don't. Drink it yourself.'

'It's no fun on your own. Come on, pretty please.' She shook me again.

'No, really, Clare. I was asleep.'

'Come on, be a sport. Not an old killjoy.'

We wrangled for a time, she urging in a wheedling voice, which she made no effort to keep down for Mother's or the lodger's sake, I holding back in low whispers.

Suddenly she grew annoyed. 'Suit yourself, crosspatch.'

It had been pitch dark in the room with the ugly blackout over the windows. Now Clare switched on the lamp, ignoring my raw eyes. I saw her get into bed in her underclothes, leaving the bedspread hanging off the eiderdown.

She poured cider for herself from the square bottle on the night table between us. She'd brought up two of Mother's cut glasses from the dining-room cabinet; not caring they were kept for best when Father was alive. Then she lay back on her two feather pillows stacked up against the iron bars of the bed-head. She lit a couple of cigarettes, presumably intending to give me the second, then smoked both herself, puffing one, then the other.

She was in her silk petticoat and nylons, part in- and part out-side the eiderdown and bedspread. Her petticoat shone in the low light as if glistening wet from some starlit pool. The ends of the cigarettes smouldered red.

Deep damask of a glowing tiger moth.

I watched her, my eyes almost closed and the sheet below the blanket pulled up against my face. I pretended to be asleep.

She usually had a look both alluring and appeasing, mainly for boys of course: come in and let me come in, said her prettiness. But now, tonight, it was her unself-conscious self-satisfaction that fascinated me, her indolent self-possession as she passed smoke through her slack lips. As if there could be nothing better than her world and she within it. Then she stubbed out the cigarettes in an old jar of Pond's cream, already half full of ends. She went on drinking from the glass, carelessly with one hand, the other smoothing the inside of her thigh where she'd pushed back the bedclothes. She dribbled a little of the liquid and I saw it mark the bedspread. Her chin glittered like her petti-coat.

I shut my eyes against the sight. It pained me in the pit of my stomach.

Mid-July 1976

Since water is rationed, we pour what we've used for washing up into the lavatory to flush away. We do what we're told – knowing hardly anyone else will. The careless benefit from other people's obedience, the frugal pay for the profligate: that's the Welfare State.

During the war we were told to have baths in five inches of warm water to save on heating. Anything more was wasteful. To be clean above those inches was to be unpatriotic. Like crying for lost iron railings.

The government should ration air, so little to breathe. Some people don't mind pulling the musty stuff into their throats, air that's grown old and flaccid passing in and out of wheezy lungs, air that's as hot and stale as they are.

I *do* mind. I say we need a great wind from some giant with belly trouble and a tendency to eruct. Better one monstrous organism fouling with a single huge belch than these petty lungs repeatedly sullying our common breath.

Having no memory, politicians, newsmen and journalists chat to each other over dinner parties in Hampstead and Kensington. 'Unprecedented' weather, they murmur, deciding what we're to think. (I used to yearn for London. No longer. It's just a scramble of little Nortons, the only difference that Londoners think better of themselves.)

What *could* the weather portend? Probably very little. In old times, sandwich men from the Pentecostals would warn of the Day of Wrath, men with the light of Armageddon in their eyes and placards with fiery texts in blood-red paint: Prepare to meet Your End, Doom or God. All gone with the station horse and rag-and-bone man.

Later we dreaded the Hydrogen Bomb and built nuclear fall-out shelters, stocked them with tins of Campbell's condensed soup and corned beef, remembering to put in more than one tin-opener. (If the bomb *had* exploded on us and the shelter were private and snug, it could have been peaceful down there – after the twelve million souls above ground had dissolved. Not the Government of course. Or the Royal Family.)

Everyone's forgotten the H-Bomb. *I* think of it. It must be kept somewhere, like those leftover canisters of poison gas for which our war had no use. Maybe it's underground, stored with the other toxic wastes of Coventry.

Wasps are dying at the window, their dry corpses falling to the sill.

Depression's in the house. Not the snarling or glamorous sort. Not the 'nervous breakdown' that demands other people pay attention. Just a melancholic clutching at foundations, a drooping lowness beyond the reach of bromide or valium or whatever drug's in fashion. Beyond licensed coaxing on an expensive couch or baring one's breast and full bladder in a hotel ballroom. It's here, fogging the hot air; in the bricks and bathroom linoleum and tiles – and in my Maud. I can see her stumbling over furniture maliciously placed to do most harm.

Not uniquely mine, then, not something I hug to myself or shrug off one bright morning. We're both hobbled by it.

I accept it, seeking no reason. But you, Maud, were you trapped in the loose threads on Phyllis's vulgar butterfly settee, entangled in that insolent mane of hair, so tightly you believe you now have cause to deflate and shrink? But surely you must know your home is here, in this commonplace house; neither of us can live without its special oxygen. Whatever's been the past, we'll not now be tempted outside its walls. We're all exiles. No need to feel defeated by a counterfeit world.

I used to sleep soundly. Not for a long while. I'm often up four or five times a night. Then, beyond Mogadon, I need a sound of words, jumbled, repeated, winding through my brain. Any words, so they quiet the past or present. 'The moan of doves in immemorial elms, And murmuring of innumerable bees', the long murmuration.

Last night I awoke at 3 a.m., no chance of coaxing further sleep with Mogadon or muttering magic words from *The Golden Treasury*. Painfully getting up without Maud's help, I drew the bedroom curtains apart and heaved the window up on its sash. I put my head out and looked at the world beyond, trying to ignore the unlit street lamp. The dark was everywhere.

The sky at night has a special odour and feel. It enters the room and presses its soft fingers against the ceiling and against my face. I breathed it in.

Switching on the light, I caught myself in the triple fan mirror of the dressing-table. With no make-up I was haggard, deep frown lines across my brow and round my mouth. I squinted a one-eyed look in hope of mellowing contours in the angled glass. Then I wasn't there at all.

A triptych of mirrors on her kidney-shaped dressing-table let Mother see herself from all sides. She was multiplied and flattered by the excess. Only *I* could disappear in this mysterious tripling. No reflection.

The war house

Our home came with Maud, came *for* Maud. Without Maud there'd be no home nor I in it, disappearing.

Not meaning it doesn't excuse you, Maud.

Once Phyllis told Maud that I ought to refurbish the house.

You can't refurbish your life, Phyllis. You'll discover slip-covers transform nothing.

Bob's dad found it for us to rent in Norton, a dismal town, neither village nor city. It came through a friend of a friend when houses were scarce, so many flattened or cut to bits by unscrupulous bombs. Two bedrooms and a box room, an inside lavatory and bath, an occasionally functioning geyser. Much, as everyone said, to be thankful for. No struggling under the bed for overflowing chamber pots, no sharing of taps in a common courtyard with water running out like long-brewed tea, no resorting to the public baths at eightpence a go. Of course, there'd have to be more than one lodger, a baby's cot not requiring a separate room, even a box one. Also, my pension wouldn't nearly cover the rent.

Many people in worse need than you, my girl!

'Without your luck,' pursued Uncle Harry, 'when the war stops, the baby would have to be farmed out and you be a live-in housekeeper nearby, getting, at most, a quid a week.'

Mother started a snort at the idea of my keeping house and pleasing anyone, then blew her nose. Tears—for me, for herself, for the woes of the world? – suddenly filled her eyes, now slightly sunken. But Uncle Harry still admired them.

Looking back, I think that perhaps she was, after all, a little ill;

that her supposedly fragile constitution, her prating of shooting pains when refusing titbits of food, was not all malingering but a symptom of the heart attack that took her off when she was still pretty enough to be looked at. Just as well, for she'd never have managed old age. Unlike Aunt Laura, who's taken to it like a duck to water in her 'home', having practised for it her whole life.

What if the baby were stillborn?

'You'd have to sell the second-hand pram.'

Uncle Harry stepped from foot to foot, rubbing his hands as Bob's dad explained about monthly rent. The men weren't social equals: Mr Kite called Uncle Harry 'sir'. Yet it wasn't so many weeks since they'd haggled in clear equality, indeed with some advantage to the lower party.

He spoke for us as the man of our family. Despite, perhaps, an inkling of her shortcomings, he was grateful to Mother for nurturing his Clare in those years with his indifferent wife and was eager to show a virile appreciation.

We moved into 14 Ackroyd Close still in one body. Bob Kite already dead, not missing, not presumed dead, just dead.

The telegram came days after. Glad it wasn't 'passed away', 'passed over', 'gone' or 'taken'. He'd been 'killed in action' in Operation Plunder. His tank regiment had suffered heavy losses, said Bob's dad with paternal pride, enjoying the army euphemisms.

I shed no tears as the telegram lad slouched off leaving the 'Regret to inform you' message in my hand. I was thought unfeeling, but I knew the future with or without that news. At least no rain-stained headstone to tend, then neglect, then forget.

Later I was sent a photograph of a cross in a field and five shillings from the sale of his possessions. I sent the photo on to 'Mum and Dad' Kite and kept the five shillings. I was entitled to a War Widow's Pension: the amount depended on the rank of the deceased.

After I'd made some mordant remark, Clare of all people said, as she dashed off through my blistered front door, 'You are *so* lucky. Thousands of women would give their eye teeth for this place.'

Yes indeed: let's collect those eye teeth and lay them out on a platter, divide up the square feet of this devoted house in proper exchange. Bury those teeth and watch them grow into bricks and slates rooted to a spot, as my own eye teeth never were. (By then one had already been sacrificed for the child, for the house, and all my 'luck'. I didn't yet have the plate, so I had to keep my mouth shut. Best thing.)

'Luck' like Sindbad's burden or Christian's sin on a bent back in *Pilgrim's Progress*.

Oh, Lady Luck. Teeth on a plate. You don't expect *life* on a plate, do you?

Out of store came Aunty Gertie's grandfather clock, the hand sewing-machine and the framed *Ophelia*; added to these, some kitchen equipment from the old home Mother didn't use or want. Then, on her death, a stove and mangle (now abandoned), the ladder-back chair, a tallboy in which – and this surely is comedy – she'd left that dirty old book from Clare, *Forever Amber*, some glasses and cutlery, and the birch-wood double bed. I gave it a new mattress and padded headboard, tearing off the old pink and green stuff with my nails.

Bob's dad came across the dining table and chairs in a dead friend's home in Stoke-on-Trent; second-hand furniture was rationed as new, but no one was the wiser for this backstreet transaction. Of course Uncle Harry paid over the odds.

'Thank your uncle,' said Mother as if I were still a three-year-old.

'Thank whatever gods may be,' I whispered.

'*Thank You Very Much*': put it on my tombstone, Maud. Do graves do irony?

Brooms and dusters you can get as you go along, some thin saucepans, light enough to ignore the call: 'Turn Your Pots And Pans Into Spitfires And Hurricanes.' Clothes and a few oddments came in two trunks, including my few books – *Palgrave's Golden Treasury*, but not *Pilgrim's Progress*, misplaced somewhere in the earlier move – and Father's *Dictionary*, too big for Mother's book-case which she preferred to fill with glass knick-knacks. She left one trunk for me to store blankets in and things I didn't want. When opened, it smelt of dried-out lavender and camphor from mothballs; I've left it empty. Muriel gave me a shorn sheepskin rug someone passed on to her; I washed it over and over before it resembled wool.

Uncle Harry helped with the move. A fine, tall man I noticed now, looking at him closely, taller than Father, growing fat where his cummerbund was worn, perhaps already the tumour masquerading as prosperous flesh. A colonial type, wonderful with natives but not so good with folk at home. Whatever he'd been brought out of mufti to supervise in wartime hadn't gone well and corroded him just a little, though he never spoke of it.

Grunting and nodding his head a lot, he looked but didn't often express his thoughts.

Though he didn't like me, in general he was a kindly man – 'a trump', Mother called him. Not really disposed to tolerance, he must have been relieved it was I, not his flighty, beloved Clare, who so urgently needed half a house. In that he was fortunate, for, though admiring Mother's style, even he must have seen her deficiencies as chaperone. (She'd had no other evacuees. Maybe the Distribution Board realised one child couldn't supervise another. Or our suburban village never quite counted as 'country'.)

'She really is grateful,' said Mother, 'she just has odd ways of showing it.' For I had said – as I would later say to the doctor who admired breastfeeding – something that intentionally grated. To the man who had engineered the wedding, the house and most of its scruffy contents, I remarked that I might, when war was over, take a course in something or even work for Higher Cert, possibly go to . . .

Before I'd finished, he exploded. 'Your place now is in the home with your child.'

Mother was appalled. I displayed that faint, peaceful, irritating relief I'd riled a man.

'Very snug,' remarked Uncle Harry when he'd regained his equilibrium and perhaps achieved some pity. 'Soon be shipshape. A home in no time I'll be bound.'

He'd brought over a present of a shell egg from Clare, carefully wrapped in crepe paper. Clare came a day or so after. 'It's really quite comfy and cosy,' she said in the breezy way she'd adopted since leaving Mother. 'Oodles of space. And a garden. You must plant flowers for next year if you can grab any. It could be sweet.'

I'd polished the cheap furniture to make it passable. 'Crikey,' she exclaimed. 'Everything I touch gets smeared and smudged, and here you are in your own home with all things gleaming. You'll be a proper little housewife in no time.'

Through her laughing eyes I saw the pathetic homeliness of what I'd tried to do.

'Must dash now. Pitch black round here but sort of wonderful. Like walking off the end of the world, so mysterious. You should try it at night.'

'With a pram?'

She swung out of the house and off to her small flat in the centre of Birmingham and all the Veras and Irenes whom you really wouldn't believe, they're so hilarious, and a host of encroaching Rogers and Dicks.

Tea in Bed

No one leaves openings and orifices undefended in this house. Phyllis will never enter again, I've seen to that. No one is here without my say-so. Why then, when I can hardly drag my legs upstairs, did I watch my body carry a Prince Albert cup of tea on a small silver tray to Phyllis?

Phyllis of all people, lounging in my bed that wasn't exactly my bed – too yellow – hearing her say quite audibly, 'I myself would never take tea to a man in bed. I have more pride.'

Where was Maud in this ghostly farce? (She must have said something to trigger a curse and deliver this nightmare.)

The tea in the cup was thin, refined and amber-coloured, though I know for certain Phyllis takes milk. Gold-topped milk. Sugar too. And uses mugs instead of cups. I've remarked it with distaste.

'You go on writing, writing,' she said before she lapped up the tea with her protruding tongue. 'It's not good for a girl.'

Absurd of course and, like hallucinations and dreams, all my creation, I'm well aware. Everything in this house trails out of my mind, from the wing chair to the Audubon prints to the spin dryer to Maud. But never before has it formed such repulsive drama. As if Phyllis has crawled into that vulgar spin dryer and the pair of them have prodded the green imp to concoct a new scene just for me. Defecating right there inside my very own unexploded head.

I blink and blink, twist my neck and roll my eyes, but the dirty scene lingers.

Each morning Father made tea for Mother. He brought it up in a small flowered pot on a dark-brown-wood tray with brass handles. While she lolled there in the bed they shared, he poured it out into two cups. Then he'd climb back into the high featherbed and they'd sip the tea, leaning against the padded green-and-pink headboard. Peeping through the door, I saw it all.

Later Mother would throw on her red, blue and black kimono and prepare breakfast (well, take it from Megan's hands). Usually only toast and an apple or pear, for Father disliked fried things such as bacon, pork sausages and black pudding, which Aunty Gertie loved (and which she and Mother must have eaten daily with their siblings in that faraway Hereford home with its pigs and single dairy cow). Father always thanked her. She left the plates in the sink to be washed up by Megan, who also took the brown-wood tea tray from the bedroom before making Mother's and Father's bed.

After they married and moved into the London house, Nick

bought Clare a Goblin Teasmade. They could have tea without Nick needing to pad down to the basement kitchen to fetch it on a dark morning. Alerted by the alarm, they'd heave themselves up from sleep, ready to face the day with a hot cup and no bother. Once Clare forgot to position the pot below the funnel, and boiling water spurted out on to the bed. On to their new latex mattress.

'It was an absolute hoot!' she said.

I've never had tea in bed made by a man. It was not what a bloke did in his neck of the woods, said Bob Kite.

When I made the tea, he wouldn't drink it. He said piss was hotter and stronger.

We had a twenty-four-hours' honeymoon, hardly worth the taking. We went because Bob had a sliver of leave and his dad had paid for it, Uncle Harry paying for everything else. One had to be grateful. *Didn't I know . . . ?*

The shabby hotel was almost empty. Little choice of food and Bob Kite was fussy, as such working-class people are, liking neither fatty pork chop nor cottage pie Oxo-cubed into taste.

We kept silent through the thin soup and into Oxo pie. I heard him chew, basting his food in saliva. To interrupt the sound, I urged him to talk of his 'mess' and his kit and – of all things – his padre.

He'd no idea what he'd do when he stepped out into civvy street, and who cared?

I hurried that bleak look off his weak face by making another eager noise about his future (my own quite cut off). Every part of me rebelled against the effort.

He might go into insurance, except it'd be boring sitting behind a desk. He wasn't one for an office. Then again, it would be a fag going round doors to badger people into buying what they didn't want.

I cared nothing for his puny future. Though it was only a week on, when he'd gone, that it gripped me: I'd be part of his sour time of peace. I stood still, then, on the carpet in Mother's sitting room, iced to the bone.

God make the war last for ever!

If I'd told Muriel, she'd have said, 'It takes all sorts.'

I could never have told Clare, to hear her laugh, see her eyes shed teasing sympathy.

The hotel bedroom strove to be genteel, pictures of rural cottages and fox hunts on the walls. I'd brought a book, Struther's *Mrs Miniver*, vignettes of stoically decent upper-middle-class life for us to admire. It was chosen with care, something even dull mother Kite might have picked up if she ever read anything beyond *Tit-Bits*.

'Is that what yar goin' to do?'

A hint to keep the book closed. Instead I busied myself with anything to hand. In the dining room I'd tried to ease things with my encouraging questions. Only once I'd forced myself lightly to touch his arm. He winced. (Noting the reaction, the lame, elderly waitress sensed some romantic incongruity: how thoroughly she misjudged the case!) Now, in the bedroom, I took out the black nightie Mother had found, heaven knows where, probably under the bed in her stock of unwanted gifts. It had to go over the bulge, so would have been a tent on her trim figure. I brushed my hair into a shine and dabbed on the eau de Cologne

Clare had wheedled out of some chap in the PX. Then, seeing a button fall from his pyjama top, I took out my handbag sewing set and fixed it on. (Recalling the heart of needles and thread Maria once gave me – long ago, when I was still a child and knew nothing.)

I heard him peeing into the toilet bowl in the bathroom next door. Like a poisonous toad, polluting the whole ocean.

He came back from the corridor smelling of shaving cream and scraped-off hair. Something rose in my throat; I pushed it down, then swallowed. I was used to the manoeuvre by now. Wham, bam and down.

I sat still in the bed. The room was warm enough, but my flesh was goose-bumped. He got in beside me.

'It's late already,' I said, clearing my throat of encroaching phlegm. 'We'd better have the light out.'

He swivelled his eyes, so that I caught an almost smug expression. He reached out and switched off his lamp, with those surprisingly long fingers.

For a moment we lay there, still as marble figures on a tomb. Then his pyjamaed leg fell clumsily on to my bare one, a hand took my neck, moving roughly down, a face lurched into my hair.

'I wonder,' I said, 'what'll happen to Hitler when war's over. Probably he'd rather be shot than reduced to size.'

He jerked away, letting out a loud, thick breath, on which lingered the thin meaty meal he'd so despised.

I went on, I couldn't stop, I shouldn't stop. Will you try to get a motor car when it's all over? What sort? Or a motorbike? With sidecar? Do your friends play cards? What games? What concerts, your favourite singer, band? Newspaper? No? Comic book? That mess, your comrades, pals?

218

It took time and persistence and a trembling fear he'd grow annoyed at such obtuseness in the face of his – *his* – desire. Or perhaps, if he was blessed with any imagination, he'd think it a maidenly modesty, a proper feminine fear. Well, in part it was – he wouldn't have been wrong there – the fear, that is.

Whatever there was, and I think it more to do with body than mind, only further aborted gropes followed, and palpable ripples of irritation. So, for better just then but potentially far worse in future, my rushed medley of topics was working. The striped leg fell off mine and back on to the sheet.

I dreaded it dawning on him what I'd been about – instinctively to be sure but no less culpably. It would have been the same had I planned a campaign. When the feeble win anything, there's the devil to pay for victory. But, for the moment, it set him on the right course.

I heard of the Joes and Jacks who could do wonders with a pack of cards and a couple of strong beers inside, how the lower ranks had a raw deal and how the padre joined in so well, one of the lads really, a good sport. The food in camp fit only for pigs. 'Swill' was the word. Give it to the Hun, he'd say, it'd finish the war in a jiffy.

Then – this was unexpected – long before that December morning began to dawn, he brought up 'the nipper'. Sometimes it was 'the poor blighter', once 'the little bastard', never a baby.

It should be reared as he'd been, he said. You couldn't do better than ask his mum and dad who'd raised three without a hitch.

'They're good parents,' I said, as he wanted me to. Trembling by now, at saying the wrong thing, to have wasted that effort of breath and in the end be defeated, to have to endure justified

219

anger, to have to be even more meek when – what? – when I imagined murder.

But he went on. At that moment in that nasty bed in that nasty hotel it felt like a miracle worthy of any church. I'd prayed in my way – if desperation's a form of prayer. He wasn't pious, he told the padre, but he'd a robust reverence for the C of E. A child should be brought up with Sunday School, no sweets and respect for parents.

Then – and only excessive gratitude for a miraculous reprieve could have allowed such momentary loss of control – I heard myself mutter, 'Why not wait and see if it wants to go to church.'

'What yer say?' He twisted his face towards me.

Without looking at him I repeated what I'd said.

'It's parents what choose.'

'Not in my case.'

He sniffed. 'Yer nowt to 'old up.'

He spoke testily, his body tensing. The rest of his life and the night's emptiness perhaps for the first time touched him. Elsewhere and until now he'd had a war to take his mind off what was to come.

My fear evaporated under a wave of bleakness. I had no care for what he was thinking. Why should I? This isn't a world where women should pity men. They chose their wars. We didn't. Pity, sympathy, empathy are all pathetic when felt by the vulnerable.

He spoke again. 'The first thing 'e'd better do is learn from 'is dad. No goin' wi' girls till 'e knows what they're about. Bloody 'ell!'

I whispered something. My momentary recklessness gone; chronic wariness restored, though less complete. My throat was clogged.

Whatever I said then or failed to say annoyed him and kept him silent. I feared what he would do.

And not do. Millennia of conditioning, after all: I was mortified that, with my struggle at improving mind and body through a short, unsatisfactory youth, with all this – the brutal boy didn't want me enough to persist.

Then he began. 'Reg's wife gets 'er way by turning it on and off. Like a bleeding gas fire. Yer put in money, it goes; yer stop, it switches off. I wouldna stand for it. A man's got rights. 'E's payin'. 'E should 'ave what 'e wants.'

'Perhaps she doesn't always want him,' I said. Gently I thought, not disagreement, just suggesting one might look from one's own place and see differently. But in the end, if it went as it commonly did, why then, just agree, give in, surrender, whatever's usual between a man and a woman.

'Then 'e shouldna pay,' he said, proud of the swipe. 'Makes me boil to think of 'im out there riskin' 'is fuckin' life, and 'is pampered bitch at 'ome being coy when 'e comes on leave for a few fuckin' days. "Too tired," she says. For good reason I could tell 'im. I'd give 'er "too tired" on her backside.'

We wrangled on vulgarly. Then suddenly – it was nearing morning by now – he was fast asleep. As though it were the most natural thing in the world to sleep through one's wedding night. He even snored.

Outside, ghostly waves came in and out, over and over, up and down the shingle.

My eyes were wet. I glanced through their mist at his pale lashes and almost white, streaked hair. Tears came so effortlessly, enjoyably even, diluting, at least for some instants, this parody of an evening, this travesty – or perhaps honesty – of a wedding night. (Ah, Phyllis, do you hear this echo? Is it why you stood at my front door and lounged in my bed? Were you a virgin when you got off your butterfly settee and headed for Coventry? Were you 'frigid'? Have you learnt the repertoire of chains and manacles?)

Finally, I too went to sleep.

In the morning, though it was still dark, I got up quickly to give him his tea. I'd heard it being delivered outside the door. Hot water, a brown teapot, milk jug, some sugar in an egg cup, and loose tea leaves in a small bowl.

He was morose and sluggish. He asked me peevishly why I'd got up. His thin fair hair looked sticky. He was more raw adolescent than man. Whiskers had grown irregularly in clumps on his cheek. Near the bed I saw his uniform and underclothes, soft and intimate in the dim light.

'I've made you some tea,' I said.

It was too weak and cold to drink, he said. 'Piss.'

Later we walked along the deserted cliffs past a few stunted, salty trees. The wind was strong, fluting our faces with every gust. The sea swelled thick and petulant like saliva that can't be swallowed.

Seaside in a wartime winter: damp menacing clouds, wind, rain, choppy water and mist swirling from sea on to land, the town quite dead. Even in daylight peace times, this was no jolly, bucket-and-spade place, more a matter of hard prickly walks for retired people in stout shoes along eroding cliffs, high above rain-polished pebbles.

One elderly pair, out for their morning constitutional arm in arm, smiled at us when we passed. I returned the smile as they expected.

'It's good to see a young couple these days,' I heard the woman say.

Nothing left of him now but Maud's pale hair and eyes, and that inch or so over me.

Perhaps the long fingers. The teeth.

She's never asked much about him. Have she and Phyllis speculated? Girls together criticise their mothers. But Maud and Phyllis aren't like other girls.

I don't mention him, I keep no photo on the mantelpiece or in a drawer. Once Maud did want to know when exactly we were married. She'd seen school friends make cards for their parents on their wedding anniversaries.

I told her.

She didn't respond or openly calculate. There was little I could add. Yet something might have mattered to her, some aspect of how he'd looked or acted then.

Maybe at the time I was too numbed to see shades of grey instead of black and black. Him and Me. He may have said, or someone from his side have said, 'Why do you have to have it? There are ways.'

He did have the grace not to say, 'How do you know it's mine?'

Or the gracelessness, knowing by one look at me it could be no other's.

He had the supreme grace to die.

When she was a young child, Maud knew her grandparents, Albert and Sis Kite, by the trashy presents they sent for birthdays and Christmases. Then came their bankruptcy and in shame they moved from Stoke back to Newcastle where they'd come from. We weren't much in touch. By then they'd other nearer grandchildren.

As he, then she, died, I sent letters of condolence and money for wreaths. The first time, sister Kath sent back a printed card with general wishes written by hand at the end; the second, she didn't reply though we had a card at Christmas with sparkly snow on it, by way of thanks I suppose. We heard no more, though for two years I sent decent cards to her and her family.

We didn't need them. I've raised Maud with sweets on Saturdays and no Sunday School.

Perhaps with an urge to repeat the grim 'honeymoon' visit, like pressing a sore tooth with one's tongue, I took Maud – she'd be about four or five – on a short holiday to the same South Coast, despite hearing tales of sewage and dead gannets round polluted English shores.

The sky was only intermittently blue, though not as dismal as when I'd come before: at least sand was scattered in front of the cliffs and a jaunty, slightly dilapidated pier stretched into a bright grey sea. It was August and the waves were scaly.

Before we descended the concrete steps to the beach, I bought Maud some pink candy-floss; it attached itself to her plaits and gave her a moustache, made her like other girls. On the sands I urged her to ride a donkey, but she drew back and the donkey man had no way with shy children.

The icy water was uninviting. In any case Maud couldn't swim. I hadn't let her go to the public pools to learn for fear of infantile paralysis (far worse than infections caught from velvet cinema seats), a crippled life in leg irons for the sake of a few breast strokes.

Near us a portly man stood in the shallow water, with the trousers of his striped suit rolled up to his knees. His feet must have been freezing. He was looking out to sea.

At another seaside resort in the West Country, Father tumbled me in the cold water to splash Mother and make her laugh, for I was a small round baby. Despite the cold from sea and wind we were all so warm.

That was another touching. I'd forgotten that till now.

Maud was making sandcastles, putting tiny shells on the walls, wrinkling the sand round the edges. She pushed her tongue on to the outside of her mouth to concentrate. Her woollen bathing costume sagged at the crotch. Little thin shells and bits of sand stuck to her bare thighs. She was shivering.

I sat on a tartan blanket on the sand. Breeze ruffled the pages of the old *Life* magazine I'd brought along to read. I rifled through articles and pictures. Then I pulled the cork out of my Thermos and emptied some of the tepid tea into the plastic cup. I stared at the weak liquid without drinking.

In the distance from some rundown café on the promenade, Fred Astaire sang 'Night and day you are the one, only you 'neath the moon or under the sun.' I continued to hold the plastic cup of tea in my hand, gazing up at the shiny grey sky till my eyes hurt and sounds blurred. I blinked hard before I heard again the noisy water and shouting seagulls. I poured the tea on to the sand.

Why doesn't Maud look quizzically at me? She must know what I need. Why doesn't she ask why I'm writing, instead of staring at me through her blue eyes?

Late July 1976

Her summer holidays threaten her. She didn't stay late on her duty day – didn't they need her? Has she been seeing Phyllis privately instead of going to school? Do teachers play truant?

It can't be: the woman's married, quite dead to her.

Perhaps it's just the warmth getting to Maud. After all, the bed, the house, the cul-de-sac, the whole town, nothing's made for this weather. She's no different from all the other miserable pale folk formed for quiet drizzle.

But why should it be worse in the holidays than in termtime when she must prepare for work and go back and forth to school with such expense of effort? That new unfriendly headmistress?

She's keeping something from me. I ask, to see if she'll respond. She's silent and seems unmoved by my question.

In truth, I don't need to be told.

So thin.

Phyllis *will* be part of the trouble. She used to badger Maud to come round, go on trips, do something, anything with her – but not this summer, not these hot months. Just invitations to Coventry apparently, telephone calls, some flowers in brown paper left on the doorstep. Nothing much else.

When you murder someone, you don't go to the funeral. That will be her thought.

'Who was it?' I asked last time the ring sounded and Maud picked up the receiver.

She hesitated as if trying to recall. Who else would it be?

'Phyllis,' she said finally almost in a whisper. 'She heard from Helen in school I looked ill.'

'Do you?' I said. 'If you do, it's because you aren't eating properly. You've always been pale. People often thought you anaemic.'

'Yes, they have.'

'Well, what happened to make anyone remark now?' I spoke quickly as one does to slow, plodding talkers by way of hurrying them on.

'Nothing. I felt faint in the staffroom. Only a moment.'

'Why don't you see a doctor?'

'I don't need to.'

'You should. Though it's probably just this heat. It's upsetting everyone.'

Again she waited to reply. 'When would I go?'

'There's a surgery one evening. You could manage that.'

'You'd be on your own.'

'I could cope. I'd want you to do what's right for yourself.'

After a pause she said, 'Phyllis says she'll come to see me now it's holidays if I'm not able to visit her.'

'Why did she say that?'

And when?

Did Maud stand in the urine-soaked kiosk by the Post Office to talk to Phyllis? Once, long ago, I saw her through the soiled glass pane. If she did stand there, she'd have done it to spare me.

'Were you encouraging?'

'Of course not, but you know how insistent she is.'

'Oh,' I said, 'she hasn't bombarded you with attention these last months. I haven't seen her standing on the doorstep.'

'She's telephoned school sometimes.'

'Why? Is she afraid I might speak to her if she rings the house. You can tell her not to worry about that.'

Maud was silent.

A couple of times I'd picked up the phone when Maud was out. 'Is that you Mrs Kite?' said the voice.

I replied that it was, but I was busy. As I was.

Neither Maud nor I spoke for a while. Then she said, 'Do you want an orange when you're in bed?'

'Thank you. That would be nice.'

She brought up the orange on a blue and white plate with a serrated knife on the side. 'It was the last one downstairs,' she whispered.

She cut the skin of the fruit into sections for peeling, then loosened the segments and, as I gazed at the orange and its peel precarious on the plate, she removed the unwanted skin and placed it on the tray. Then she handed me the cut, prepared segments. They were juicy and, when I'd finished, she fetched a damp flannel to wipe my fingers – with care since they've begun to ache.

I can see the sweat glistening on her face. I don't believe she likes me writing. She wanted it at first but she must have changed her mind.

Actually, Phyllis did stand on the doorstep, but only once. I didn't let her in. Why would I? Why upset Maud by telling her?

At first she pretended she thought Maud would be here, then changed tack.

'May I come in Mrs Kite?'

'No,' I said. 'The doorstep does very well for you, Mrs Payne.'

'It's a hot day. We'd be better inside.'

I was in the shade of the frame, she in the sun. Let her stay out there till her snaky hair ignited. 'Maud's not here,' I said.

'It's her late-duty day I know. I can see *you*, though, Mrs Kite.'

'If you have something to say to me, Phyllis, say it here.'

'Right.' She took a deep, self-important breath. 'You're destroying Maud.'

'You're very frank, Phyllis. Is this what marriage does?'

'I've always tried to say what I think, Mrs Kite.'

'That's quite a boast, Phyllis.'

'We both care for Maud . . .' she began.

I cut her off. 'You think your flimsy friendship – which, by the by, I see hasn't survived a wedding – can equal a mother's tie to a daughter?'

'It's different but equivalent. You know I love Maud.'

I looked at her levelly. She was shielding her face against the sun with her hand, but our eyes locked. 'That's a strange thing to say, Phyllis. And you a married woman. But I doubt your selfishness is dented by a ceremony. Do you listen to yourself?'

She was rattled. 'You know very well what I mean, Mrs Kite.'

'Oh yes, I know.'

She harrumphed and recollected herself. I stood my ground on the doorstep.

'I care for Maudie very deeply, whatever you say.'

'Maudie? Her name's Maud. Does "care" include poking your nose into our affairs, giving and taking what and when you wish?' I paused to let the question sink in. 'I know your sort. You think you can get inside a person like a tick, then dare her to tear you out and spill her own blood. You disgust me.'

'Whatever are you saying, Mrs Kite . . . ?' she began. She was surprised at my words. Two can play the frank game.

'Don't interrupt,' I said. 'I'm telling you. You've no notion of

229

the life we lead, Maud and I, and have always led, despite your scheming.'

'What on earth are you on about?' She faked surprise. 'Do let me come in. You mind about being respectable. You mind what the neighbours think. Here we are wrangling on your doorstep like fishwives.'

That fired me. How dare she mock my world! If Maud has betrayed our life to her, I forgive Maud. I have to. Once Phyllis accused me of being house-proud, 'finicky', I remember the insult.

'No,' I said, 'we stay here till we're done. Nothing indecent in that. Why have you come?'

She'd taken control of herself despite sweat gathering on her brow, running like tears down her cheeks.

'I heard on the grapevine that Maud isn't well.'

'Grapevine?' I said. 'Is that a modern word for gossip?'

She brushed this aside. 'Is she ill?'

'So you listen to other people, not Maud?'

She slid out of this one. 'I listen to both, and I think she's unwell.'

'In mind or body? You always taunted her for her normal life.'

She squinted at me. 'What do you mean?'

'You understand me, Phyllis. You prod and mock, give her suggestive books, and press your modish ideas on her. You think to pry her loose from where she's safest.'

'I'm not here to argue, Mrs Kite.'

'Oh, but I think you are.'

I heard her swallow. The heat was getting to her. Good, I thought. She'd not worn a sunhat, thinking to walk right into my sitting room.

'I just want to ask you how Maud is, and if there's any-thing . . . ?'

I interrupted again, 'There's nothing. I'd be obliged if you'd step away from my threshold, Phyllis.'

I began to close the door. She was too quick and, before it shut, she wedged in her foot. I pushed but the door didn't move.

'I have nothing communicable to say to you, you little minx. Get out of Maud's life. You've done enough harm. Don't think you can worm your way back in.'

'For God's sake, Mrs Kite, you're mad, do you know that? Cruel and mad. You should be hanged for what you're doing.'

'Just go.'

I pushed hard, but she's stronger than me and, though the door must have hurt her sandaled foot, she held her ground. Then she stretched out an arm towards me. Why? To hit or touch me? I shuddered and pushed harder.

Suddenly she jerked her foot free. The pain must have got to her. I slammed the door and leant against it.

I went into the sitting room and looked through the net curtain. Phyllis went down the path, got into her car, and sat a moment. Then she roared off, aiming to startle the whole neigh-bourhood.

Good riddance, I muttered. I was exhilarated and shaken. Shaken but satisfied. No need of reproach.

Yet, would Mother, would Aunty Gertie, have conducted themselves in so vulgar a manner?

Irrelevant, they inhabited a pre-war world. Remember what you've fought for – and lost.

I've recorded this. Perhaps it happened just so, perhaps not. I doubt anyone can really repeat a whole conversation. (I'm always suspicious when I read those biographies that quote mutters in boudoirs and taunts in council chambers.)

I'm certain of the tone though, the threat, the malice, so much else. She was on the step. I'm almost sure of that. If she was, I kept her out. The foot was in the door. I would have mutilated it into splinters of bone had I had the strength, then picked them up and laid them tidily in cotton wool.

Why didn't she try harder? This marriage of hers has made her feeble. I clenched my eyes against Maud's sadness.

I feel enraged.

No, 'rage' isn't quite the word, something less vivid, more insistent, twisting and costing the heart and mind. Hatred, repulsion, repugnance, abhorrence, disgust? Not quite any of these. Shame? Oh yes, shame, in part: a squashed-down, sat-on, shat-on, terrifying, yearning shame.

It's not the sensational bottom, I know that. Not W.E. Henley's black pit for vainglorious fools, not the cellar with the rag-and-bone man and idiot son. Nothing so dramatic, neither glory nor grievance. Just a place that demands one stand on one's hind legs and shout: 'No.'

If one were that kind of person.

Early August 1976

Does anyone sentient simply give herself away?

Answer without moving your mouth, Maud! You can have an opinion. After all, you as good as murdered me.

Who, knowingly, would become slave to a burping, defecating, urinating, vomiting, wailing thing; be cannibalised by needs that can't be ignored or ever filled? Who would march to another's beat for the next twenty years? Who'd abandon independence before it's been grasped, before any life or youth? Who'd accept such entrapment, such demolition?

You'd have to be a very brainwashed person, wouldn't you? No one in the Nazi death camps or Soviet Gulags more contingent.

'You never were young,' said Clare. 'You were born old.'

'And you were always a child.'

Who had the better life?

You make your bed, girl: you must lie on the lumps.

Not at once. Taking the matter into my own hands: those girlish, unspotted hands, though there was dried blue ink under the nails and the arms had a few faintly parallel scars left over from pre-war years. (Yes, I was a girl once, whatever cousin Clare says. Once even a schoolgirl who came second in the class – not first, eh, Swottypotty?) A young girl, with a thin metal coat-hanger, its hook straightened with the iron curling-tongs Mother used on my hair.

I worked it gingerly at first but already with excruciating pain, then with more force. All the while pulling with one hand at the unlocked bathroom door. Mother thought it not worth mending the latch: one reason Clare wanted to move out.

I'd thought it might be no different, except in intensity, from scratching an arm. Not so. One can position an arm; it knows the open air. Down there flesh is secret and secretive, yet so welded to the skull it's as if it sat behind the eyes. Pain streaks through your sky in thick crimson and black.

Girls are told to scrutinise themselves. Then what: roll over in repulsion? Seen or unseen, spoken or unspoken, the terrible place exists.

Did you ever look, Phyllis, like Ms Greer said to do? Look down there? No wonder you ran away from yourself to Coventry.

The hanger stuck in raw pain before it got near where intended, before it came close to touching that bundle of cells and nerves that was threatening to eat up my life. Stuck in some soft and twisted spot, so that wrenching it out brought blood. My blood, not its; no earthly point in that. Agony, yes, but no destruction, no killing. Not even infection.

The thing was pitted against me and was winning.

It was serious now. Nothing would do: no coat hanger, no scalding bath, no malt vinegar or lemon juice or Epsom salts or castor oil or earnest tumbles down stairs that were always too short or had unexpected kinks or obdurate banisters bulging out to ruin an accelerating fall, no shifting of heavy wardrobes and chests at home or iron filing cabinets at work. No use at all, except to magnify the impotence of a feeble body against an unwanted immigrant, the cancer that had grabbed a hold and wouldn't be cajoled or forced to move out.

Why then, I had to take more grown-up measures.

It was a man, 'Mr Smith'. The address came from Rachel in the Food Office.

One day as we went down the corridor with bundles of ration books under each arm, she with the recovered stolen ones and I with my duplicates, she'd turned to me and looked from my face downwards. Then she gave me a cocked-head smile.

An artificial look, for there was in truth nothing to see inside my belt buckled tight as usual, no evidence of a 'bun in the oven' as the vulgar say. I think she'd heard some retching in the outside lavatory and put two and two. Indeed, she said as much when I admitted it with a shrug.

'You of all people,' she said, but low enough to keep the gossip trapped in our part of the corridor. 'My, but aren't you the sly one!'

From what she'd hinted later, as she furtively handed over a torn piece of used-up ration book with an address scribbled in pencil, I'd expected a woman. Perhaps someone she or her friend Edna had used themselves, for they were wild, tough girls. A peasant type, high-coloured and round-faced in white apron, keeping, through her kindly, illicit trade, a child in rural nursery or naughty daughter draped in silk in the wicked part of town. That was my thought, not Rachel's. I just misheard 'she'.

'Mr Smith' was a stout man of at least fifty in a black waistcoat, bobbled wool in front and shiny cotton in back. His shirt sleeves were rolled up to the elbows as if he worked all day on the docks shifting dirty cargo.

A mild early-winter afternoon when I went to that address in Bordesley Green, a dilapidated terrace with bomb damage at one end and neglect everywhere. I mounted the stairs into a back apartment, stuffy, with blacked-out windows. I saw two desks and two split leather chairs; I smelt carbolic soap and something like new linoleum improperly glued to soiled boards, dirt and adhesive interacting. (One day I'd be sticking linoleum on to a stained pine kitchen floor, and the smell would take me back where I never ever wanted to go again.) One side of the room was hidden by beige curtains hanging unevenly and not quite pulled tight across the space. Through the gap I saw a windowless area, a horsehair couch and a basin; an electric light bulb dangled on a cord from the ceiling.

I'd dressed smartly but without make-up, to show I wasn't some street girl in trouble for the umpteenth time: I wore an old but respectable brown frock, long dark-grey coat and a hat off the brim with a felt rose attached by a feathered hatpin.

'Are you sure?'

'I think so.'

'What sort of life?'

I was silent. 'Mr Smith' grew irritated.

'Only once,' I said. 'It was only once. It seems impossible.'

A child's tale.

'It only takes once,' he said. Of course he did. 'It'll be expensive.'

'I know.'

'You can get the money?'

'Yes.'

'No mum or dad, I suppose.'

'No, but I work. I earn.'

'Where?'

'In a government office.'

'You're nobut a kid.'

'I look younger than I am.'

With a nod of his head he signalled for me to go through the curtain into the other part of the room.

I went, then stood with my back to him waiting for him to follow.

From behind me he said, 'Hitch up your skirt, wench, drop your knickers.' He spoke like someone from Walsall, but I wasn't sure.

The suspender fasteners stuck when I tried to loosen them from the stockings. My knickers were clean. They always were. I took them off and waited.

He'd put a worn green apron over his head, then tied it slackly in front. He glanced at me without interest. 'Hurry up. 'Aven't got all day.'

On the couch was a towel, washed I think since there was no odour from it. I would have known, all my senses being horribly acute. But it was stained. A striped tea cloth was slung over the end. A wooden clothes horse nearby was etched in brown blood. Or so it seemed. A washbasin with a square bar of carbolic soap by the taps, no soap dish. A threepenny bit stood on one of its flat sides by a leg of the couch. Something dark beside it.

'How long?'

'Two months,' I whispered.

'What? Speak up.'

'Ten weeks.'

'Hardly time to know. Better wait.' He turned away.

'But I do know.'

'What do you know, wench?' he sneered without catching my eye, then raised his chin. 'All right, I'll look since you're here.'

He gestured for me to get on the couch. I clambered up. My legs had begun to tremble; they no longer felt mine. I lay on the towel and tried to straighten them, willing them to be still. The light bulb hurt my eyes. There could be no wind in this stuffy room but the flex swayed.

'Some soldier, I suppose? Move your legs, girlie. Spread them.'

Abruptly like a butcher breaking the pelvis of a cow's carcase he jerked my legs farther apart with his two hands. 'Loosen up, missy. You're tight as a boxer's fist.'

237

'I'm trying,' I said. My voice squeaked.

He snorted. Then, without warning, he jabbed into me a long thick middle finger with a short male nail on it. Razor sharp. I bit my lip.

'Hurts, eh?'

'Yes.'

'You're closed as a clam. Too much imagination's your trouble.'

'No, really. But I told you it was only once.'

'Was there blood?'

'Yes.'

'How long was it?'

'What?'

He gave me an impatient look.

'I don't know. It hurt.'

'Like now?'

'Yes, but worse.'

'Not the fun and games you expected from your soldier boy. Never thought you'd have to pay for them nylons.'

While speaking, he moved his finger with its razor nail in and out of me, scraping the flesh. 'The first time, eh?'

'Yes.'

'What for?'

'What for?' I echoed.

He shot me another impatient look.

'I don't know.'

'A bit half-soaked, are you?' He laughed with a stale-beer sort of laugh. 'Soft in the 'ead? Should've had more sense.'

He jerked his finger out, giving a final harsher scratch to my soft flesh with his terrible nail. Then he wiped his hand on the tea cloth in the way one shouldn't do. (A tea cloth is for dry-ing fine china, a towel for drying skin. Remember that, Maud. Arafat wears a tea cloth on his head to distinguish him from other men.)

He turned away and said over his shoulder, 'You couldn't have had much out of it.' He snorted again, then repeated, 'Closed as a clam. But he didn't get much for 'is money neither.'

He waved his middle finger at me. Although he'd wiped it on the cloth, it still looked bloody: congealed, mud-coloured blood under the jagged nail, indelible perhaps from iterations, so many sad girls. I looked away.

My blood. Not its.

'Go home and wait, girlie. Ten to one there's more wish and willing than truth in your story. If not, come back in thirty days and bring the money. Two guineas.'

'Yes.'

He went over to the basin to wash his whole hand. Soap-ing just the one as women do in public conveniences. Then he turned back to me, pulling off the apron. 'Get your knickers on. Sharp, wench.'

I pulled them up. They felt cold and strange. My skin was lumpy and ridged. I caught gobbets of flesh in the suspenders for my hand shook in fastening them. Where his finger had been on the edge of me and inside I felt sore and raw, as I had with the straightened hanger. It was hard to bring my legs together to walk.

I stepped through the curtain back into the larger section of the room. I'd kept my hat pinned to my head throughout.

'Thank you,' I said.

'Mr Smith' didn't turn around.

239

I waited a moment, then put on my coat and tiptoed towards the door. My legs were obeying me. They'd stopped shuddering, but other parts of me trembled. I was afraid of doing something dreadfully wrong and being trapped before I reached the street.

I pushed at the door. It was locked. I panicked. Before I could exclaim, I sensed the man behind me. Touching my arm as he reached out his fingers – those fingers again – with a key, he unlocked the door.

He said nothing. I said nothing. No looks were exchanged. I stashed a few coins into his hand. He accepted them without counting.

Going down the stairs, I noticed the anaglypta painted dark brown, the flowered linoleum pulled away in patches leaving lighter squares of scuffed floor. I saw the smudged, stained-glass half-moon over the front door. I went out, gulped the air, and pressed the palm of my hand against my arm where his fingers had scalded through the coat.

It had taken root and wouldn't shrivel or die. You were rooted, Maud.

Had I come from a country family with many siblings – been in touch with those Hereford aunts who'd had numerous children and could easily have hidden another – or had we been a city clan with some anonymity, had I possessed a mother in whom I could confide – though even now I find the notion strange – or one who had some skill beyond self-fashioning, why then I might have been packed off somewhere and the baby put up for adoption at birth, with no one the wiser. Especially in wartime when people weren't so concerned with other people's business. If Father had been alive and seen the disaster threatening the tranquillity of his wife.

If Clare had not been Clare. If she'd not invaded our home, pressed on me that burning orange frock and scalded my life, I'd not have exchanged my future for a cruel child.

When Mother heard, she cried a little. 'What can't be cured must be endured,' she said finally, dredging up this bit of folk wisdom from Aunty Gertie and a distant childhood. Then she turned to Uncle Harry. With him she cried a great deal more.

During the family encounter that followed I was to be silent and sit alone on the pouf at the far end of the sitting room. Mother knew I would do no good by talking when it came to persuading a man to take up our cause.

He was the only person she had left to turn to, she sobbed, the only *man* – she stressed the word – who could advise her now she was a poor widow, take off some of the burdens too heavy for her slight, still pretty shoulders. (Bertie Shaw was clearly not a man of Uncle Harry's calibre.) Ashamed, heaven knew. What sort of mother was she that this could have occurred? She'd asked herself a thousand times since learning of the calamity. It couldn't have happened if the child's father had been alive. Women alone were so helpless, quite unable to give a girl the guidance she needed. There must be a man for that. She glanced at me in the corner huddled over my still discreet bump. 'And who's to say, who can possibly say how much her fatherless state has pushed her into this dreadful mess?' She should have done more earlier, she knew. But there was so little domestic help now and indeed so little money since her beloved Jack died that her days had been filled with cooking and cleaning (the 'girl' Gladys proving quite useless), all the looking after that young people required.

While speaking, she followed Uncle Harry with her eyes, hoping to catch his as he paced up and down on the carpet that had, a few short months before, been covered with sweating bodies, spilled liquor and one discarded wedding ring. The look was to remind him of Clare, for whom she'd taken more successful trouble, hadn't she?

In due course, he stopped pacing and caught her look in his manly way. 'Certainly!' he said. 'No one could blame you, Isobel.'

Then, after a pause, he grunted something about trying times, confusing everyone, boys scarcely out of their teens dressed up as soldiers and loosed on towns to swagger like men. But, he added forcefully, for my sake, 'Nothing can excuse it. A girl has responsibility for herself. She disgraces her family by such stupidity.'

Did he think the error would rub off on Clare and Mother?

I had no desire to speak. I stayed hunched in the corner of the room. Apparently, the hunching was not enough.

Mother took the hint, stopped weeping, and looked crossly over at me. 'Yes, indeed, Harry. I've told her and told her. She's sorry. Not that it helps,' she added.

Was I detecting in her voice the first sign of real discomfort at her – as well as my – role? Most likely she simply noted again the wisdom of not trusting me with my own apology and defence.

She went on rapidly now in a high singsong, 'She is *so* sorry. She's grateful too for a kind uncle willing to help. I don't know what we'd do without you, I really don't.' She dabbed the corner of an eye with one of her lace-edged handkerchiefs.

Uncle Harry cleared his throat and paced along the carpet once more, trying to subdue his obvious pleasure and look stern. 'Well, well, I'm not sure there's much I can do. But I'll do what's possible. A man can't do more.'

He glared over at me. 'Common sort of people I suppose?'

I could think of nothing to say except that they probably had very fair hair and long teeth. 'I don't know really. I don't know anything about them.'

'You know him, don't you?' said Uncle Harry. Then he shot out in a louder voice, 'Or do you?'

'Yes, I know him.' I made things worse but had to add, 'They all look alike in uniform. How can I judge?'

'You should have judged a man who'll be the father of your child,' said Uncle Harry with sudden outrage.

'He had a vulgar accent if that's what you mean by "common",' I said.

Uncle Harry glared at me again. 'You must marry him if he'll agree,' he said at last. 'No help for it.'

'Yes,' I said. 'I suppose not.'

I couldn't think of any other way either. Nothing that could disturb the dreary momentum. Nor could I see beyond a wedding. No home life, no sharing of beds and breakfasts, just a seedy ceremony in an ugly Victorian church in Birmingham, I with a few browning chrysanthemums and Mother dressed too poshly in pre-war finery. I tried not to think of an infant with a wide, mocking Cow-and-Gate smile.

Then a trip by myself to Uncle Harry's. He'd demanded this, so I could give particulars about which he couldn't ask in front of my lady mother. Invalid Aunt Laura upstairs in bed, so we whispered.

I couldn't say what I felt: that the boy was repugnant to me and would be more so out of uniform, which always added a menacing grace. What were personal feelings to demands of society? What was this war for if not to defend our standards?

Why say anything at all, so ambushed, so totally defeated by a body whose entrances I'd failed to guard?

'Is Your Journey Really Necessary?' screeched the poster.

Returning on the train with its blacked-out windows, I watched a young woman sleeping. She'd said she was going where I was. As the train came to our station, not its last stop, I tiptoed past her then glanced back to see she was still sound asleep. I went down to the platform. The year before I wouldn't have done this.

The loose curtain cord behind the back of Mrs Patterson and her cronies, the dollop of cream unremarked on Phyllis's nose.

It's not an excuse. Just how it is.

According to his own account, Uncle Harry controlled himself well when he went to Stoke-on-Trent, his first visit to a town he never wished to set foot in again. He sat upright in his military way on the Kites' cheap settee, wishing both of them damned to hell.

He could vouch for it, he said firmly when they demurred in the common manner for which he'd prepared himself.

They argued, of course. They were vulgar about money and their 'young lad'. Such a good son until this. But boys will be boys, especially in wartime. Risking danger for the safety of us all. They have to have some relaxation. Not excusing it, mind. But you could understand it in times like ours, and it's hard that a lad giving everything for his country should have to pay with his whole life for one fling with a lass who should have known better. Indeed, who was probably no better than she should be.

Uncle Harry hated the narrow Geordie vowels and dropped aitches with which they delivered this graceless speech, taking turns at argument and misery. He deplored the identical fawn cardigans they wore as they sat in their worn paisley-patterned chairs. He agreed right enough with their sentiments, but despised them when expressed in such rough accents, such wheedling tones. He'd come for a purpose and would see it through, even as they jangled his nerves almost to breaking. So I later heard him tell Mother.

By the second meeting he knew they'd agree to a wedding. As he reported to us, he was quite aware which way the wind blew through their little grasping minds. They were not likely to say 'Bugger off' now, though their faces had leant that way when he first stated his business at their front door. Good church people, they said they were, never condoning immorality, but they didn't dislike having this man of military bearing in his smart blazer on their settee asking them a favour.

Uncle Harry returned from the final distasteful visit. We met him at the station. All had been concluded.

'Thank your uncle,' said Mother.

I did but it was not enough.

'She does appreciate it, Harry,' Mother assured him afterwards in my hearing. 'But she feels ashamed.'

'I'm sure she does,' said Uncle Harry, mixing irony with outrage. Then he looked at Mother.

If, years back, he hadn't had a poorly wife and shrew-eyed daughter, who knows what Uncle Harry might have proposed to his brother's widow? Rich Bertie Shaw never held sway like Uncle Harry.

No help for it. Yet on many mornings, after a restless night, I hoped I'd wake up with the blessed blood staining my skin or running wet along my thighs and caking the iron leg of the bedstead. Sometimes I sensed between sleeping and waking that the thing slipped out and fell, floating legs and arms on the rag rug by the bed, then flailing in the air like a marooned sea anemone till it flopped and died.

After returning from the Food Office, I'd sit in the room I no longer had to share with Clare and knit with bits of coarse rationed and unravelled wool. Nothing was soft as I remembered: that supple velvety touch on pliable baby skin so very long ago. Now, any Angora and Merino there was had to be reserved for generals' vests. Despite the springtime when it would arrive, I knitted vigorously as for the harshest winter: three pairs of mittens, a matinée jacket and leggings with feet like flippers: in the event, nothing went inside this coarse casing. I should have stuck to socks for the troops.

'She's making the best of it,' said Uncle Harry in a mellow moment during one of his frequent evening visits to Mother before I moved out. 'I'm sure my Clare will come when she has time.' He chuckled, imagining his daughter's whirlwind, coloured, anchored, lucky life.

Mid-August 1976. Is it?

Getting up in the morning daunts me. More and more I lie limp on the damp slippery sheets, a whale beached on blush-pink cellophane sand. Most often I stay upstairs until lunch when Maud comes in to help me dress. For such a thin girl, her feet tread heavily on the stairs.

I go on writing in the notebooks. Each one is the same

common type. Maud brings a new one out when I tell her. Did she know at the outset I'd need more than one?

He said. She said. I thought. I wrote. (Whose words am I using?)

Was that evening bitter chill or infernally hot? What care I? I have borne rain, wind, frost, heat, hail, damp, sleet and snow.

All the words I use once lingered in other mouths; all are grimy and thick from overuse, zapping about in muggy air between lungs. If they detonate at all, it's feebly. So, go on, scratch away with Maud's slovenly Biro on the lined pages, spilling out just a little second-hand absurdity. I do myself and the world some service.

As the spin dryer says on Mondays: 'Just fuckin' do it.'

Day and night Maud goes on reading to me from the few books left in the house. We've stopped going to the public library and she's returned our last volume. (Mrs Jenkins wasn't there to receive it, she reported; a plump, epicene young man told her the librarian had had a fall on the basement stairs and gone to stay with her sister in South Wales. Mrs Jenkins wouldn't have approved: giving away too much.)

Does Maud know I don't listen to what she reads? Maybe so, for the last book might have been one of her old French ones. Possibly even absurd *Forever Amber* from the tallboy, kept under the linen sheets we no longer use. It's Maud's presence and rhythmic rumble that soothe, something human but not *too* human, hinting at mixed music and speech. She could read Father's *Dictionary* if she wanted to, but the volume's too big to hold upright.

Sitting there in a half-light late at night when the brash sun seems finally almost out of sight, though its stench lingers – you can't tame that – her hands and face assume a gentle glow; the down on her bare arms, more than I remember, is luminous, her pale, limp hair heavier. The long dusk softens all her blemishes.

She rubs her eyes; I see the twitches that never quite leave her. Controlled tears gleam in her eyes.

Sometimes Maud has a milky smell about her, of pale white orifices; sometimes of congealed sick. When she's anxious or hot, beads of sweat spring above the pale hairs on her trembling upper lip and on her wide chalky forehead.

She has straggling reddish pubic hair. I hear her sometimes in the bathroom, the splash and hissing, the tentative spurts. Just occasionally in the past, she left thin streaks of blood on the lavatory bowl. Not now. But she still deposits flecks of toothpaste on the washbasin and mirror and lets pale hairs, more and more of them, dangle from the bath plug. No one can leave nothing behind. There'll be traces in Phyllis's old flat, traces of Maud and Phyllis, as in an emptied tomb.

She's 'broken up'. She need not rush out to school, or anywhere else. Everything's leisurely. No earthly hurry in the mornings.

My first tea comes calm in its thick cup with no slopping into the saucer. There's time for everything; time can be bent as we need.

She's brought home her personal things, her indoor school shoes and her lumpy grey cardigan with its scalloped, old-fashioned buttons. It's been in her locker for years until it's taken on the musty smell of mushrooms kept in a paper bag.

The yellow car is off the public road. We won't have to pay for a new tax disc.

We're all snugly compacted.

We don't need to talk. I know what's happened.

Maud manages the house when I tell her what to do and when to do it, or when I glance at her and wince. Then she knows what she hasn't done or done improperly. No need to smack her. As I've said, she's grown more sensitive than she used to be.

Occasionally she shops for a little food. I see her stop on the threshold like a timid animal coming from cover, sniffing the air for predatory beasts, her nose twitching while she stands motionless. She flinches if she sees another front door start to open. Then, if nothing further happens, she thrusts herself forward on to the pavement, looking neither to right nor left as she slouches past the alien semis. She crosses the road if she sees next door's husband coming towards her, though he'd never accost her.

When she returned from town last time, she said, 'There are three crows on the roof.'

'Yes,' I said, 'I can hear them cawing. The blocked chimney amplifies the noise.'

'They look like vultures.'

'Vultures aren't black.'

'They're sitting close, touching beaks.'

'A murder,' I said.

She looked at me, her thin face damp and expressionless.

'A murder of crows.' I added. 'They kill each other if they have to.'

'Like cock robin,' she said after a long pause.

Soon the downstairs floor will blister against the fitted carpet, like the cheap, shifty pre-war paint that used to bubble up on the front door and window frames. We've not wasted water on the philodendron, and it's dead. Perhaps the room it lived in has stopped breathing.

The front garden has given up too. It's dried out to little more than caked, cracked mud. Even the forget-me-nots that always caught the dust before growing leggy, even those hardy vagrants among superior flowers, needed water. All dead on the bleached patch, just bare dusty rose stalks remaining.

The centre of the house has moved upstairs, leaving the sagging armchair in the sitting room. (Did it always sag? I rarely observed it from an angle to judge. It was comfortable and I imagined elegant. I know different now since I'm less disposed to sit in it. I see how its arms are worn.)

I thought the bedroom might be cooler by day, however oppressive at night. But no, it's the heart of the jungle.

Maud staggers in with her tent skirt of gingham check round her legs and her hot emaciated face bare of make-up. She brushes my damp hair and I exact one hundred strokes, fifty on one side, fifty on the other. At the end, it falls lanker and thinner than before. Dark and grey strands clog the bristles of the brush. Soon I'll be a match for bald Melinda.

I've always admired Maud's hands with the long fingers. So gently she strokes my neck and later, as day wanes, my lower abdomen, rubbing and easing the pain that comes and goes, so subtly one can't tell whether it's real or remembered. (Where's the core of the body or the mind?) I close my eyes, the sweat pouring down both of us, or is it just mine in front of my eyes?

Her face when I look is preoccupied. What she thinks or feels I can't tell. Does she have that sweet orange-coloured juice coursing through her brain and rake of a body – or something quite out of my reach? Out of Phyllis's too I shouldn't wonder, Phyllis with her bush of coarse Medusa hair, the snakes that bite whatever they touch. They'd turn any sweetness to gall.

Downstairs, Maud is preparing the infinite egg, promoted from breakfast to form an evening meal. She's taking out some blancmange from the fridge.

No sound from the spin dryer. It only talks in the mornings in its rough way. 'A little bit of what you fancy,' it said last time I listened. What could I fancy?

For supper, the egg is poached. Not the freshest. Our boy milkman doesn't deal in the best produce, but we're grateful he brings anything nourishing at all. (Why doesn't his silver-topped milk sour on the doorstep in this heat? Is it real milk, the kind selfish Clare splashed on her pretty face? Probably as far from cows as Crimplene from living flax. Not even blue tits peck the top to drink it.)

Maud sets down these light inconstant things. Her hand trembles from the effort, lines on her face deepen.

Put your hand in mine, I almost say, so white and thin, never to be doctored or plumped up with food or nonsense. I understand. Everything is too coarse for you, Maud. Phyllis and Aunty Clare, both coarse and cunning. They knew what they did – snatching the golden lemon and silver orange – but you never needed either gaudy tinselly thing.

I lean into the pillow against the headboard and shut my eyes.

With the fork she cuts through the egg and softened toast below. She lets the yolk ooze out into a thick smoothness. She sprinkles salt and pepper from the blue china pots. She hands me the fork. I take it in silence. Ears ring with hot tingling pressure.

'Sit with me,' I tell her. She leans against the same headboard.

I stop eating. The egg has stained my lips. Turning slightly, she lifts the serviette and dabs my mouth. Every movement aches and only stillness comforts. Why move when moving brings pain? It shoots like fireworks through all limbs, cascading into my chest and abdomen, exploding in colourful sparks.

You can't fight that.

'I'll help you,' she says seeing what I need. She spoons up the blancmange. When my mouth grows slack, I take it in, letting it ease its way down my burning throat. She wipes my mouth again, checking the slimy white stuff as it begins to froth.

Lying flatter in bed, I wait for her to arrange the shiny top sheet. She's already plumped the pillow. Only my head and hands are bare. Come close again, Maud, to stroke my hair, brush off the humiliations.

Through half-closed eyes I see the top sheet, almost white: the once lurid colour has seeped away. Often washed, the Bri-nylon has taken on a slight roughness, even snagging in places. The fault – or gift – of that vulgar spin dryer? Could these sheets ever be cosy in winter, ever feel like linen or pale soft wool?

Rub too my neck, I need relaxing.

Maud rubs gently, her face hidden. Lower she goes, extending her hand and arm so that her head lies on my breast below the modest, still shining, chemical sheet.

'Just so,' I say. 'Just so, Maud. Let yourself be.'

She rubs and strokes and folds until pain rises to the surface, to be sloughed off like a scab softened in water. Her hand's tiring. Her fingers, so stiff at first, go limp. I raise the sheet for her to breathe more easily and close my eyes from the effort. The moist skin is mine and hers.

'Go now,' I say. 'Go.'

Go so I can sit up, reach for the Biro, and write. Writing's part of life, scrawls across the years like cuts on a child's arm. Now it lies obliquely over everything, distorting memories, soothing, fooling them into going 'poof', creating new blank spaces. So I must have hoped and hope.

Aren't we all just waiting to forget or tamper with memories by some means or other? Senility wouldn't serve, there'd be fragments even in a lost mind, not choice ones either. You can see that truth in the bitter eyes in geriatric homes. Writing's better. Not writing as screaming – that would be trashy.

13 August 1943

Mother went out – she had to, she said. Bertie Shaw's spirits needed chivvying, the lamb, he'd had a hard time with his house in smithereens. She went, knowing Clare planned a party.

A Friday night. Invited were a few friends from 'work'. Mother would be back early because it wasn't proper for young people – even though she knew, giggling, Clare and I were no longer children – to frolic alone. No knowing what they'd get up to. And in a war too, when almost anything goes. Clare didn't want me around, but it was Mother's house and she couldn't do less than invite me.

'No,' I said, 'my party frock needs mending.'

With Mother listening, Clare chirruped, 'Don't be a chump, wear my old orangey one, the top's slack on me. It would fit you to a T. It'd go with that green necklace you wear, from young Joe.'

She caught Mother's eye.

'Mmmm,' said Mother. Turning to me, she added, 'I'll use the curling tongs on your hair, give you a front curl. Like Jean Harlow.'

They sniggered. My face flushed, furious.

Then what?

I remembered the red and black discarded frock I'd tried on in secret. Should I humble myself again – or hope for better? I didn't know.

Did I relish the idea of being Clare for an evening? Was there a twinge of excitement at wearing her frock, though resenting every second? Perhaps.

So it happened. Mother was delayed – as she should have expected when roads were a mess of rubble and holes, buses were erratic and cars collided in the dark or broke down for lack of spare parts.

Clare had her party unchaperoned. The blackout curtains were closed and the central light bulb was draped in red muslin, so the ordinary sitting room took on a louche, dissipated air. The party was a hectic event with too much drink.

Yanks came: where there were Yanks there was always plenty of everything: cigarettes, chocolate and alcohol. I liked looking but didn't want to talk to them. They spoke in loose-limbed accents, like people in the pictures, smiling so their whole face opened to expose their even teeth. They chewed gum even when drinking. I'd hoped there'd be a darkie since I hadn't seen one close up. One of the American officers told Clare he was amazed the way English girls danced with – a word we can no longer use apparently. White girls back home wouldn't have acted like that.

Not even with Paul Robeson? I wonder there.

For Clare, a room must be jam-packed for it to be fun, every space up and down filled, no landing or cupboard empty. This night there were too many men, not all officers; a few, uninvited, were just recruits from RAF Ansty, with corporals and a private from the 4th Infantry Division and a tank regiment. Not enough girls to go round, even though Clare asked all her hospital mates – and me. Six men at least to every girl, the younger ones raw and awkward, just boys until they'd gulped down a few beers.

They smelled gamey, of leather and grease, a masculine odour that mingled with cheap girls' perfume, talc and sweat. The house was pulsating with gramophone music, popular swing, big bands, Snakehips and 'You'll Never Know...' – the kind Clare adored.

Cool late summer, but too warm where so many were squashed together. I was perspiring along my hairline, in my armpits and under my bosom where Clare's frock was tight – I had heavy breasts, not compact, fashionable ones. The bodice was held up by slender straps which didn't fit me; I felt almost naked in this unaccustomed décolleté. I leant against the wall in the sitting room, holding a glass awkwardly in one hand, a cigarette burning in the other. The lock of curled hair fell over my forehead. I felt like a grotesque doll.

Fixing a smile on my face as well as I could, I sipped the burning liquid someone had poured into my glass. I inhaled my cigarette too deeply, then coughed. Remembering the previous time with Clare at a party, I longed for the easy camaraderie of Muriel and Olive, even Rachel. But I had nowhere to go.

I heard the odd snatch of war talk. Germans were OK to English prisoners but ghastly to Russians and the Pole. Leave their bodies by the roadside when done with them. Beastly Huns. Beastly, beastly. Collapse before too long. Mark my words. Look at Sicily. But mostly it was male eyes searching for female nipples and loins. And not enough of either to feed those hungry eyes.

I kept my smile rigid as I watched Clare's arms clasp a handsome oldish American officer, forty perhaps, her high heels exaggerating her height so that he and she were almost on a level; they could kiss with ease, rocking on one spot, less in dance than in lascivious public embrace. The great yellow buttons sewn with green thread to the back of her navy frock stood out like beacons.

'Goodnight, Sweetheart.'

On the settee swooned an incongruous couple: diminutive, dishevelled kitten girl and huge, shaven-headed soldier.

'Want to Lindy 'op?' said the boy. He bared his teeth; they were too long, one missing. I suppose he meant a smile on his pointy face. A winter fox.

'No thanks, I don't know how to.'

'I'll teach yer.'

'I'd rather not.'

'Yer'd rather not.' He mimicked my posher accent. 'What sort of talk's that in a war? Come on. What's yer name? Mine's Bob Kite.'

'No, really. I want to stay here.'

His head was still, stealthy like an animal's, while his glinting blue eyes swivelled round. Three or four men stood joking in a corner, slapping backs and gulping drinks. The girls were all entwined by uniformed arms or huddled in chairs with men leaning over them, fingering what they had to offer.

He grabbed my glass and put it on one of Mother's little rosewood tables, almost toppling over with empty bottles and brimming ashtrays. He stubbed out my cigarette, then pulled me into the centre of the room. Under one thin shoe I felt a ring on the carpet. I moved my foot and looked down. It glinted. A wedding ring? Pulled off in haste and dropped by a Yank – couldn't be one of our boys – making a story for the evening.

Why was I there if I didn't want to 'do nowt', the boy was asking. I too. The dizzying liquid frothed in my throat like vomit that refused to go up or down. Why had Clare persuaded me to wear her loud frock and Mother forced her curling tongs on my hair before she'd tripped out? For what exactly?

I trod on his foot with my light court shoes, and he trod on mine in his heavier army ones. He'd no more idea of the steps than I, but I said, 'Sorry.'

I'd been taught to apologise whenever someone else offended.

Suddenly he jerked me with his long fingers. 'Yar stiff as a pole,' he said. 'Let yersell go.'

I tried.

'I'll get yer summat else to drink.' He picked up a used glass from the little table.

I was already light-headed. I recalled Father's slightly embarrassed Christmas Eves, Clare's sleepy disordered cider, some tainted whisky illicitly passed round in a mug by Edna at the end of a Food Office day, making us all giggle before going home.

'Gulp it down,' he said. 'It'll loosen yer.' He grabbed himself another bottle of Brown Ale, not bothering with a glass.

I did as I was told, then spluttered. The liquid had a nasty, heating, scouring taste, worse than the first drink. Like fiery disinfectant.

'I don't really enjoy this sort of thing.' My voice sounded stilted, hoity, coming from far down the road.

'Why not? Yer frigid or summat?'

I still didn't know the meaning of the word, though hearing it a second time. (To this day I don't know, *really* know: chilled, self-hoarding, frozen-loined, private, free, independent?)

The boy didn't say his t's and d's, they disappeared down his throat. It wasn't a Brummie accent.

'I just prefer being alone,' I said. 'I don't like lots of people, crowds you know.'

He was still ugly though not as ugly as I'd first thought when my eyes saw more distinctly: the harsh, raw contours of his face had tempered, even his pale hair had taken on a wheatish hue from the thickness of air below the red, filtered light.

He smirked. 'We'll try again, eh prude? Yar warmed up.'

We left the safe place by the wall and he held me tighter this time, no effort at any particular steps, my head reaching his chin, my face pressing his rough khaki chest. He lurched back and forth, rocking sideways, pushing his loins against me so that I could feel a swelling even through thick, coarse trousers.

Perhaps there existed no one but me in that hazily lit room who would not have understood at once. That something terrifying could grow from something weak.

I was dizzy, hot and fearful, not liking any of the sensations. The boy was warm: he disgusted me.

'Tired?' he asked through the screaming music.

'I don't know,' I said, my voice high and prissy.

'I know though. Come on, sit down. Yar stiff. Need relaxing.'

As he pulled me along, he kept that touch of his hips to mine, the awful swell pressing into me.

The settee was still taken by the incongruous pair of lovers. Possibly others there too, for more legs flopped out than fitted a single couple. Clare was in one of the chairs, flirting with her older man. His hand fumbled about her as he laughed. Perhaps his had been the trampled wedding ring. His fingers had a naked look.

'Come upstairs. Show me yer bed. This yer place?'

'No,' I said. 'We should stay downstairs.' My words were slurred, or was I imitating his horrid accent?

'Nar room 'ere.'

His face had altered again, slightly softened, as faces do when they close in. He brushed his hand below the top of my dress in a way that almost hurt, then urged me, pushed me up the stairs. The Kelly Oil Lamps Mother used in the hall were flickering.

I moved as he wanted, yearning only to lay down my dizzy head.

I spied the outline of a couple on Clare's bed, the rotting smell of male feet rising from it. My bed was in such disorder and darkness I couldn't tell if bodies were there or just thrown-off clothes.

My feet stumbled as the boy pulled me along.

Mother's room was full too. How upset she'd be when she returned from somewhere clean and refined with Bertie Shaw! She was so particular about her bed. Clare and I never disordered it.

The little guest room at the back of the house was empty, the once deskbound lodger having miraculously recovered health and flown off in his Hawker Typhoon. Another reject from the front would soon be billeted in there but hadn't yet arrived. So the small iron bed was made up and empty. No bodies, just discarded scarves, jackets and bits of flimsy apparel left strewn around, mostly on the floor.

The boy pushed me on to the clothes and shiny green bedspread. I was glad to lie down. The room around the bed tipped and slanted, then stayed awry. I closed my eyes, my body stuck in a right angle. I wanted to go to the lavatory but couldn't move. (That lavatory with its wooden seat of which Mother had been so proud when she first moved here – Father thought it unhealthy to have a privy inside the house.)

When I opened my eyes, I saw him unbuttoning. I knew then, of course, I must have known, but I did and didn't. Heavy and tired and unable to move, feeling stupid and so longing to be clever and not 'frigid' – or so frigid I'd be all power and ice.

I pushed him away a few times with hands smaller and stubbier than his. Again I noticed that. And weaker too. Much weaker.

He took it as a game, then grew cross.

His left hand fingered me hastily with new, unexpected roughness, while his right covered my chin and mouth; casting down my eyes, I could see the veins on the side of his hand standing out in a raised pattern. My throat was full and dry, something congealed in it, the green glass necklace pressed against the skin. I shivered, fearful now that it would and wouldn't happen, that I'd be humiliated by the act or absence of it, by my response or incapacity, weighed down by it all, by all the burdens of my age and place and voice and body, and his clawing fingers and boy's strength.

Such heat then, too, such pressure in the head below his right hand, too heavy a heartbeat and breathing so close to pain.

'Stop,' I said into the hand. Why didn't I kick and try to scream? Did I whisper? 'Stop, please, please, stop.' Muttering words like a child, words only I could hear.

He withdrew his fingers from scrabbling below but kept his right hand over my mouth, ready to press down. I felt his wrist digging the sharp necklace farther into my neck as the strap of the frock broke. His face was monstrous and bloated now, his mouth huge, vicious like a cinema villain's. The long fingers reached to my nose, taking away my breath, tearing my sight to strips.

He lunged at me with the blunt engorged thing between his legs. I could see it only dimly along the line of my stomach and rumpled dress. Big, blind, horrid slug.

I struggled with the trivial strength girls have, straining head and chest against him. I bit the flesh on his hand and tasted rust and salt, so must have drawn blood.

We wrestled together, perhaps serving his purpose, until the sensation down there grew so intense I felt myself splitting open with a splintering of bone and flesh and gut.

Then pain fell away to burning. He shuddered, stopped, and grew heavy on top of me.

I was wet, scarred, soiled, with a thick liquid trickling from me.

I pushed him off. He fell to one side and closed his eyes, his breath curling thickly out of an open mouth.

'Get up, get up, go away.'

'Awright, keep yer 'air on,' he mumbled but didn't stir.

'Go away. You're horrid.'

In the dim light I could see he grinned slightly without opening his eyes, his lashes so fair they hardly existed. He felt for my hand, pressed it and murmured, 'Yar awright, pet.'

The room was still and shouting.

*

Someone left the bathroom as I lurched in. My stricken face expelled another girl who'd been there trying to clean herself up after more harmless fondling.

There was blood all along my inner thighs. My torn cotton knickers dangled from one leg. I tugged them off and dropped them on the floor, along with the dreadful orange frock, now smeared with blood and something else. I ripped off the cheap green necklace. It too had blood on it where it had pierced my throat.

I was now less dizzy, but my mouth, still tasting blood, was parched. I held a white flannel between my legs, while trying to swallow away the gritty pain. I took the wooden top off the bath and turned on the tap, filling the tub with cold water as far as I could. When I stepped in, the level was so raised that water tumbled down the overflow.

I knelt, seeing my and his filth surface and float. I wanted to duck my face underneath and wet my throat but couldn't. I could hardly breathe as it was.

Someone poked a head in, said, 'Whoopsie,' and withdrew. A long way away I heard people leaving. The music stopped. I made out Mother's voice remonstrating mildly with Clare. She hadn't yet seen her bedroom.

'They're just going,' said Clare. 'A bit rowdy. Sorry, Aunt Izzy.'

My legs were shuddering, rippling the scummy water.

'Is that you in there?' Mother called once.

'Yes,' I said.

'Are you all right?'

I couldn't answer.

'It's been a bit of a wild evening,' she said.

The door was unlocked. She mustn't come in.

'Having a long bath?' Mother said hesitantly

The luxury of running water upstairs, she used to exclaim, the luxury of a tap that spurted out the stuff just like that!

I unfolded my numbed legs and sat on in the cold bath. My flesh had shrunk and withered as I trembled and shivered. Veined and sagging, it was heaped now in its own dirt. I couldn't move. Then Clare rattled the door and started to open it.

As always, that night I laid my dressing-gown on the bottom of my bed and folded the bedspread over the chair. Then, before I got into bed, I went along to the small spare room. Its green bedspread was smeared and soiled. In the early morning I used a flannel, soap and a cup of cold water. The worst dirt – blood and that something else – came off but it remained smudged and creased. I ran a bath shallower than the night before and stepped into the cold water. Again, my legs shuddered noisily at the out-rage. No one noticed since the geyser didn't light with its sound of exploding gas.

Mother was vague and not unkind, though she nagged me about my hair – I should use the curling tongs more often, it had made such a difference, especially the front curl. If I spent more time on my hair and less in that cold bath I'd be better off, she said. For it wasn't just two days but every day I lay there soaking in that water chill as an arctic glacier, my legs thudding beneath the scummy surface. I scoured but there was always more dirt. As August became September and September October.

Clare was annoyed because it overlapped with the time when she wanted to use the washbasin mirror to make up her face. She didn't put up the sort of fuss one might have expected from her.

She was about to move in with a crowd of girls from the hospital and wanted to part from her Aunt Izzy on smiling terms.

I continued to work at the Food Office. I never felt clean, however many minutes I soaked and shuddered in that cold water before the new lodger and Mother got up. Inside my handbag I kept a flannel within a little oilcloth pouch; I took it to the outside lavatories and used it, over and over.

Whenever at my working bench I thought I felt an oozing down there, I rushed out, then dabbed away with the soaped flannel, scoured and rinsed and scraped once more. Each time. The flannel was never quite clean, always faintly smelling like custard. But I went on until any part about me that had been smooth or slimy grew clear and coarse. Often there'd been nothing there in the first place, just misjudged sensation, a violent hope.

After the first numbing weeks, a desperate hope.

There it is.

Years of temperance and restraint erased in a night by a stupid violent boy – but more by a flighty girl who should never have entered our house. A girl who let in the war as it really was, the thing itself. Not Spitfires, Pride, Battles of Britain and heroic 'Blood, Sweat and Tears', but Recklessness, Division, Flippancy, Contempt and Despair, the real blood, sweat and tears of the world.

'Really,' Mother would have said if she could hear inside my head, 'don't be ridiculous.'

'She's always histrionic,' Clare would have responded.

And I would have had nothing to say but, Sorry, so very sorry. As I'd been taught to do.

And as Madeline says to flushed Porphyry after he's raped her on St Agnes' Eve.

I've cut no classic record here with my tale. Nothing is eased or cleansed by describing this petty, common drama. Some time later, I read a magazine article by a robust matron reminiscing about the war.

'Rapes and incest, cruelty and torture happened on the home front during those savage years,' she wrote, 'and if everyone who was harmed set up for a lifetime of selfish woe there'd be no end to it. Rape can, after all, be an act of love.'

'You have a comfortable home,' cousin Clare once said to me, 'what more do you want?'

Why dwell on a random act?

Late August 1976

With the sun outside banging the window, who can know what happens in our shadows?

Sherry was all we had. Father would have been proud. (No gin and vermouth, no posh wine for us to 'use'.) I told Maud to fetch some.

She went downstairs, squelching sweat in her thick wool slippers.

Why not kick them off?

She doesn't like the feel of squashed ladybirds under her bare feet. She imagines them crawling half-dead over her skin.

The ladybirds have assumed way too much bulk and importance in our lives. Their eyes and memories are small.

She returned with the sherry in one of Mother's cut glasses intended for whisky or brandy. She handed it to me, her fingers transparent against the brown liquid with its yellow and amber lights.

'You could have put it on a tray,' I said.

The first swallow caught my breath, then burnt my throat as it slid down. Was I too sensitive or had the stuff coarsened with age? I sucked in more, letting it wash between gums and plastic plate. I eased myself into the pillows and closed my eyes. The burning lessened the pain in my chest.

'Would you like another?' Maud said.

I didn't answer. The empty glass rolled from my hand on to the floor. It wouldn't break on the sheepskin rug.

Maud stooped to pick it up. As she bent – she had to peer, for it rested slightly under the bed – my hand, so heavy beneath the unnecessary sheet, was freed; it jerked out in a careless blow to the side of her face. She reeled back and dropped the glass.

'Pick it up,' I said, my eyes still closed under their red, pulsating lids. A shouting, deafening type of stillness round the bed.

When I opened my eyes, I saw Maud's thin face close to mine, beading sweat. Rare tears were coming through the lashes, those pale, pale lashes: sweat and tears joined together and bathed in rivulets her hollow cheeks. Blue lines of veins were taking blood from her heart. A slight pink flush appeared on one side of her face.

I gazed at her. Then, unsmiling, I put my hand on her fair, thinning hair that's never back-combed out of its lank honesty. Those pale gold strands, the colour of French irises.

She shivered and a larger tear oozed from her left eye. I felt her slender hand hesitatingly reach up to stroke my head. As it came down over my face, eyes, nose and mouth, the long fingers gently, kindly, tore my sight and breath.

'Yes, I'll take another.' Despite the indigestion it caused – or because of it. Pain is so sly, so seductive.

She picked up the glass and held it, kneeling for a moment. Then she stood up to go downstairs.

Later she read and read, though as usual I heard no distinct words. Maybe the same ones over and over, not reading at all, reciting perhaps her shabby French.

Under the ebb and flow I grew drowsier, full and heavy, suspended, dozing in a tepid, torpid world where my rubbery flesh had no edge but merely thinned out and frayed beyond sugar into glutinous air. Not threateningly, despite its pain.

I'd drunk tea and sherry and more sherry, and now become a blob of hot thick liquid suspended in thinner agonising fluid. I seeped into it, my body closing and unclosing like a sucking baby's unformed mouth, not even trying to cope with the shock of being born.

I'd cuffed Maud a little, just playful. Her cheek was paling again. On my neck and shoulder, her hand was gentle and soothing; unbitten and smooth, her nails didn't snag. Turning my head, I smelt the eau de Cologne she'd dabbed on a white handkerchief and placed on my pillow. The strands of her pale hair sparked and sparkled, or perhaps my eyes distorted the world.

Her fingers were sure, faltering only when, dizzy with too much purity, she leant a moment on her white bony elbow and looked towards my face through her sunken eyes. The breath in me caught as I sucked in air. It shot downwards. Melting pain.

Come closer, Maud. Lie on me, weightless in your skin and elegant bones.

Yet, not weightless. Those bones are heavy. I could hardly breathe.

A strange, disquieting smell rose above the eau de Cologne, a whiff of Aunty Gertie in memory. Maud so clean; how can it be, Maud?

On my breasts I felt her skinny chest as I pushed her head down. Down to where her thin mouth brushed against my nipple, which sprang up like a small cannonball to meet her tongue. Licking and sucking, so that the waves in the room rolled and tumbled, then fell in the darkest place where pain grows moist and secret.

There by the laughing belly of the station horse in this rag and bone of a life.

I pulled her face with its closed eyes towards me and felt for her beneath. Her lean quiet loins where nothing swells and all is clean.

I jabbed my nail into her. She winced and cried out. The cry came from a dry mouth, tongue no longer wet. She was beyond subterfuge. Bravo, Maudie.

'Mother,' she whispered.

Or I did.

We were all once inside each other. Push time back and we're re-joined in that pink, pristine, moist space. We're migrants, we don't necessarily belong here. Maud can come home when she wishes.

September 1976

Over of course. The sky, once panting for air, grew so full of itself it couldn't contain the tension. Waters broke, gushed in torrents, battering our drab, tottering house.

Tut tut. What a show!

Women are indoors again, burnt red flesh covered in old cardigans, painted toenails squashed into cruel high heels, noisy transistors back on kitchen window sills, toddling children in playpens and dogs like rugs in front of electric fires. Limp lettuce, tomatoes and ice cream binned in favour of more sustaining fare. All the loose habits heat allows abandoned.

England grew bored with a sun it only pretended to want, then shooed it away. Sun and heat, writing and reading, all become so tedious. Everything's a mere record of loading up, of rising pressure and heat, of bursting, melting, staining. A person, a people, a world.

'Go on with you,' the spin dryer would say if I could hear its common tones. But it stays in the kitchen far off.

Through the window I watch as the sky is daubed with a dirty brush. It carries muted colours. An unkind rain streaks down the glass like a swollen river, capturing on its way dust from weeks of drought. Thunder shakes the house and makes its shoddy rusting joints skittish and unstable, its floorboards crackle. The unexpected coolness limps around, heat flops away. Where the bedroom window's open, the curtains breathe in and out against the leaden, water-damaged sky.

I can hear the air again, as I used to, clasping, rasping, like tinnitus in the earth's ear.

It's all far too late. Soon it will be autumn and falling leaves, particles of trees broken off from the mass.

Surely one may fall off a twig without disgrace, like any yellow thing. Is anyone watching and judging? (*He* was supposed to notice the sparrow? But there's no evidence.)

I've taken up the Biro to write this and sense a transformation. Nothing, no outer sound at all.

'Maud, what on earth has happened?'

'Aunty Gertie's clock has stopped.'

'Are its arms spread wide?'

Big Ben has stopped too. The wireless says so.

They'll start Big Ben again and put its tinny chimes back on all the nation's wirelesses. But Maud and I will leave the grandfather clock unwound. We have inner time. It goes round and round, dissolving and folding, another order altogether. Big Ben's imperious rule doesn't reach us.

Just waifs, we cling to our semi-detached raft as waves roll gently or fiercely up the sides: our sole at-homeness in this sliver of history. There's only ever been room for two women on these frail, quarantined planks. No one lies in that spare bed with the clean, unstained bedspread pulled neatly over.

What a privilege! Three upstairs rooms for two ageing women. How Phyllis must have envied us our shoddy together-space, she with a mother who cried with joy at her sacrificial wedding, seeing off an emptied daughter to a man's house in roaring, damaged Coventry. When all the while she wanted nothing so much as to lie in yellow irises fingering yellow hair.

Now the sweat no longer oozes out, my hand has regained its old congealed look, blotched, death-freckled and slightly gnarled with little grey-blue veins. It's abrasive on the page of this cheap paper in this last half-full notebook. When I stop writing I'll place the book neatly with the others on the bedside table, its corners aligned to make a tidy pile. Then Maud must take it downstairs in her thin, pure hands.

I'll 'Shut the Fuck Up, Bitch', as the displeased Yank said to Rachel.

If one finds things unavailing, may one not be unavailable? If one hasn't been accommodated, one need not be accommodating. Surely that's just.

All the books in the house are grimed. Even Father's great *Dictionary* and *Palgrave's Golden Treasury* are mouldy from long closure. Has Maud ever explored them, ever been like me? Of course not.

Tonight, as I lie here in the unaccustomed cool, I'll tell her what to read for herself, to herself. Later. Alone.

'Fair do's' as Aunty Gertie used to say – for Maud brought home the notebooks, put them in front of me and then, when I was near stopping, inserted this slithery Biro, forcing me to remember or pretend to. Now the Biro can roll where it will, lie by the shaming teeth, under the bed, I really don't care.

She'll learn what she didn't know before – *if* she didn't – note the date of the only anniversary in our life that mattered and know her own story's already happened.

Then she'll come back upstairs and slip quietly into the double bed beside me, seeking the nourishment she so long refused. She'll stay – as surely she always meant to do – as my pain floats flamboyantly through arms and chest. By then her eyes will have grown blurred in her gaunt face, the residue of unshed tears lurking beneath those transparent lids. We're Siamese twins now, organs stuck together.

271

Oh Maud, my dear, isn't life such a . . . ? Do you think it's time to laugh that belly laugh? Who's to say we don't share a joke in this 'black pit' of ours?

Invictus. In spite. Best not look down.

Phyllis carries the notebooks upstairs without examining her motive. Emotions jangle and collide.

She's skimmed Joan Kite's writing, often feeling murderous towards the woman, but occasionally grasping a sadness behind petulant words, a cheerless self-absorption that doesn't elicit much sympathy.

She's startled at the picture painted of herself as schemer and wrecker, but even more of darling Maud as prisoner and slave. Now, while the silence and smell press down, an overdue thought strikes her. Could silent Mrs Kite be dead? And, if dead, by her own hand? – or someone else's?

Only two women in the house.

Phyllis pushes the door of the main bedroom and enters.

The face on the bed sags, the mouth hangs half open. Teeth leer from a rug beside an upturned glass. Clenching stomach and bowels, she almost drops the notebooks.

Joan Kite looks dead, yet the eyes are open and yellow. At least one eye sees.

A stroke or heart attack? Phyllis knows too little to judge and is too shocked to try.

The face is distorted, a hand dangles limply; a crumpled sheet and stained bedspread cover the body.

The seeing eye fixes not on Phyllis's face but on the notebooks under her arm. The crooked mouth jerks, Joan Kite is trying to speak.

Overcoming her horror, Phyllis bends towards the distorted face, then recoils, even now dreading some vile remark. But the look, as far as it's controlled, is pathetic, pleading. Putting her ear near the dry mouth, she makes out a single word: 'No.'

Steadying herself and leaning back, she catches Joan Kite's seeing eye swivel towards the notebooks, then sink back in its socket.

She understands.

The notebooks by the grandfather clock had been tidily stacked before she scattered them with her feet. Maud lacks her mother's precision, never placing knives and forks, mats and chairs just so. Phyllis has joked about this when she and Maud were alone in her flat, away from the suffocating house. So, if Maud carried them downstairs in their tidy pile, as must have been the case, she couldn't have opened them, then restacked them so neatly.

It's obvious to Phyllis: Maud has not read them.

Nor need she. Phyllis prides herself on being quick and resolute. She's not taken in every word Joan Kite wrote but she's read enough to know the story told is not all the truth of 14 Ackroyd Close, not by a long way. For a start, it's not Maud's story.

The seeing eye on that bed had spoken to her, Phyllis. She's certain of it. The inference is clear: the final recipient of the importunate notebooks is – and must be – herself, not Maud.

She's never doubted Mrs Kite's selfish love for her daughter. The sadistic intimacy confessed in the notebooks is a perverted kind of loving; self-loving as well, but loving. So obvious, so natural perhaps, though not at all to Phyllis's taste. Of course, the incest is imaginary, on a level with Joan Kite's absurd fantasies. Imaginary because Phyllis knows full well Maud's astonishing purity, the untouchability that's kept her friend yearning for over a decade.

Maud couldn't possibly have caressed her mother's body. No woman could. It would be corrupt, revolting. Phyllis shudders at the image of her own skinny, sentimental mother, foolishly adoring her only son.

*

She's hated Joan Kite so long – in a way she still does – but now she sits on the bed, places the books on the blanket beside the body, and takes the clammy hand. Her head whirls as her own stubby fingers displace Maud's slender ones. Tightly Phyllis clenches the hand, unaware it lacks feeling.

She goes downstairs and half fills a glass of water. Then she returns to find Joan Kite dead.

Making no move to shut the eyes, she retrieves the notebooks.

The air in the house is still rank but less fragile and ominous. Back in the hallway, she calls an ambulance and gives the address. Now at last she can breathe deeply.

Maud is and always will be the love of her life. No fading Transformation Training can obscure the fact. Yet she'll likely keep to the new route so gratifying to her parents.

There's been strife between Joan and herself – both are clear on this point – but wars can end too abruptly, leaving the combatants depleted and uncertain. Phyllis knows this, as Joan Kite must have done. She also knows that, when a war is won, the victor had best run away, abandon the loser.

The morning is fully present. No need to think longer of the dead. Phyllis steps through the front door, closing but leaving it on the latch. The notebooks are under her arm. In the car, she lays them on the passenger seat. Ray's house has an attic where lives can be stored discreetly.

She hears the siren of the ambulance approaching as she reaches the end of Ackroyd Close. She turns the car towards Coventry. She hasn't driven far before pausing. The engine idles. 'Maud,' she whispers, 'Maudie.'

Acknowledgements

This novel has had a long gestation. Living in the USA through the late 1960s and 1970s (except for 1976), I visited England annually and noted its huge social and cultural changes. People far from the centre of power and politics were expected to assimilate with little help and no demur. The insecure and aspirational lower middle class of the twentieth century has often been mocked through figures such as Reggie Perrin and Hyacinth Bucket; I have tried to create in Joan Kite not a sympathetic but an understandable character. For the portrait I drew on a few memories of post-war life, especially rationing, but the characters, situations and locations are entirely fictional.

It seems presumptuous to thank people for helping with a book that may or may not find favour, but I must mention my usual supporters and critics, my friend and publisher Katherine Bright-Holmes, and husband, Derek Hughes, both of whom have read more versions of the novel than I (or they) care to remember. Many, many thanks to both. For his heartening appreciation of the work, especially the voice of my central character, I owe much gratitude to Art Petersen, met in Houston and rediscovered in Alaska some forty years later.

A selection of Janet Todd's previous works

The Revolutionary Life of Mary Wollstonecraft
(London: Weidenfeld and Nicolson; New York: Columbia University Press, 2000; London: Bloomsbury eBook, 2013)

Rebel Daughters: Ireland in Conflict (London: Viking, 2003);
Daughters of Ireland: The Rebellious Kingsborough Sisters and the Making of a Modern Nation (New York: Ballantine Books, 2004)

Cambridge Introduction to Jane Austen
(Cambridge: Cambridge University Press, 2006)

Jane Austen in Context (edited)
(Cambridge: Cambridge University Press, 2006)

Death and the Maidens: Fanny Wollstonecraft and the Shelley Circle
(London: Profile Books; Berkeley: Counterpoint Press, 2007)

Jane Austen: Her Life, Her Times, Her Novels
(London: André Deutsch, 2014)

Lady Susan Plays the Game
(London: Bloomsbury, eBook 2013; paperback, 2016)

A Man of Genius
(London: Bitter Lemon Press/Fentum Press, 2016)

Aphra Behn: A Secret Life
(London: Fentum Press, 2017)

Radiation Diaries: Cancer, Memory and Fragments of a Life in Words
(London: Fentum Press, 2018)

Jane Austen's Sanditon: With an Essay by Janet Todd
(London: Fentum Press, 2019)